TRUST HARRISON

a heart warming tale about a public rights of way revolution

NICK COWEN

Privately printed for
Nick Cowen
trustharrison@kingsoflounge.com
(all enquiries to the author at this email address)

by The Hobnob Press
30c, Deverill Road Trading Estate,
Sutton Veny, Warminster, Wiltshire, BA12 7BZ

Design and typesetting by John Chandler. The text is set in 12 point Doves Type, leaded 2 points. Doves Type is a digital facsimile, created by Robert Green, of the celebrated face made by Edward Prince in 1899 for the Doves Press, based on Jenson's 15th-century Venetian type.

ISBN 978-1-906978-34-1

¶ DEDICATION

My Mother, who saw the worth in Harrison from the start, which was encouragement enough.

¶ A DISCLAIMER

PART 1 HARRISON FINDS HIS FEET

1
HARRISON APPEARS

ON HIS FIRST morning I found Harrison in the yard awaiting my arrival. He stood motionless with his back to me before a muddle of railway sleepers, signposts, spare off-cuts of timber, bundles of wire, heaps of stone and abandoned punctured wheelbarrows. I felt slightly ashamed by his scrutiny of my disorganised accumulation. He had the familiar slouch of so many people of his age and as was customary his trousers were in the slow process of falling down. I explained that there was a bit of sorting out to do in the yard and perhaps he could help. Harrison did not respond to this suggestion or even turn around but I pressed on and continued to list some other things that he might assist me with. I concluded by saying that having inhabited my office for the last twenty seven years then that also was in need of a good sort out. I joked that I still had Christmas cards from parish clerks or even grateful members of the public who were probably long dead by now. We continued to survey the disorganised wares of my profession and I found myself getting rather irritated by this young man's attitude. I was about to inform him that it was only good manners to face the person who is addressing you when Harrison suddenly turned around. He lifted up his loose woollen hat whilst plucking out two small ear phones by their wires to let them dangle around his neck and then half raised a hand in acknowledgement of my presence.

He had obviously heard nothing of my introduction nor even

realised that I had been standing behind him. I looked around to see if any of the road maintenance crew, with whom I share the yard, had witnessed this rather embarrassing scenario but all was quiet.

"Well, um Harrison, good morning, shall we go and have a cup of tea then?"

"No fanks."

Having established that Harrison did not drink tea he also declared that he had no interest in making it either. I explained that it was just the sort of thing that a new employee, or a young addition to any team did. They made the tea, it was traditional.

"I ain't gonna make no tea," said Harrison.

From the outset, I could not see how this relationship was going to work.

There had been no formal interview before Harrison's arrival on that first Monday morning. Two weeks earlier he had wandered into the yard and pressed the buzzer for reception, requesting to see me.

"I wants to work with you," he said, after being shown in to my office.

I found it hard to gauge this lad's age at the time and I am still not entirely sure but I would place him at about twenty three. He was short and wiry and had a curious silent confidence about him as if he did not really require my approval to his suggestion but would play along with it for now.

I asked after his experience and qualifications and was he a graduate?

"Yeah everyone's bin to uni but there ain't no jobs. I've been helpin' out. In a park. In a zoo. In some gardens. I can do fings."

On the face of it, it all seemed a bit vague. I have had a number of helpers over the years and whilst some have prospered others have just drifted away but common to all was the need to impart a lot of information and practical knowledge regarding the management of public rights of way. Also common to all, once they reached a stage where they became useful, they then left. Yes there is a responsibility for good employers to nurture the aspiring youth but was I prepared to spend time nurturing this rather reticent individual?

"How did you find out about me?" I asked.

"In the dentist."

"You'll have to explain."

"Where you waits, this magazine said you 'ad the best job in the world so I come to check you out."

At least two years ago the article had appeared in a free local monthly magazine that consisted largely of adverts and group photographs of florid faced solicitors and accountants attending some business function or other. In an attempt to give the publication a bit of reportage credibility the reader is offered a glossy two page spread on some local character who they hope might be mildly interesting. Quite how they ended up with me I'll never know but they made a big deal about mine being the best job in the world. The piece had been titled; "A job to die for, 25 years on the right path; meet Victor Wayland, your public rights of way officer." I had tried to explain that it was just a job like any other with its own pressures and problems but they hadn't included that bit.

"Good photo of you man in that magazine fing," said Harrison, "made you look cool..you know, younger."

I recognise it now as flattery but in response I must have nodded or displayed some kind of positive indication towards the lad.

"Fanks man for giving us a try, see you in a couple of weeks."

With that he raised a hand and left the office and two weeks later appeared in the yard and refused to make me a cup of tea.

There was no time to mess about this morning so Harrison had to accompany me in the van now that he had appeared.

Whilst we drove to Difford I thought that for once I would not begin to trot out the long and well worn summary of what rights of way are to the uninitiated. Instead I would wait for him to ask me if he was truly interested. There is an awful lot to learn and to put it bluntly I needed to know whether the effort was going to be worthwhile.

I am so used to travelling alone about the county it was odd to have a passenger, especially a silent one who I knew nothing about. I was determined that he would crack first and after a few miles I must have forgotten that he was there.

"She's got a lovely bottom and I prize it highly."

"What was that Mr Wayland?"

"What was what?" I asked.

"What was you singing about a lovely bottom?"

"I wasn't aware that I was singing."

"Was it that lady that we just passed on the horse? Did she make you fink of it?"

I did not know what to say and felt myself growing hot around the collar.

"Cool that the fire is still burnin' Mr Wayland."

"Thank you," I said.

As we had nearly reached our destination I made no further reference as to why I was absently singing snatches of Jake Thackray songs.

In the farmyard everything had the same dull hue of cow shit and there was an old tethered sheep dog kennelled above the shoreline of liquid cow slurry. It barked savagely in no particular direction but then broke off periodically to chase back and forth with a broken plastic bucket in its mouth. I was not going to get out of the vehicle and the farmer, now successfully alerted to our presence, drove a small tractor through the lagoon towards us. After causing a brown bow wave he drew level and cut his engine, throwing open the flimsy cab door whilst I turned off my engine and wound down the window.

After an initial fruitless struggle between two quietly spoken men trying to make ourselves heard I soon realised that I was no longer shouting and the farmer was reclining in his seat with his arms folded rather than straining forward to be heard. The dog, which was chained up out of my sight on Harrison's side of the vehicle, was now still and silent and we were able to conduct a sensible conversation.

The farmer pointed to the centre of the yard where the public footpath ran through the lagoon of cow slurry.

"So I says to 'er, you'm welcome to carry on but she didn't get far. We had to pull 'er out. Spec she wrote to you after that?"

I nodded.

"Well.." continued the farmer "..seems a daft thing to do if you ask me. I've had the Agency round."

"About the slurry?" I asked.

"Ah, says they wants a new pit. Summat about a water course, cause we can't 'ford that. Can't 'ford to divert thit path neither."

We chatted for a bit longer as was customary and the farmer then nodded towards Harrison in the passenger seat.

"Was goin' on with thit dog, reckon ee's put the fluence on un?"

Harrison turned to face us, breaking his gaze from looking out of the passenger window and the dog began its barking and bucket antics to make any further conversation impossible and I signalled to the farmer that I was off. He waved and reversed through the lagoon whilst I backed into a gateway to turn around before driving away.

"So what 'appens now?" asked Harrison.

"We're going to look at stuff and I've got a meeting later on."

"No, what 'appens to the footpath through all that cow shit?"

"It's a working farm. Nothing's going to happen."

"But isn't you supposed to sort it out?"

"Yes, but some things are not solvable. In time circumstances will change and Mr Maskew who has no sons will eventually give up and sell. There is little profit to be had for all the hours that go into running a small dairy herd. These are people that operate within a very small area for most of their lives. This was how it once was and they are a dying breed.

The footpath itself goes nowhere, it is a cul de sac path that stops altogether on the county boundary. It has become a point of principal and when people's rights come into it, it all gets a bit emotional. Footpaths are the charting of the routines of our ancestors and quite rightly they should be cherished but they must also serve the living and be of some use."

Damn, I was not going to even begin to explain about public rights of way to Harrison.

As promised we now spent a few hours looking at "stuff" which is my preferred term for the mass of unfinished business out there on the public rights of way network. There are plenty of loose ends; things that landowners should have done by now, things that we should have done by now and things that are never going to get done by anyone.

To knock one problem off the list, I had put some bridge decking boards in the back of my van last week but had not managed to get to site to repair a footbridge. I try to cluster my visits and inspections so that I am not darting willy nilly about my area and so today we were able to attend to it as my next visit was only a bit further down the road.

I parked at the end of the path and between us we carried a pot of four inch galvanised nails, a short wrench, a few decking boards and a hammer. The footpath was raised on a slight causeway and crossed a broad water meadow system. On an old footbridge a few planks had lost some of their width through the edges of the timber splitting and becoming detached. The sight of the river in spate flowing beneath your feet was probably a little unsettling for some walkers but there was no imminent danger of anyone falling through. Six decking boards needed replacing today and I made a mental note to renew the rest by the end of the summer but for now we would just patch it up.

With the wrench I levered up one of the planks and using the claw end of my hammer I prised out a nail that had stubbornly remained in the beam below. The cross beams looked in a reasonable condition but they only usually decay where they rest on the abutments at either end. I removed the neighbouring board to leave a larger hole in the middle of the bridge and was about to fit two boards at once when a jogger appeared behind us.

"I reported that before Christmas," said a lean man in his mid forties who began jogging on the spot at the end of the bridge and fiddling with his wristwatch, "I can step over the gap if you'll let me pass."

"We won't be long," I said.

"But I can squeeze by."

"Honestly, a couple of minutes, that's all."

"I'm going to step over, it's not a problem."

"It would be a problem if you fell through the hole, then you would be suing us quickly enough."

"Don't be a jobsworth, I'm coming through," he said.

Harrison moved to the side to let him by. Reluctantly I began to haul myself up and as he edged beside me he kicked the handle of the hammer as it lay on the bridge sending it spinning around to topple through the hole and plop into the river.

"Oops..." said the jogger, as he pranced across the gap, "..that was your fault, if you had let me through in the first place that wouldn't have happened."

Having left the bridge he then sprang away up the footpath and I swore at him under my breath but he obviously heard me as he raised two fingers behind his back.

"That was my only hammer," I said to Harrison, "god I hate the public sometimes."

"Does you really?"

"No, of course not, but they can be so bloody.. annoying."

"Isn't you a public servant?" said Harrison, "that's what it said in that magazine fing."

"Yes and thank you for reminding me," I said, "I've had that hammer for years."

Harrison walked along to the hole in the bridge and peered down at the full and silt clouded river below.

"We can't leave it open," I said, as I handed Harrison two new planks to place in the gap, "just in case our jogger friend comes back and falls through the hole. Now that really would cause a lot of extra paperwork."

We returned to the van to see what else I could use to hammer nails in with and luckily I unearthed a lump hammer that I had forgotten about and we were able to finish the job without further hindrance.

My final visit of the day was to a remote farm that had changed hands again and the new owners had requested a meeting about the public footpath. The yard and outbuildings were busy with contractors and I rang the door bell of the old farmhouse. A tall, slim lady talking on her mobile phone opened the door and ushered us into the kitchen.

"Yes, I will..look I'd love to but we are up to our eyeballs in it. Oh it's wonderful. I've got to go. Bye, yes bye. Ah hello Mr Wayland..

and?"

"Harrison," said Harrison.

"Yes..Harrison..would you like a cup of tea or coffee?"

"No thank you," I said.

"No fanks."

"Right, well, thank you so much for coming all the way out here. We could not believe our luck when this place came up. It is just what we have always dreamt about."

"That's nice," said Harrison

"Shall we get down to business then Mrs Knowles?" I asked.

"Yes, well, if I can't tempt you with a cuppa, let's go, my husband Peter is about somewhere."

I had visited the farm on a number of occasions and it has had at least three owners in my time. They were all farmers but the last had diversified with a small livery yard. The public footpath entered the property through the main gate then ran up the drive passing the front door of the farmhouse before angling away through a gap in the buildings where it intercepted the bridleway.

"You see Mr Wayland, sorry, calling you Mr Wayland sounds so formal?"

"It's my name."

"Yes, well, you see I am now a grandmother, goodness knows how that happened, but my daughter will be living in one of the outbuildings, you know after it has been made suitable. Well, we just do not think it is safe to have the public footpath running right through here, you know, when the child is playing, when there are strangers about."

The husband appeared and marched across the yard, breaking from his discussions with the contractors.

"Ah, Mr Wayland, thank you so much for coming all this way ..and?"

"Harrison," said Harrison.

"Peter Knowles."

I shook hands with Peter Knowles but Harrison did not respond when it came to his turn, keeping his hands firmly buried in his pockets.

"They didn't want tea darling."

"I see, well let me show you about, isn't it a fantastic place? We saw a red kite yesterday over there above the escarpment, fantastic."

"I have been here a number of times and I do know where the footpath runs," I said, to save a bit of time.

"Ok, well we're now grandparents, though goodness knows how that happened and our daughter.."

"Yes, Mrs Knowles explained."

"Oh, well what do you think?"

"About what?"

"About moving the footpath to somewhere more convenient and safer. I'm sure walkers don't want to find themselves snooping about when they come through here."

"They'll be walking, not snooping," I said, "what did you have in mind?"

"We thought that it could go in the field behind the house and with a few right angles your paths could all join up somewhere over there."

"Do you own the field behind the house?" I asked.

"No, it was sold off separately, but it has to be a better option."

"Better for who?"

"Well, for everyone."

"Not for the owner of the field for starters and if my memory serves me correctly it is always a very wet field, so not for the walkers either. Anyway it would require the consent of the owner before you could even consider an official diversion."

"Yes well that's the trouble Mr Wayland, it's Victor isn't it, can I call you Vic?" said Peter Knowles.

"Shall we stick with Mr Wayland?" I said.

"If you insist, it's just that the owner's likely to be a bit prickly about it all. We haven't exactly hit it off with the neighbours so we thought that you could ask them?"

"I see. There is already a perfectly serviceable and popular path through here that runs on firm dry ground. You were presumably aware of the status and location of the public footpath before you bought the property?"

"Yes, but.."

Mrs Knowles then offered her view.

"But this is the kind of place we have always dreamt of, to make our home for succeeding generations of our family and it just won't work with a footpath trampling through the middle of our lives. Oh Peter what shall we do?"

"Don't worry darling, I think Mr Wayland is being a bit inflexible, I've met his type before. Do you have any other suggestions Mr Wayland?"

"No," I said.

"Well we don't seem to be getting very far and I am a busy man. Can you see these gentlemen out darling? I am going to take this matter higher until I can find a reasonable person who demonstrates a bit of sense."

With this Peter Knowles marched back across the yard to resume discussions with the contractors.

"See you later," said Harrison.

The tall, slender and distinctly less friendly lady directed us vaguely towards the direction of the gate and after turning in her driveway we drove away in silence.

"You was not very helpful there," said Harrison eventually.

"Oh, I think I was but they did not like what I had to say."

"Why can't they move that footpath?"

"There's nowhere to move it to. I went over the same thing with the previous owners. It is not our problem if they chose to ignore the fact that there is a public footpath across the property when they bought the place, a well used and useful footpath incidentally."

"Why didn't you want a cup of tea from the lady, I fort you loved tea?"

I now had more explaining to do despite my initial resolution not to.

"Do you know what Mr and Mrs Knowles are?"

"Rich?"

"They may well be rich but they are property developers."

"What's wrong wiv that?"

"There's nothing wrong with it, if they are straightforward with me but I am not going to be bamboozled by all that "we're going to live here for ever" nonsense. It happened to me a long time ago and I was taken in by it. I once helped these people as much as I could, I liked them or I was charmed by them. What they were proposing was against the will of the parish council but they got their diversion in the end. It caused a great schism in the village. Of course once they got their diversion and the place was developed, they sold up. To remove a public right of way from running through the Knowles' yard would put thousands, perhaps tens of thousands on the value of the property. I am certainly not going to help them get richer, not at the expense of the public who use the path."

"He was cross wiv you, that Mr Knowles."

"Yes he was. What he does not yet realise is that at some point in the near future he will have no option but to march back across that yard and say something like; "Now Mr Wayland we got off a bit on the wrong foot last time..let's have a chat over a cup of tea." Well, I do not want their tea and I shall be equally bureaucratic next time and nobody ever calls me "Vic"."

The previously unremitting grey sky now relinquished a welcome pale wash of late afternoon sun. Harrison placed his minute earphones back in his ears and I was happy about that as I felt that I had done enough talking for the time being.

About three miles from town I paused at a cross roads and Harrison asked to get out.

"What here?"

"Yeah."

"But it's in the middle of nowhere."

"Fanks for today Mr Wayland."

Harrison grabbed the plastic carrier bag that had contained his lunch and leapt out slamming the door behind him.

"See you tomorrow?" I called out after he had gone.

I watched through the passenger window as he trotted away with short urgent paces along the verge of the main road and I wondered whether I would ever see him again. I reflected on the day as I drove back to the office and regretted swearing at the jogger in front of Harrison. Perhaps I have been doing the best job in the world for too long.

2
HYDE PARK CORNER

"AN INTERESTING DAY yesterday?" I said to Harrison after he breezed into the office and found a perch.

"Yeah."

"In at the deep end really."

"I guess."

I was rather surprised to see Harrison this morning but as he had turned up I thought that I would test him on his level of relevant knowledge, basic stuff really.

"Tell me about "the right to roam.""

"Is that somefink to do wiv the pope?"

"What? No, roam not Rome, you know, as in roaming about."

Harrison shrugged.

"How about the definitive map?"

Harrison remained inscrutable.

"So what course did you do at university?" I asked.

"I didn't."

"You didn't go to university?"

"No."

"But you told me that you did."

"I don't fink so exactly."

"Not a good basis for a trusting relationship?"

"I was blagging, it ain't lying. You can trust me Mr Wayland."

I was not entirely convinced by this distinction.

"Either way, I get the impression that you know nothing about public rights of way."

"No, but you does."

"I know I do. But what are you, Harrison whatever your surname is, going to bring to the table?"

"Give us a week," said Harrison.

Another silence ensued as I thought about the situation wondering why I should consider this at all. He had, however, presented himself on an entirely voluntary basis and nobody else in the authority knew about Harrison as it stood.

"Three days," I said, attempting to exert a bit of control on proceedings.

"A week."

"A week and you make the tea."

"I ain't gonna make no tea."

There was something about his uncompromising approach that made me remain silent and by this silence I knew that Harrison now considered that we had struck a deal.

On the outskirts of the town of Moldbury I had a long overdue visit to make to a caller who had concerns about an area of neglected woodland near a sports field that seemed to attract the local youth. There was a footpath through the middle of it, hence the call to me but at the outset I did not believe that his issues had anything to do with the right of way. Harrison joined me as I rang the doorbell of a bungalow at the very edge of a large council estate.

The male tenant kept us on the doorstep, pulling the door partially closed to keep his dog inside and it was only really the man's head that I could address. I showed him my identity card which he ignored and glowered instead at Harrison throughout our brief meeting.

"They set fire to a heap of plastic just over there. Little shits. They broke a load of branches off the trees. Little bastards. They pulled the planks off the side of the cricket pavilion in the playing field over there. Little shits. They dug a big hole and covered it with branches. Little bastards. They ride an old moped around the woods in the middle of the night. Little bastards..."

After a short time I lost the thread of the specific complaints and found myself trying to anticipate whether the next misdemeanour would be attributed to the "little bastards" or the "little shits" as if there were in fact two different gangs operating in the woods.

"They shine bright torches in your windows. Little bastards.

They set fire to the dog waste bin. Little shits."

After an unexpected end to this litany of antisocial behaviour the head around the door prompted my response.

"Well?" he asked.

"Little blighters?" I suggested, but there was obviously no place for a third gang that sounded like some rough boys from the Enid Blyton era.

"No, they're little bastards and little shits," insisted the man.

I pointed out that these were really police matters and not something that we in public rights of way had the powers to deal with.

After a final terse lipped scowl at Harrison the man's head disappeared and the front door closed.

"Anuvver satisfied customer Mr Wayland?" said Harrison as we returned to the van.

"Don't be sarcastic, he is obviously quite annoyed about it. The police will already be aware and I guess we were his last resort."

Before we embarked upon some physical work I needed to call upon a frisky horse that had been bothering the local dog walkers in a village eight miles or so from the town. There is not much I can do about one animal that doesn't like another animal as that was almost certainly going to be the root of the problem.

We parked in a narrow lane next to a house sign that read "the Old School House" and I tried not to block their access. The frisky horse was in the next field through which the public footpath ran and I had mapped out in my head a short circular walk that we could do to check up on some other issues whilst we were about it. I informed Harrison of our route just in case he thought that we were going to be wandering about aimlessly.

"From the Old School House we'll pass near the Old Mill House and the Old Blacksmith's Forge and return by the Old Orchard then it's left at the Old Drover's Inn before returning to the Old School House. Ok?"

Harrison shrugged.

We left the Old School House and crossed the field towards

the Old Mill House and the frisky horse could not have displayed less interest in us. Perhaps I should borrow a dog for such occasions as it was almost certainly the local dogs that caused the horse to react. At the Old Mill House the footpath had been diverted nearly twenty years ago to avoid the residence and we crossed the stream by a footbridge that had been erected to take the new route. I tested the bridge by stamping up and down on it and tugging at the parapets. We could hear from a distance but not see the powerful sloshing of the water as it dropped to pass beneath the old stone building. I have always enjoyed the earthy smell and the exhilarating tingle of the negative ions if you are able to stand directly above breaking river water. With the path redirected it was now just an alluring sound and I blame myself for this loss as I had agreed to the diversion all those years ago.

I kept this recurring frustration to myself and we set off along the footpath where it emerged onto a minor road next to the Old Blacksmith's Forge which was undergoing further expansions and renovations judging by the number of contractor's vans parked outside.

After fifty yards or so we turned down a narrow lane where I had received a report that the footpath signpost was missing at this junction and we searched for it in the hedge with no success. Continuing down the footpath we arrived at a property called the Old Orchard which was a large converted barn with a proliferation of glass and a renewed black clapperboard exterior. Part of the building also appeared to be some form of design studio. Two small yappy dogs emerged and in no time they were gazing up at Harrison in quiet expectation.

A door opened and a lady studied us with suspicion.

"Can I help you?" she asked.

"Well, perhaps," I said

The owner called her dogs but to no avail.

"Torvill..Dean... can I ask you what you're doing down here?"

"Walking the public footpath."

"There's no path down here. Torvill..Dean..come.."

"Oh really?" I replied, "that's strange. I would have thought that you would have known that this is a public right of way being that you live here?"

"No, it was done away with and there's no sign now."

"I was going to ask you about that," I introduced myself and walked across to show the owner my identity card, "do you often challenge people when they are walking the public right of way? If you do then that could be construed as intimidation which is an offence. Secondly, there was a sign at the end until fairly recently until it disappeared. Here's my card and I would appreciate a call if you witness anything suspicious or anyone tampering with the sign as that is also an offence."

"Dean ..Torvill...come here for chrissakes."

"I can send you a copy of a plan with the path on if that would help?" I said.

The lady left the barn to snatch up the recalcitrant dogs and carried them inside slamming the door behind her.

"What is it with you and dogs?" I asked Harrison, "anyway, let's hope that the footpath sign does not go missing again once I get around to replacing it."

We carried on along the footpath until we met with another road at the Old Drovers Inn which was boarded up with shiny metal sheets across every window and doorway. I had heard that the parish council had requested that the brewery replaced the metal sheets with wooden panels in case it jeopardised their future participation in the best kept village competition later in the spring.

Another five minute's walking and we were back at the Old School House where I had parked my van. I decided to call in at the garage on the main road as I fancied some peanuts. Harrison shook his head when I asked him if he wanted anything.

I took the small packet of peanuts up to the counter and the young man scanned them.

"How much?" I asked, squinting at the electric display on the till.

"Two thirty five."

"I'm sorry but I can't pay that for a small packet of peanuts."

"That is price."

I replaced the peanuts on the shelf and the young man watched me depart.

"No peanuts boss?" asked Harrison.

"Not at that price."

A man was walking towards the garage on a worn trail across a grass paddock from the direction of the village.

"Look Harrison, there's an example of a convenient new path forming out of modern necessity, or should I say desperation as there is no other shop in the village. It is not a public footpath yet but it could end up as one if it were claimed some time in the future. One day when this business closes down and gets turned into a house called the Old Garage, the new residents will be stuck with a footpath running up to it. Some things don't change."

"This is a weird ghost place," said Harrison as we left the village, "there ain't no ....soul."

To emphasize this statement Harrison beat his clenched right fist against his chest.

"That's your heart," I said.

"Same fing."

The difference was too subtle to call.

"You're right," I said, "let's go and do some digging."

We had a drive of twenty minutes or more in a westerly direction and I maintained my pledge of non explanation and silence which did not seem to bother Harrison. We took an interesting route along minor roads through small hamlets and villages and I resisted singing out loud to myself.

Our destination lay at the foot of a long chalk escarpment and we made our approach by a narrow lane flanked by stark hedges that offered little hope that spring was on its way. Rather than take the van on further, up the steep and unsurfaced incline to the downs, I parked in a small car park at the bottom.

Whilst still behind the wheel I handed Harrison the key to the back of the van and asked him to get out two spades and a couple of pairs of gloves. I wanted to establish whether he knew the difference between a spade and a shovel as that would tell me a lot about his practical knowledge and experience. If he got it wrong then there really was no future, not even to the end of the week, as his grasp of rights of way knowledge appeared negligible. At the very least, to be any kind of asset to me, he had to have some practical skills and experience. If he knew he was being tested he did not let on.

As I got out of the van he handed me back the keys. I walked around to the rear of the van where I was pleased to find two spades leaning up against the tailgate. He held the two pairs of gloves in his hand.

What lay ahead was actually a considerable amount of digging. All the way up this steep byway were narrow ditches cut through the deep verges where the gathering rain water could be discharged onto the lower slopes of the downs. If the fallen water was allowed to accumulate from the very top of the hill and gather in volume and momentum, then with one heavy storm the entire track surface could be washed out and become dangerous and impassable. This was valuable preventative work to ensure that the ditches could accept the water all the way down. Once in a while I got in a small excavator to re-establish the profile of the ditches but today it was down to manual labour.

Adjacent to each of these ditches and running at an angle across the track were raised humps of tarmac that acted as water deflectors. Without them the water would not be encouraged to one side of the track and away into the ditch.

Before I start any manual labour I like to undertake a few warm up exercises. It is taken for granted in any level of sport that you are supposed to throw a few shapes and go through the motions of preparation even if it is, at an amateur level, just a bit of a gesture. Certainly in my cricketing days we did it out in front of the pavilion to intimidate the opposition after firing down a couple of pints in the pub beforehand. Harrison looked on impassively and said nothing.

Having concluded my warm ups I now donned my gloves and rammed the spade into the mouth of the small ditch, loosening a heap of the accumulated silt. By demonstrating the correct ergonomics, I then shifted forward and raised the loaded spade to cast the dug material onto the verge on the lower side of the ditch. It was on the second push with the spade that I felt a slight niggle in the lower back. I left the spade on the ground and stood to rub the troubled area.

"Is you ok Mr Wayland?"

"Yes I'll be fine, just a little stiff."

"Shall I 'ave a go?"

"Well just for a bit, I'm sure it will ease off."

After my solitary demonstration of what was required, Harrison seemed to get the hang of it pretty swiftly and he is blessed with a lower centre of gravity which must help.

An hour later and we had worked our way half way up the hill clearing the small ditches as we went. Harrison had stripped down to a T shirt whilst I was operating purely in an encouraging capacity.

"Have a break," I said

He indicated that he needed a drink from the van and returned with a bottle of water and an apple. We surveyed the view across the flat lands below, chequered by vast square fields displaying the uniform pale green of an identical crop at an identical stage of its growing cycle. A large tractor pulling a spraying boom with the wingspan of a jumbo jet raced about these same fields. The released mist settled behind the machine and it really was the perfect day for spraying your crop with no wind to cause any drift of the chemical application. How different this view would have appeared before the ripping out of hedgerows and the amalgamation of small fields to accommodate modern agricultural efficiencies. I wondered what Harrison was thinking as we looked out upon the same scene but I am not so foolish to believe that everyone shares my same preoccupation with the past and of the ways things used to be.

Harrison crunched on his bright green apple that had been flown across the world as chilled freight and tossed the core over the fence onto the lower grass slopes below. He picked up the spade to resume digging and I thought I should really have another attempt myself so I carried on further up the slope with my spade to the next ditch and cautiously ran it along the base of the narrow cutting. As long as I took it gently, it was not too bad and Harrison, having finished the ditch below, now began on the next in the line, on up the hill. In this fashion we leapfrogged each other, so to speak, and after another forty minutes or so we were very near the top.

An old milestone was positioned just above the final ditch and I could see Harrison studying it and tracing the engraved wording upon its face with his finger.

I felt a sense of pent up relief as he called down to me.

"What's this?"

I had to be sure not to go overboard with my explanation. I wanted to tell him everything about milestones, turnpike roads, the old road network, travelling by stage coach but I stepped back from the brink and took a more measured approach.

"It's a milestone," I called out up the hill.

"What's it sayin'?"

"Well, this was once a major road, a long time ago."

"Oh."

He picked up his spade and began scraping away at the base of the ditch, lifting out the silt and banking it up on the verge.

The giant tractor that had earlier been careering around the fields below had moved on but another engine noise could now be heard. In time two vehicles ascended the track, one an old Range Rover and the other I did not recognise. Each had a passenger in the front and they were obviously out driving the byways. Beyond this long slope there was a ridgeway track that ranged for a good five miles and sections of it were in a very poor condition. I carried on with my slow digging but Harrison straightened his back and turned to watch as they passed. He put up a hand in response to the driver's acknowledgement.

"Is they allowed up 'ere?" he called down to me.

"As long as they're road legal, yes."

"Cool."

I could feel my resolve cracking and he had asked the question after all.

"It's a byway. A byway open to all traffic. As I said, it's an old road."

I walked the ten paces or so to stand beside the milestone to avoid the need to shout.

"Obviously there weren't motorised vehicles back when this milestone was erected but a road is a road and today's vehicles can still use it. It's a big issue and a lot of people think they should be banned because of the damage caused."

I pointed to the indistinct markings on the face of the old milestone.

"It says it's one hundred and three miles from Hyde Park Corner."

"No way?"

"It's one of the earlier routes emanating from London and Hyde Park Corner was where they measured it from."

"Sick."

"I should imagine most of the passengers were at some point on their journey," I patted the old upright stone, "there was a whole network of improvements carried out in the eighteenth century by individual acts of parliament. They were called turnpike roads and travellers were charged to use them to fund a better standard of travel. It was a boom time for roads, until the canals and then the railways came along. Interesting times."

Harrison nodded.

"I wanna go where those dudes were going," he said, pointing up the byway, "where is that?"

I thought that it was too good to be true that Harrison was actually interested in the origins of our road network. I was going to reply "Hyde Park Corner" but instead I briefly mentioned the ridgeway track with its problem sections before stating that we were now finished and we set off back down the hill.

We ate our lunch sitting in the van and he asked me whether I had some workers who normally did the digging and any physical labour.

"You think I'm past it then?" I said.

"No, well yeah, a bit. Your back don't seem so good."

I conceded that I would not have undertaken that task on my own anymore.

"I used to, I'll have you know. There is a work gang from a

local charity that come out and they're pretty good really with a good supervisor. I'd be up the creek without them but they're not available today. There is a heavy storm forecast for tonight and I knew this needed doing badly so thank you for your help."

Harrison shrugged.

"I'm glad you knew the difference between a spade and a shovel by the way."

"I don't."

"But you got out two spades?"

"I know, you said we was going to do some digging and you can't dig wiv those other big fings."

"Shovels?"

"Yeah, shovels."

On such slender threads doth our future hang. Don't try to find this quote by the way as I just made it up. Somebody must have said it at some point throughout history.

I am not certain but I think Harrison may have fallen asleep as I drove around to look at some stuff whilst out this way. Later on he asked whether I could drop him in town and as there seemed little point in his returning with me to the office for half an hour I duly obliged.

3

THE DIRECTOR'S CUT

THE PROBLEM THAT presented itself on this rainy Wednesday morning was what to do with Harrison when I needed to spend time in the office?

For a local authority that aspires to operate a paperless system I seemed to have accrued an inordinate amount of the stuff. I occasionally encounter slick and virtuous fellow local authority workers who can slip into any available space where they can plug in a laptop and that constitutes their office. I believe it is called hot desking. Their ascetic working life is unencumbered by the physical and they drift about inhabiting a parallel world to which I shall never gain admission. Goodness only knows what their job actually consists of and if a piece of paper should enter their orbit they shrink away from it like a vampire being offered a slice of garlic bread. They tend to avoid my office. There are still members of the public who write me letters and I eventually write letters in reply. There are also reactionary members of our own staff who send me nicely stapled paper reports. I would not be surprised if the hot desking tribe were planning to hunt these unrepentant sinners down and threaten to burn them at the stake upon a pyre of any remaining reams of A4. Anyway, I have paper in my office, lots and lots of paper.

I introduced a nonplussed Harrison to my overflowing filing tray and after explaining its relationship with the well stocked filing cabinet I left him to it. It was painful to watch. I could now get on with hammering my computer keyboard as if it were a 1950's typewriter whilst Harrison sought audio refuge with his ear pieces plugged in under his woollen hat. He may have refused to make me a cup of tea but he could not very well dodge what was essentially a work task but he would however take an eternity about it. Not on the face of it the most appealing aspect of the best job in the world I would have to agree.

When it came to leave the office Harrison expressed his relief by slamming shut the drawer of the filing cabinet. On our way out to the van I asked him what his name was.

"Harrison."

"No, your surname."

"Why does you want to know?"

"I just think I should."

With no information forthcoming I tried a different tack.

"Harrison's an interesting name."

"Is it?"

"Is it a family name?"

"No."

By this time I had lost the will to pursue the matter of Harrison's surname any further and we drove away in silence.

Before Christmas I arranged for a quantity of stone to be delivered to surface a muddy footpath and some weeks later it was now going to be laid on the path by the work gang. I had sensed a bit of trouble brewing and I wanted to talk to Michael the supervisor who had been on intermittent sick leave. The Gilbert Trust are an organisation that provide shelter for the homeless but they also operate two work gangs undertaking community based projects. The footpath gang are regulars and are generally not homeless but more the long time unemployed and the same faces have been appearing for the last few years. Today there were four "trainees" as they are called; Nigel, Council Peter, young Ollie and Knocker. Nigel was a huge somnambulist, immensely strong but on permanent heavy medication and would fall asleep on his feet gently rocking to and fro with his chin on his chest. Council Peter did not actually work for the council but always wore a faded yellow fluorescent jacket and if it was not a market day in the town he would be in. On market days he would collect the fruit boxes from the stalls and clear up the rubbish for which he was paid by the stall holders. He was probably in his late fifties and wore a stainless steel hook that was strapped onto his left elbow. The story was that he had been struck by lightning as he sheltered under a tree when he was a child. Ollie was a short round chap who probably could find himself a regular job but he could spend days sulking over the most trivial matter. He had an appalling diet of multipacks of crisps washed down with litres of diet coke and the very presence of Harrison was likely to send him into a sulking tailspin. And finally, the faithful Knocker who had been the longest serving member of the gang. Knocker had long grey hair and a long grey beard and wore a black gabardine coat belted tightly at the waist. He was the self appointed quartermaster and when the gang arrived on a job he would extricate the necessary tools from under the seats of the work van and woe betide anyone who tried to interfere.

"Hoi, ghedout, thas moi tankin' job."

Once the tools were in play he was very reluctant to handle them again until it was time to feed them back under the seats and move on. To Knocker his role in the organisation was clear cut.

"Thars yer tankin' tools, now tankin' well ghed on wid it."

To be fair to Knocker he had been unwell for some time now but recently with a bit more colour in his cheeks he did seem to be getting involved once the tools had been distributed.

Michael had been the supervisor for about two years now and we had built up a good working relationship. I parked the van on the verge and there did not appear to have been much activity so far this morning as the pile of stone had not diminished by very much. Michael strolled across to meet me.

"Michael, Harrison. Harrison, Michael."

They both nodded to each other and with the introductions over I gestured to Michael that we should move away from the group for a chat. Harrison wandered over to where the work gang were either sitting in wheelbarrows, standing up asleep or leaning on tools.

Michael had obviously been doing some work as he had taken off his coat and was wearing a pair of old work gloves.

"I find that I am doing it all, it's the only way to get the job finished. It's far easier just to get on with it rather than trying to chivvy along four immovable objects. Wrong I know but that's what it's come to."

It was a familiar tale. The supervisors generally lasted about two years and to be frank, Michael's time was up and I could see it in his eyes. There was obviously something else on his mind that he was yet to mention, a contributing factor that could tip him over the edge.

"Is it the clingfilm?" I asked circumspectly.

Michael shot me a look as though I had been spying on him or talking about him behind his back. I raised my hand to show that nothing untoward was going on.

"How did you know?" he asked.

"Just a guess."

He dropped his head and let out a long sigh.

Clingfilm had done for the previous couple of supervisors before Michael. It was the last straw. The final realisation that all was not well.

"Yes, it was the clingfilm," he admitted, "my wife caught me and she wondered what on earth I was up to. I knew then that I had come to the end of the line."

I should explain about the clingfilm before you get the wrong idea.

Lunchtime for the Gilbert Trust team always takes place in the van, even if it is the sunniest and warmest of days when they could all easily laze about on the grass. It has to be conducted in the van and despite all their willpower and resistance the supervisors end up in the van as well. The seating arrangements are always the same. Ollie rides in the front or he'll sulk and not appear at all. Nigel, the somnambulist, sits behind the driver emitting a strange whistling sound through his nostrils. Council Peter sits by the near side sliding door and Knocker is positioned centrally behind them at the back. Once the food has been consumed it is essential that the driver does not look in the driver's mirror. The view in the driver's mirror is of Knocker and his clingfilm folding ritual. Once he has extracted any rogue crumbs from his beard he shakes out the squares of clingfilm and flattens them one at a time across his bony knee. This involves smoothing out all the creases with numerous passings using the palm of his right hand. Once he is satisfied he then meticulously folds the clingfilm into tiny squares and stows these carefully in his aged lunchbox. There might be four or five squares of clingfilm to be preserved in this way and the whole ritual might take up to ten minutes to perform. I have witnessed it myself and your eyes are inexorably drawn to the driver's mirror even if you have a good book or a cricket report in the paper to read. It is going on behind you and you will end up watching. The same cling film is used over and over and over again. Any stretching qualities have long gone and it becomes gossamer thin, so much so that you are drawn to wonder whether it is all an illusion. What if his hands are in fact empty and there is no clingfilm? After weeks and months of this the final stage of the process is to find yourself smoothing and folding clingfilm and I could hear the relief in Michael's voice now that this was out in the open.

"Yeah, she said, what an earth are you doing that for and of course I couldn't explain. I just found that I physically could not make myself come to work. Pathetic isn't it?"

"I understand. Unfortunately I've heard it all before."

Our attention was then drawn towards the work gang after hearing an unfamiliar sound.

"What's that?" asked Michael.

"I think it's laughter."

"Crikey, what's going on?"

I shrugged but the next thing we noticed was movement and Knocker and Nigel had begun loading wheelbarrows with stone whilst Ollie and Harrison were shipping them down the path and tipping them with Council Peter raking the heaps level.

"What's got into them?" asked Michael.

"I'm not sure."

"Is Harrison a trainee?"

"I'm not sure what he is. He just turned up on Monday morning."

"Seems to have got them moving which is no mean feat."

I suggested that we left them to it and took a nice circular route that would eventually bring us back along the same path from the opposite direction. We talked about this and that and I thanked him for his contribution over the last two years.

"I love being out here," he said, "it's a fantastic county that I knew very little about..it's just..who will supervise the gang next after I leave?"

"Well I guess they'll have to advertise it and hope they find a suitable replacement. It obviously takes a while to get used to the job and find your way around and there's the working with the lads and the ..you know."

Michael took a deep breath of fresh air and said that he felt so much better after our chat. We had now returned to the far end of the path that was being surfaced and halfway along Council Peter was guiding the handle of the rake back and forth through his steel hook as though it were a pool rest.

"Not nuff stone," he observed gruffly.

I said that he was probably right and I would order some more and they would have to return on another day to finish it and I apologised for getting the volume wrong.

"Nuffink like," he grumbled.

Ollie came towards us with a laden barrow and we backed against the fence to let him pass.

"You didn't order enough stone," he puffed.

"No, I'm sorry," I said.

By the time we got back to the dwindling stone heap Harrison was just moving off with another barrow load whilst Knocker was leaning on his shovel to greet us.

"Not enuff tankin' stone," he said.

"More stone," agreed Nigel.

I had now been thoroughly chastised for messing up on the original order.

"I'll order some more," I said.

"Soon be lunchtime," said Michael.

"Ahh, when we're tankin' done and not afore," said Knocker.

"I'll leave you to it," I said, once Harrison had returned with an empty barrow, "I have to get on. See you next week."

"Yes, one more week and that's it," said Michael, "thanks Harrison."

Harrison raised a hand as he wandered away.

As I unlocked the van I looked back towards the path and Ollie had stopped in his tracks with the wheelbarrow upended and Council Peter had cast aside the rake. Nigel's head now rested upon his chest to signify that he had fallen asleep whilst Knocker was making his way towards the work van. I could see Michael looking around and scratching his head at this sudden halt in proceedings. It appeared as though things had returned to normal.

"Where to now boss?" asked Harrison as he got in the van.

We undertook a couple of minor tasks but by mid afternoon I announced that I had an appointment in town. I explained to Harrison that there was utterly no point in his coming to meet the new director of my department but he shrugged to suggest that he would tag along anyway. The director was doing the rounds to meet the staff and ignoring all sensible advice to stay put in castle County Hall and pull up the drawbridge. We stopped at the edge of town avoiding the need to buy a ticket to park and walked the rest of the way. Most of the traffic wardens would be at the meeting but you couldn't bank on it and they liked nothing better than to stick tickets on a county vehicle if the opportunity arose. The venue for this ill advised occasion was the town hall and I was keen to find a seat right at the back. There are so many services now under one managerial umbrella that I had met very few of the rest of the audience of perhaps one hundred and fifty people.

The new director's name is Lucian Poole and he was raring to go.

He raised a hand to signal that we should quickly settle and be quiet. He then introduced himself. So far so good.

"Ok, any cricketers here?"

I certainly did not respond and nobody else seemed keen to draw attention to themselves.

"Surely..come on?"

A few tentative hands were raised.

"OK, it has often been said that the three most important aspects of batting are..?"

Silence.

"Well, I'll help you on this one, it's footwork, footwork and footwork. You've got to get your feet right and the rest will follow..."

For the cricket purist he then demonstrated a shot on the off side, just forward of point, and paused to admire an imaginary ball crossing an imaginary boundary rope. I instinctively felt sorry for the imaginary bowler.

"Stay with me here, following this thread, let's talk about the new corporate focus. Yes it's the three P's and now its over to you, so you tell me, what are the three P's?"

An audible shuffle could be heard of people trying to sink further into their chairs.

"P.P.P.P," continued the director, "Peter piper picked a peck of pickled pepper. P?"

By concentrating on one or two unfortunate individuals who had been forced to sit at the front by virtue of arriving late the director managed to coax out some mumbled suggestions.

"Polite?"

"I hope we are always polite but no that's not what I had in mind."

"Partnership?"

"That's another good one, any more?"

By applying a combination of wide eyed staring and an unrelenting maniacal smile some more reluctant voices could just be discerned.

"Practical?"

"Hmmm, yes."

"Perspiration?"

"I should keep your arm down if I were you, no."

"Perfection?"

"That would be nice.."

"Politics?"

"Ahhh. Horrid word, get thee behind me.."

After many more erroneous attempts to find the elusive P the director's grin now deserted him as he scanned the averted gaze of a silent workforce.

"Am I to believe..," his staccato whisper barely audible, "that not one of you ..are aware.. of our new ..corporate.. focus?"

I was startled by a movement at my side as Harrison suddenly rose from his chair.

"THE PEOPLE," Harrison shouted out loudly, as a statement of intent rather than a tentative suggestion.

The director spun around and buckled at the knees.

"YES. PEOPLE," he cried, punching the air, "People, people, people, the three P's."

The director ran across the open floor and then dodged between the seated workforce to give Harrison a celebratory high five.

"Well done that man. What's your name son and what do you do?"

"Harrison. Rights of way."

"Well go to the top of the class Harrison. People, people and people. I am a people person. Harrison here is obviously a people person. Ask yourselves now, are you a people person too?"

This was exhausting and I decided that I would have to give Harrison a sharp dig in the ribs if he tried any more stunts like that again.

"People," continued the director, "the public that we serve, yourselves the work force and we the management. All people. People, people, people. It's a funny word if you say it often enough. People, come on let's say it together..."

The director pursed his lips and conducted the workforce in joining him to experience the word for ourselves.

"One, two three..People. Louder and at the back. People. People, that's it you've got it, people, people people. Phew, we got there in the end. It's all about people."

Once we had eventually got the people issue out of the way the director concentrated on how our jobs could be made easier.

"If you have a problem then inform your line manager, there's no point in keeping things bottled up if you know how improvements could be made. Nothing is set in stone."

Having loosened their vocal chords the workforce now seemed

prepared to exercise them further.

"I've got a problem," said the lady with the earlier "Perfect" suggestion.

"Ok, well have you informed your line manager?"

"The problem is my line manager."

"I see, perhaps you had better talk to me afterwards."

"I've got a problem," said the "Practical" man.

"I'm not sure how we can get on if you all start listing your individual problems. Have you informed your line manager?"

"Yes."

"And?"

"He's had a nervous breakdown."

"I see," the director looked about for a suitable distraction, "now take Harrison over there. He strikes me as a positive sort of chap. There's a good word beginning with P that you all missed earlier. Positive. What does it say to you?"

"I've got a problem..." said a hitherto unheard voice.

"Yes, we've now moved on to the positives," interrupted the director.

"..I empty all the dog waste bins. I didn't join the council to empty dog waste bins but I got shoved across. I've told my line manager and he said that I have got to empty the dog waste bins."

"Ok, someone's got to do it."

"Well, I don't want to. Would you? What if someone told you that you're not going to be the director anymore and you've got to empty the dog waste bins instead."

"Well that's not going to happen.."

"Why?"

"Well..it just isn't."

The director's earlier gusto had now deserted him and he was looking decidedly exasperated.

"Let's move away from dog waste shall we..."

"I'd like to but I'm stuck with it, day in and day out."

"Positives.." began the director.

"There's nothing positive about dog waste."

"WILL YOU SHUT UP ABOUT FUCKING DOG SHIT.. OR..OR..GO AND WORK FOR SOMEBODY ELSE. JESUS CHRIST."

After this unretractable outburst the director clamped both hands to the stable door of his horror stricken mouth and remained stock still in the centre of the room. Quick to seize the opportunity and with barely a backward glance the workforce made a hasty exit from the building and once outside dispersed in all directions.

"That went well," I said to Harrison out in the street, "he probably won't be leaving County Hall again in a hurry."

On our way back to the van, I asked Harrison what he meant by his earlier intervention.

"The guy needed help."

I had to agree with this assessment of the situation.

"The trouble is though he's going to come away with only one name in his head and that's your name and you don't even work for the authority."

"It's all about the people," Harrison reminded me.

"Don't start that again."

Once we got to the van I unlocked the door whilst Harrison kept walking.

"See you later," he said.

I stooped down to check the time on the clock on the dashboard and decided that I would probably now just call it a day and head for home.

When I looked up Harrison had already turned the corner and was gone.

4
NICE BOOTS

On the Thursday morning I was late arriving to work. It had stopped raining briefly but still threatened which probably ruled out a tidy up in the yard so I was still faced with the problem of what to do with Harrison for an hour or so. I entered my office and Harrison had already arrived but to my surprise he was not alone. A girl of similar age was leaning against the far wall.

"Hi," said Harrison.

"Hi," said the girl.

"Good morning?" I said, intending this to be more of a question than a greeting.

No explanation was forthcoming and I took off my coat and hat and sat down at my desk to log on to my computer as if everything was normal.

I had been playing the waiting game all week with Harrison and so I decided that I would let him make the first move as to explaining why there was a girl in my office. I even found myself whistling which I never do and I was struggling to think what I could actually whistle. The chap from the other end of the building popped his head around the door to tell me that there was going to be a fire drill in fifteen minutes when we all had to go and muster by the main gate. I thanked him and he paused briefly to scan the office whilst I carried on whistling as if it were perfectly normal to have two young people hanging around.

"This is Dolores," said Harrison finally.

"Oh, I had forgotten that you were both there. Hello Dolores."

"Hello," said Dolores and she gave me a little wave across the office.

I found myself waving back. What was I doing?

"Dolores said she would..you know, do that fing," said Harrison nodding towards the filing cabinet.

"What, filing?" I said.

"Yeah," said Harrison.

"Yes," said Dolores.

"Really?"

The chap from the other end of the building popped his head back around the door to inform me that the fire drill had now been cancelled and I thanked him again.

Harrison then explained to Dolores what he had been doing yesterday morning and Dolores made a start. Harrison now leant back in his chair, inserted his earphones under his woollen hat and closed his eyes.

I asked Dolores whether she particularly liked filing and she shrugged.

"It's all right."

She was certainly a lot quicker at it than Harrison but after a couple of minutes we were interrupted by the fire bell.

"We'd better go outside," I said.

Dolores stopped what she was doing and followed me out. We got as far as the front door until we realised that Harrison was not behind us and must have remained oblivious plugged in to his music with his eyes closed.

"Oh, leave him, we'll be back in a minute, it's only a fire drill," I said.

The office manager was feeling pleased with himself that we had all been fooled by the cancellation and as we mustered by the front gate the heavens opened and we all ran back inside.

"Oi," he shouted after us, "I haven't done a roll call yet."

Back in the office we were now dripping wet and I tried to brush off the rain from my clothes and hair. Dolores did the same and she flicked her fingers at Harrison who flinched and opened his eyes. He looked from one to the other of us in frowned puzzlement.

"Tell him he's now in hell after being burned alive in the office," I suggested. I then asked Dolores whether she was very wet.

"I'm ok but it's dripping on your paperwork," she said.

"Sorry about that, well never mind about the paper work. Just leave it. I don't want you catching a cold," I said, summoning up some hitherto untested parental concern.

"Would you like a cup of tea?" I asked

"Yes please."

Harrison pulled out his earplugs.

"What's going on? Why is you both wet?"

"You're dead," replied Dolores.

Ten minutes after the ridiculous fire drill a figure appeared at the window wearing a bobble hat and a man bobbed up and down trying to peer beyond his reflection to see whether there was anyone inside. Having satisfied himself that there was, he now gestured to be let in. I recognised him as Mr Watt who did not belong to any organised walking association but was more of a maverick operator who prowled the public rights of way network and then sent me heaps of reported problems and issues. I was able to deal with some of them but others were just an annoyance to him or where he had had an argument with a landowner or householder.

Having been escorted through the labyrinth to my office he now launched into his latest bête noire.

"East Chase golf course. You know it?"

"Well, I know the path that crosses it," I said.

"Exactly, well I was out that way a few days ago and I nearly got hit by a golf ball."

"Oh?"

"Well I was crossing, you know, what do you call it, the long bit between where you hit the stupid ball and where you try to get it in the stupid hole."

"The fairway?"

"I suppose so. I noticed that my boot lace had come undone and I stopped to tie it up."

"On the fairway?"

"If that's what it's called. Well, there was this idiot waving his arms at me to move and so I thought blow you I'm going to take as long as I like tying up my laces. I retied the other one as well whilst I was about it just to be sure. I was on the public footpath for goodness sakes which has been there a damn sight longer than the wretched golfing thingy. Anyway the next I knew this bloody golf ball whistled past my head so I waited for this idiot to come down and gave him a piece of my mind. I was jolly cross."

"Do you not think that it would have been better to cross the fairway and then do up your laces?"

"It's a public footpath. He should have waited for me. Bloody silly game, a good walk spoiled and he bloody well spoiled mine as well. I've a good mind to go up there and walk backwards and forwards on the path all day. That'll show 'em."

"Hickman V Maisey," I said, leaning back in my chair.

"Pardon?"

"Hickman V Maisey 1900. It's old case law. A journalist was walking up and down on the same fifteen yards of footpath eyeing up the form of the race horses whilst they were training on the gallops. The Court of Appeal ruled that he had exceeded his right on the footpath and he was trespassing."

"Well I've never heard such rot. I don't believe a word of it."

"It's true, I've got it here somewhere," I said, reaching for the rights of way bible.

"Don't bother. If I want to walk up and down on a bloody footpath I bloody well will. I suppose you're a bloody golfer to, you're a bunch of local authority wasters and I'm paying for you all," said Mr.Watt.

"You ain't paying for me," said Harrison, who had unplugged his earphones to listen to our conversation.

"Or me," said Dolores.

"I'm clearly wasting my bloody time here," said Mr Watt, as he bobbed back out of the office and opened the door to the boiler room in his attempt to leave the building.

"Bloody hell."

Eventually Mr Watt passed my window again on his way out of the yard, scowling at his bobbing reflection

I decided to give the golf club a quick call to see whether they knew anything about the incident.

"Well come on over tomorrow if you like," said the club secretary, "you can have a coffee and we can take a look to make sure all's above board. I've not heard a dicky bird."

I made a note in my diary to a call by mid morning as I would be out that way.

Half an hour or so later I had to go out and I explained to Harrison and Dolores that there was simply not enough room in the van for three people.

"That's ok," said Dolores and she informed me that she only lived down the road and would be happy to finish the remainder of the filing another time.

I told her that I was really grateful and thanked her as I showed her to the front door so that she could avoid the boiler room.

"You certainly do it quicker than Harrison," I said.

"Well, he can't read can he? Bye," said Dolores.

I was stunned by this news and the fact that I had made an illiterate person do my filing for me. No wonder he was reluctant and that was why he had delegated the task to a friend of his.

"Nice girl," I said to Harrison as I returned to my office.

Harrison nodded.

There followed an awkward silence but he probably didn't notice.

Out on my rounds there was stuff that I had to sort out and look at and I found myself apologising to Harrison as it must have been a rather boring three or so hours. He did not seem bothered and I explained that we had one final call to make.

On a farm not too far away I had been having trouble getting any response from the owners as they did not appear to pay much heed to the public rights of way across their land or their legal responsibilities. After a number of grumbles from locals and also from the parish council it was about time that I paid a visit and sorted them out. I explained to Harrison that from past experience they weren't the easiest people to deal with and here was one of those situations where it is important to exert a bit of control at the outset.

I had not made an appointment but most farmers return home for lunch between one and two 'o clock so I expected to find them in. We pulled into the farmyard and we were greeted by a variety of dogs barking and chasing around the van and I did my best not to run any over.

"I don't think they bite," I said to Harrison, "you can stay put if you want."

"These dogs is ok."

A bold and somewhat risky statement I thought but strangely the four dogs all gathered by the passenger door as Harrison made a fuss of them. Whilst he diverted their attention I nipped across to the front door, which stood open and reached inside to rap upon the old stiff knocker three or four times as loudly as I could. After a while a young girl wandered past me and crossed the yard to an outhouse. She returned shortly afterwards with a guinea pig in her hand and disappeared back inside the house. I knocked again. Harrison was still engaged with the four dogs which had all stopped barking by this time. Another girl, a little older, now wandered out and informed me that she had a lamb called Milky.

"That's nice," I said.

"Yes, do you want to see her? Come on."

With that she pulled at my trouser leg and as I put my hand down to extricate myself from her grip she swiftly grabbed my little finger and tugged me across the yard.

"Where is you going Mr Wayland?" asked Harrison.

"Um, I'm going to meet a lamb called Milky, apparently."

After we had stared at an orphan lamb for a minute the girl released her grip and I crossed back over the yard just as Mr Burdop emerged from the house and he stopped to give me a quizzical stare.

"I knows you," he said, scratching his unruly sandy hair. He then lifted up his hand to prevent me from telling him who I was.

Mrs Burdop soon followed from the house and looked at me and then back at her husband.

"What..?" she began, interrupting this sudden impasse.

"I knows 'im."

"It's the footpath man," shouted Mrs Burdop to her husband.

"I knows 'im, it'll come."

"Oh Christ, we could be here all afternoon at this rate. He's deaf and daft. What do you want?" said Mrs Burdop.

"I want to talk to you about your public rights of way," I said.

A female voice called out from the house.

"Mum, where are the girls, we've got to go?"

"I don't know," Mrs Burdop called back.

"One of them is in there with the lambs," I said.

"Look you'll have to talk to my husband about the rights of way until I get back, I'm only going down the road. Talk to his right ear and he might hear you," said Mrs Burdop.

The girl's mother emerged and the girls were found and herded into a car and they drove out of the yard. I was left alone with Mr Burdop whilst Harrison remained in the passenger seat of my van fussing over the dogs.

"Wayward," said the farmer eventually.

"Wayland," I replied.

"Thas right, Wayward. Footpaths?"

I positioned myself on Mr Burdop's right hand side and spoke loudly.

"Can I talk to you about your footpaths?"

"Oh ah," he pointed to his right ear, "this one's best. Speak up."

I slowly began to discuss the various issues whilst the farmer stood with his head bowed and his ear cocked towards me. He nodded periodically to give me sufficient encouragement to continue until I had recalled all the issues that needed addressing. It amounted to three collapsed stiles, a temporary electric fence across a bridleway, an unofficial diversion and a quagmire on a footpath caused by their farm machinery. Once I had finished he raised his head to look me in the eye.

"Nice boots," he said and looked down again, "them's nice boots."

After pointing his finger across the yard at an outbuilding he wandered off towards it and disappeared.

"How's it goin'?" Harrison called out from the front of the van, "all under control?"

I had half a mind just to leave now but it was not a good example to set.

"I'm going to wait for Mrs Burdop to come back," I said.

In the time that it had taken Mrs Burdop to drop off her daughter and grandchildren she had managed to work up a head of steam and her car screeched back into the yard.

"Right, lets go and have a look at these bloody footpaths. John?" Mrs Burdop called out after her husband, "oh it's useless, where is he?"

I pointed to the shed across the yard.

After it had been established that the only vehicle that could accommodate the four of us and the dogs was their primitive long wheeled base landrover, we finally climbed aboard and left the yard.

I knew from past experience that they owned odd bits of land all over the place but the area that concerned me was around the village of Samsonbury.

The ancient vehicle ground to a halt in a gateway and disgorged its load of passengers and dogs.

"Show me," said Mrs Burdop, "show me the problem and I'll show you people walking all over the place and nowhere near the footpath."

Normally I would check problems before confronting landowners as I had been caught out before. On this occasion I had received information from a number of largely untested sources. There are some people who I could trust implicitly in this regard and I would act unreservedly on their provided information. I tried to mentally scan through the origins of the complaints. One had come from the parish council clerk and I know that the parish council had fallen out with the Burdops regarding a number of planning issues and so any antipathy perhaps had its origins elsewhere. Another complaint also included an accusation that the Burdop's farm machinery had destroyed their nicely mown verges. A further complaint was anonymous so that could have come from anyone with an axe to grind.

All I could do now was look at the evidence on the ground. An old but still reasonable stile was placed next to the gate but the field gate was unlocked anyway. We proceeded into the next field through an open gate way. The dogs dispersed in all directions whilst we were encouraged to follow Mrs Burdop.

"Come on."

Mr Burdop was getting left behind at this pace and Harrison dropped back to stay with him.

"There you are Mr Wayland. There's your footpath straight ahead and look, there, there and over there are people walking not on the public right of way and with their dogs not on leads. Cooey."

Mrs Burdop waved across at one lady walking her dog.

"Cooey, you're not on the footpath. Do you know that you're not on the footpath. This is Mr Wayland from the Council and he's going to tell you that you are not on the footpath."

The lady dog walker began to increase her speed and avoided looking in our direction.

Mrs Burdop targeted another miscreant who was also not on the footpath and was therefore trespassing on her land.

"Get your dogs under control. Wait I'm coming to talk to you with Mr Wayland from the council. Stop where you are."

"Mrs Burdop.." I said."..I don't particularly want to police your field for you..it's not my.."

"Keep up Mr Wayland. Stop, we're coming over to talk to you."

A lady stopped and called her two dogs, placing them on leads.

"Is there a problem?" she asked.

"Yes, there is a problem," said Mrs Burdop, "you are not walking on the footpath."

"I always walk this way."

"Tell her Mr Wayland."

"Well, actually the legal line of the public right of way is across there from gate to gate," I said, indicating a straight line through the grass field.

"There's no markings," said the dog walker.

"Well Mr Wayland is from the council and is in charge of the footpaths. He is going to put some up and then you must stick to the footpath."

"Nobody else is. They're all over the field."

"Exactly," said Mrs Burdop.

"Why pick on me. I've just come out for a bit of fresh air and.. actually I've had a really bad day and this is the last thing I need." Her eyes welled up whilst her two dogs looked about in confusion at this break in routine.

"Well I can't help that, you are trespassing and breaking the law," said Mrs Burdop.

"Actually she is not breaking the law..." I began.

"Come on Mr Wayland there are more over here."

I paused to confirm to the dogwalker that she was not breaking the law.

"It's technically a civil trespass, not a criminal offence..don't worry."

"Mr Wayland," bellowed Mrs Burdop.

"Thanks," said the dogwalker wiping her eyes with a handkerchief.

At that moment my mobile phone rang.

I held up my phone to Mrs Burdop to show that I needed to answer it.

"Hello," I said breathlessly, "Victor Wayland."

"Hi, it's Harrison."

I looked back down the field to the bottom of the slope where I could see the figures of Mr Burdop standing still and Harrison wandering about a few paces away.

"Oh, how did you get my number?"

"Just did, in case it come in handy. Yeah, I thought you might like an excuse to stop chasing the public about the field."

"I see."

"Yeah, it's some kind of emergency. You can sort out the details."

"Yes, yes, I see. I'd better get there right away. Thank you. Goodbye."

"Trouble?" enquired Mrs Burdop.

"Yes, I've got an urgent problem to attend to...my contractor

..has ..um..cut through an electricity cable."

"Oh that is serious. Is he dead?"

"He didn't say..I mean ..I don't think so."

"Well let me get you back to your vehicle. This will have to wait for another day."

"I'm afraid it will. I'm sorry."

We all hastily retraced our steps and clambered back into the landrover and Mrs Burdop drove back to the farm yard as fast as the old machine would permit.

"Thank you," I called out as I got into my van, "I'll give you a call."

Mr Burdop walked around and held open the passenger door and winked at Harrison as he got in.

"Good lad," he said.

5
A PERFECT NOUGHT

AS TEMPTING AS it was, I resisted parking in the club chairman of East Chase golf club's reserved space and we retreated to an area near the green keeper's sheds. I have always thought that there was something other worldly about golf. There is almost certainly a green planet in another solar system where golf is all that exists across a globally tamed landscape. The inhabitants of planet golf are single minded and play one long round from the time that they take their first steps to when they finally topple into a sandy bunker and are raked over. This lifetime struggle against one's own inconsistency would hopefully be recorded in single figures on the great score card or, if they achieved the ultimate objective, a perfect nought.

If Harrison felt uncomfortable entering this Jaguar and Pringle jumper environment he did not show it. We announced ourselves at reception and shortly afterwards the club secretary strode out of his office.

"Mr Wayland..and?"

"Harrison," said Harrison.

"Please, come and sit down in the lounge."

We were guided to a table on one side of the open and spacious lounge where a surprising number of people seemed to be relaxing after golf or contemplating playing golf or just enjoying sitting amongst golf.

"Not taken it up yet then?"

"No man," said Harrison.

"I have a few other pursuits," I replied, suspecting that the club secretary had addressed his question towards me rather than Harrison, "it hasn't grabbed me yet."

"If it does, it'll never let go. I don't get out as much as I'd like. Haven't been out this year, oh I tell a lie, New Year's Day, hoping to get rid of the old Christmas tum," he said, patting his Pringle jumper. "Coffee. Tea?"

"No fanks," said Harrison.

I had already drunk three cups of tea this morning and must have appeared indecisive enough about accepting another for a decision to be made for me.

"Ok we'll go straight out," said the club secretary, "I'll grab my coat, bit of fresh air."

"'As you a toilet?" asked Harrison.

The club secretary instinctively leapt up and made a signpost of his long arm to direct Harrison to the far side of the room. I watched as the seated members followed Harrison's progress across the thickly carpeted lounge.

I was quite enjoying not explaining Harrison's presence and the secretary was sufficiently tactful not to ask; "..and who is that exactly?"

"So how's the world of rights of way?" he asked instead.

"Resources spread ever thinner," I replied. I was going to elaborate but the secretary stood up to excuse himself.

"I'm just going to pop to the office. Won't be a jif."

A couple of minutes later and the secretary was somewhat surprised to find me still sitting on my own.

"Oh. ..is?"

I nodded.

The club secretary drummed his fingers on the back of a chair. When Harrison did finally reappear the seated members in the lounge stopped stirring their coffee to stare until he arrived back at our table.

"Good," said the secretary.

I braced myself and waited for Harrison to respond as if he had been asked a question but he remained inscrutable and the secretary hastily burst into life again after consulting his watch.

"I don't know what you want to look at but let's go in the buggy."

I suggested that we checked the waymarking on the footpath to ensure that folk knew where they should be walking and then a quick visit to the tee to check that the warning notice to the golfers was still in place.

"The seventh," confirmed the secretary, "it's a par five."

"Wicked," said Harrison.

With the appearance of the sun this morning it was the best day of the week so far and the course seemed fairly busy. From the elevated position of the clubhouse distant figures could be observed across the full extent of the course. More golfers were about to begin whilst others were concluding their round, pulling their wheeled golf trolleys behind them.

I have only ever played a few rounds of pitch and putt whilst on holiday but it has always struck me as a game with frustration at its core rather than pleasure but I could be wrong, I often am. Seated in the golf buggy we trundled along a few pathways, cold under the shade of the trees but once out in the sun there was a steamy mist rising from the manicured grass.

On the way the secretary continued with his automated recruitment campaign.

"Yes golf has changed a lot. I mean it's no longer the preserve of the fusty old brigadier. There's allsorts of tradesman playing today, you know self employed chaps, plumbers, electricians there's a sign writer and of course a number of builders. Pretty good some of them. Also a lot of youngsters too, and between you and me I think they are probably some of our best players, so.." the secretary gestured with some uncertainty towards Harrison, "yes, some of them are scratch," he continued.

"Scratching's cool," said Harrison.

"Quite," said the club secretary.

Where the public footpath crossed the fairway of the seventh hole the yellow waymark arrows were prominent enough. There was also a sign that said "Walkers beware of flying golf balls" that we had agreed some three years ago to make the path users aware of the potential danger. We then drove up to the tee of the seventh hole where a group of three male golfers were preparing to tee off. We sat in silence behind them as they in turn placed their balls before positioning themselves in preparation to take an almighty swish with the club.

The first scuffed his ball low along the ground but moderately straight whilst the second hooked it into the tree line where we had just driven up. The third demonstrated a little more poise but then missed the ball altogether making the club secretary visibly wince beside me. The golfer made a few loosening movements to suggest that it had been intended as a practice effort before skewing the ball high, wide and handsome over to the right. The three golfers scuttled away, diverging in pursuit of their balls whilst they took it in turn to glower behind them as if we were somehow to blame.

"There we are," said the club secretary, as we wandered out onto the recently vacated tee, "there's your notice warning the golfers of the presence of the public footpath, requesting that they make sure that the coast is clear before they tee off. Everything seems to be in order."

I looked a bit closer at the rigid plastic sign on its short post.

"Are you sure this is the correct sign?" I asked.

The secretary crouched down and squinted at it.

""Ten quid to anyone who can hit that self righteous twat wearing the bobble hat". No, that's not right at all. How on earth..?"

He tried to pluck the sign out of the ground but found it too well secured and fumbled instead in his pockets to find his mobile phone so that he could harangue the green keeper.

"Someone's been playing silly buggers up here on the seventh tee. Get up here now and bring some tools."

After shaking his head at what the world was coming to, the club secretary apologised.

"How embarrassing Mr Wayland, I simply can't account for it."

We now returned to the golf buggy and travelled in silence back to the club house.

I thanked the club secretary for taking the time to meet us and he was still shaking his head.

"I can assure you that I will get to the bottom of this and somebody will be for the high jump. Goodbye Mr Wayland ..and?"

"Harrison," said Harrison.

"Yes, er.. goodbye."

As we returned to the van I told Harrison that I did not think that it would take Sherlock Holmes to resolve the mystery of the exchanged sign and I think he caught my drift. It is hard to tell sometimes.

Our next job was to clear a tree from a byway which involved a drive of some seven miles which gave me an opportunity to quiz Harrison on what he meant by "scratching" and I think I understand now. Not something I would be keen to attempt with any of my old records and would it even work with Jake Thackray? " Vicar, come and give a wash and brush up to me soul...me soul..me soul, soul, soul.""

We drove up the side of a steep escarpment on a minor road and turned off onto the byway at the top of the hill. I kept a slow speed to avoid the many water filled pot holes on what was essentially a level track albeit on top of a hill. I have always considered that I should set a good example and not tear around in a council vehicle, not that it looks conspicuously council with only small signs on the doors. Ahead a tractor was parked sideways across the byway and the driver got out raising his hand in a signal for me to stop. I had no choice as he had effectively blocked the route and I wound down my window to speak to him.

"Hare coursers," said the man, "I've blocked 'em in. There's a car down there. We're sick of 'em and somebody's got to do something about it. I'm the gamekeeper and I saw three or four dogs around me pheasant pens. I knew they were about so I came up to block the track. They break down fences, trash the fields, they don't give a toss. Big money changes hands."

The gamekeeper lifted his hand up to the open window and rubbed a thumb and forefinger together to emphasize his statement.

"And I mean big money. I was going to turn the car over with me forks but the police are on their way. I thought you was them."

"We'll wait here then," I said.

"Thanks," said the gamekeeper, looking anxiously up the byway as he wandered back to his tractor.

I tried to peer beyond the tractor and I could just about see a vehicle parked on the verge. I am not sure whether Harrison knew anything about hare coursing but he did not ask so I kept quiet.

We could hear distant sirens down in the valley and before long there were blue flashing lights bouncing up and down on the byway and the sirens had now been turned off as the two police cars raced towards us.

"They're not bothered about the potholes then," I said to Harrison.

The vehicles flew past us and slid to a halt on the loose stone surface just in front of the tractor. A surprisingly agile policeman leapt out of one of the vehicles and the gamekeeper began pointing further down the track.

As they talked I thought I could see some movement beyond the tractor with two people walking up towards the parked car a hundred or so yards away.

"They don't look like hare coursers to me," I mused, "one of them has a walking stick and it looks like two elderly ladies with hats and scarves on and a few dogs."

Another police car appeared behind us travelling at a more sedate pace than his colleagues and as he pulled up level with the van I recognised him as the local policeman. He got out and walked around to talk to me.

"I'm keeping my distance," he said.

"Why's that?" I asked.

"This lot are the armed response team and they have belted over here from Bulminster."

The gamekeeper reversed the tractor into a gate way and the two police armed response vehicles sped down to where the car was parked.

"It looks like two old ladies to me," I said.

"Christ, he'll be in trouble if it is."

We could hear car doors slamming and barking dogs and the game keeper who had followed behind keenly on foot now turned about and was hastening back towards his tractor. One of the police cars reversed at speed back up the track and a policeman got out and began prodding him repeatedly in the chest.

The local policeman told us that the initial call had suggested that there were firearms present hence the armed response. After a bit more prodding and no doubt a few choice words the two armed response vehicles roared away back down the track towards the road. The two elderly ladies then drove tentatively past us looking bewildered with a collection of dogs barking in the back. The gamekeeper came across puffing and blowing.

"It was just the amount of dogs I saw, you know lurchers and that, and they were all over the place. I've got me last shoot of the season tomorrow. I just thought.."

"Why did you say that there were firearms present?" asked the local policeman.

"I didn't, I just said that I look after the shooting on the estate."

"Well if you ring 999 and mention anything about shooting on an estate then what do you expect? They've just covered ten miles in about eight minutes to get here. Don't make that mistake again."

The policeman looked heavenward as he said goodbye to us and turned his car around, leaving more at the speed of the elderly ladies than his armed colleagues.

I told the gamekeeper that we were heading further down the track to clear a fallen tree but he seemed to have lost interest in events up on the byway and wandered dejectedly back to his tractor.

"It was a good job that he didn't turn the car over after all," I said to Harrison.

Hare coursers are a big problem around here and landowners now go to great lengths to keep them out by digging great linear ditches around their huge arable fields. Farmers risk extreme violence when they have challenged these gangs and intimidation is their calling card. A band of hare coursers drove into one remote farmyard in the middle of the day and just sat there glowering at the landowner whilst flicking their cigarette lighters to produce long flames. Nothing was said. Nothing needed to be said as the message was clear. Leave us alone to get on with it or we'll return and burn your barns and buildings down. I am not sure about the ins and outs of the actual "sport" for want of a better word. The brown hare is extraordinarily adept at changing direction at speed and it is only the fastest and nimblest dogs that can give chase. There is a "referee" who adjudicates as to the success of the chase in all its twists and turns and the killing of the hare is secondary to the outcome of the contest between two dogs. As the gamekeeper suggested, this extreme form of gambling goes on in the middle of someone's field.

After all this excitement it was good to get back to normal and we went in search of the fallen tree. There are thick hedges either side of this byway and although it ran along the crest of the ridge it was enclosed and strangely claustrophobic. Every now and then through a brief gap formed by a field entrance you are reminded of the views that lay beyond with the broad arable fields gradually falling away to the steep escarpment below.

Eventually we found a small collapsed blackthorn bush partially blocking the byway and vehicles were already creating a route around it by pushing into the hedge on the other side. One can never be sure from a report regarding a fallen tree as to whether it is going to be large or small until you can see it for yourself. Even though it was small it still required the chainsaw to clear it so I turned the van around and reversed back to the fallen bush to enable me to sit on the tailgate to change into my protective safety gear. I would never even start up a chainsaw unless I was wearing the right ballistic clothing and it took me a few minutes to get myself sorted out. Once I started the chainsaw, with only a handful of cuts I reduced the tree into manageable sections and wearing some thick hedging gloves Harrison tugged the pieces onto the opposite verge and stuffed them into any available gap that he could find.

In no time at all it was done and I had put the chainsaw and fuel back inside the van and was just in the process of changing out of my safety clothing when a tall skinny dog appeared out of nowhere. It was wet and gulped for air. Harrison crouched down to talk to it just as a large and fierce looking man crashed through the hedge, shouting as he emerged out onto the byway.

"Oi, get away from the dog."

Harrison stood up as the hare courser began to move towards him. In the five or so paces that this man took as he gathered pace across the byway, Harrison remained completely motionless. Events happened so quickly that I barely had time to stand up from my seated position on the tailgate as I instinctively prepared to intervene in this seemingly undefended attack. As the man committed himself to lunge with arms outstretched towards his impassive target, with the fleetest footwork and impeccable timing, Harrison stepped aside his flailing attacker. Finding no resistance to his own blundering momentum, the man propelled himself forcefully against the ground where he lay stunned and winded. From the other side of the hedge a car horn blurted and raised voices could be heard out in the field. The hare courser slowly hauled himself up and staggered to his feet as the tall skinny dog retreated back through the hedge. He lumbered forward clutching his shoulder and appeared to be contemplating another charge at Harrison. The hare courser then glowered in my direction and seeing me standing there with my chainsaw trousers around my ankles he screwed up his face in disgust.

"You filfy fuckers," he snarled, before fighting his way back through the hedge.

"Interesting," I said to Harrison, "let's get out of here."

We clambered into the van as I pulled up my trousers and slid on my boots. In no time we were speeding back up the byway with Harrison craning his neck to look back out of the passenger window.

"Stop," he shouted.

"What? Why? We've finished the job, let's just get out of here."

"Stop."

Against my better judgement I skidded to a halt as Harrison opened the passenger door and placing two fingers in his mouth gave the loudest and shrillest whistle I had ever heard.

"Wait," he said.

"We're going to get our heads kicked in if we don't get out of here. What are you playing at?"

"Wait."

"Oh, for goodness sake Harrison."

At that moment there was a blur of movement through the hedge and the same tall skinny dog emerged and clambered into the foot well at Harrison's feet.

"Ok, you can go now," he said.

"What? With a stolen dog?"

"I bet they stole it in the first place. I is just stealing it back. You'd better split man."

With my heart pumping I raced back up the byway crashing through the pot holes and checking the rear view mirror all the while. At the road I turned right and sprinted down the hill to another junction and turned into a quiet village where I observed the speed limit.

"I must ring the police, but I'll get no reception down here."

The panting dog looked from Harrison to me and then back at Harrison again.

"What the hell are you going to do with it? We're now fugitives from the most dangerous men that you are ever likely to meet. Oh god, and I can't tell the police that you've stolen a dog can I?"

"It's your van boss," observed Harrison.

"Oh, I see, I'm now complicit in this am I?"

Instinct told me to drive to the opposite end of my area where we might just survive the afternoon.

We spent the rest of the day trying to behave perfectly normally as if nothing had happened. We cleared a short section of footpath, re-erected a collapsing signpost and waymarked a permissive path around a stone quarry. The dog kept to Harrison's side the whole time and after we had given it some of our lunch it drank out of a small stream.

"Why does it keep looking at me?" I said.

"That's what they does, waiting for a signal that somefings goin' to 'appen."

"I wish I knew what was going to happen," I said.

I now considered with a clearer head that the hare coursers would have no idea of our identity or where to begin to look for their dog.

We crept back along quiet lanes and Harrison indicated that he wanted me to stop just down the road from the yard so that he could take the dog to Dolores' house.

I had been thinking about things and I had made my mind up.

"Thank you Harrison for giving up your time this week. I am very grateful but..I just want my normal untroubled life back. I'm sorry but we'll have to call it a day. You've had your week and..well..I'm sorry."

Harrison got out of the van and the dog followed. He turned before closing the door and it must have been the first time throughout the entire week that I saw him smile.

"That's cool boss," he said.

Back in the office I flopped into my chair feeling shattered. The chap from the other end of the building popped his head around the door.

"There's a message from the new director that's trickled down from county hall. He says we've all got to take a leaf out of Harrison's book. Harrison the rights of way chap. Who is this Harrison?" he asked.

"That's a very good question," I replied, sighing and shaking my head. The chap from the other end of the building shrugged and wandered off.

Why did I take Harrison along to meet the director? I tried to ignore this latest turn of events and concentrated on the prosaic business of attending to outstanding e mails. Before I left the office I resigned myself to checking the received call history on my mobile phone. After a while I was able to identify the number that Harrison had used to ring me when I was being dragged around the field by Mrs Burdop and I sent him a text message.

"Ok. See you Monday. No dog. VW."

6
PANTS

"THE COMPLAINANT SAYS that you called him a four letter word," stated the lady telephoning from our human resources department.

"Not any old four letter word," I said, "well, he did behave like a ..."

"Don't say it."

"Why not? Shouldn't we be sure that we're talking about the same word?"

"If you said it then I would have to report you as well."

"But that's ludicrous," I said.

"Anyway, he has made a formal complaint against you. We all know what the word is so you don't need to say it again. I will have to come down and take a statement."

"What a waste of time. He kicked my hammer into the river. He's the one who should be apologising."

"We are where we are," said the lady from the human resources department.

"Pardon? What's that supposed to mean? Hello? Oh she's gone. I don't know what the world's coming to really I don't."

"Is you in trouble?" asked Harrison who had walked into my office just as I had answered the telephone.

"Looks that way.. oh joy of joys, I'm too long in the tooth to worry about that sort of thing. Did you have a good weekend?"

Harrison nodded.

"No more hare coursers jumping out on you?"

He shook his head.

"Good. Where's the dog?"

"Chillin'."

"Splendid. Well at least it isn't raining. Let's go out into the yard and do a bit of sorting out."

Just at that moment the telephone rang and it was Michael from the Gilbert Trust asking whether Harrison was available to come out with them for the day. I explained that we were going to do a bit of sorting out in the yard but Harrison seemed agreeable to the idea so ten minutes or so later the old diesel van clattered into the yard and I was once more on my own in the office.

I sat for a moment staring into space until the telephone rang again and shook me from my reverie.

"Hi Victor, it's Nancy."

I should explain that Nancy is my counterpart in the east of the county. The county is divided fairly equally along a north south axis although I have a few more parishes in my area than Nancy. Nancy joined the authority about ten years ago replacing a chap who died in post, somebody who was even older than I am now and who I never really got on with. It was sad nevertheless. Nancy was fairly inexperienced at the time but I was able to give her some guidance and she has somehow retained her enthusiasm in the face of it all.

"Oh hello Nancy, good morning, that's the kind of call I like. How are you?"

"I'm fine thank you. Look I know it's short notice but you're not around this morning are you? I mean have you got anything planned?"

"Well, I was looking forward to the prospect of gurning at my computer screen for hours on end but I may be able to tear myself away, what are you up to?"

"I was planning on doing a sleeper bridge but one of the volunteers can't make it and he was the most able one of the group so I'm a bit stuck. The sleepers are on site so it's a matter of moving them a bit. I know you've got back issues and I don't really like to ask.."

"Sounds like you need a bit of youthful vigour over there. I've got a stretchy back support thingy that might help, well it might prevent a hernia if nothing else."

"Are you sure? I am meeting the other two volunteers at eleven. It's over at Marsh, I'll send you a location plan in a minute."

"Ok, I would have brought someone else along but he's just gone out. I'll explain later."

"Thanks Victor, you're a star," said Nancy.

"I know," I said.

An hour later and I pulled up on the verge behind Nancy's van and we stood together on a narrow road.

"Thanks Victor, sorry to have to ask you," said Nancy.

"Always a pleasure," I said.

Two elderly volunteers were using secateurs to clip the blackthorn bushes from a footpath that joined the road at this point. I waved to say hello and they both waved back.

"I don't wish to be rude but they are pretty aged," I said to Nancy.

"They're lovely; Helen and Stan, but yes they are both in their late seventies. They have been volunteering on rights of way for years in another county and they moved here about three years ago and wanted to help which is great."

"Did you know that I have a helper, of sorts? Unfortunately he had already gone out with the Gilbert Trust just before you rang otherwise I would have brought him along."

"That's great Victor, how did that come about? I thought you'd given up on trainees and job opportunity people?"

"His name's Harrison and he just wandered into my office and somehow I agreed that he could come in every day. Young chap, you know the sort with his trousers permanently falling down to make sure his pants are showing. Odd fellow, doesn't say much but dogs seem to like him."

"That's useful. Have you told anyone else about him yet up at the big house?"

"I can't really be bothered and I'm not sure how long it's going to last anyway. Did I tell you that Michael leaves the Trust at the end of the week?"

"No. Oh that's a shame, I like Michael," said Nancy.

Without going into too much detail I explained that he felt it was time to move on and that I was thinking of getting him a little something to say thank you on Friday."

"That's a blow. I wonder who they will get to replace him?"

"I know, I'll have to go through all that painstaking learning process again and then they'll have to get to know the area."

"I'd like to come down to say goodbye to Michael though as he has helped me out quite a few times. Where will you be?"

"I've no idea. I'll let you know. Is that where the railway sleepers are going, down there?" I said, nodding towards the footpath where the two elderly volunteers were painstakingly clipping away.

"Yes, not far, about seventy five metres."

"You're so modern, you and your metres. Seventy five metres?"

I walked across and gave one of the railway sleepers a kick.

"Ouch, crikey they're solid. These are oak, imported from Europe. Somebody once told me that they were cut from the forests for the railways leading to the concentration camps."

"Oh, don't say that. That's awful and don't tell Helen and Stan or they'll be really upset."

"It's probably rubbish, I never believed them. They are lovely railway sleepers, nice and not very straight."

"That's not true is it? What a dreadful thing to be reminded of out of the blue. How could something like that have actually happened?" asked Nancy standing with her hands together, the tips of her fingers touching her chin.

"I'm sorry I mentioned it."

"We're going to put them to good use though aren't we?"

"Yes, if we can move them at all. How did you get them here?"

"I got a couple of the highway's lads to drop them off on Friday. Actually I'm surprised that they haven't been stolen, probably because no one can lift them."

"I'm sure I could, well one end anyway," I said boldly, "I've got a sort of weightlifter's belt."

Whilst I rummaged in the van for my neoprene support and a few other tools Nancy walked down the footpath and returned with the two volunteers.

"This is Victor Wayland, he looks after the rights of way in the west of the county. This is Helen and Stan."

We shook hands.

"I've sent you an e mail," said Stan, "but I haven't received a reply yet."

"Oh, I'm sorry."

"Victor does always reply, eventually," said Nancy, nodding and winking at me behind the elderly pair, "don't you?"

"Oh yes, always." I said.

"It was about a path obstructed by oilseed rape. It was last summer, August I think."

"Ah," I said, "in that case we can be pretty sure that the obstruction has been removed, well the crop will have been cut long ago. Do I still need to reply?"

"Well, there's not much point now is there?" said Stan, "can you keep an eye on it this year though? It will probably happen again."

"You have my word," I assured Stan, "I will retrieve your e mail for the location details."

"Yes, we went on our walk expecting that it would have been cleared and of course it hadn't," said Helen, "it was well above our heads and we were like pygmies lost in the elephant grass."

"We spent an hour trying to find our way out the field," said Stan, "Nancy always seems to make the farmers cut their paths through the crop in the summer, as they are supposed to do. Well we thought that you would do the same."

I hung my head in shame.

"What can I say? I am very sorry. I will do my best to ensure that it doesn't happen again."

"Ok," said Nancy, clapping her hands, "shall we have a look where the sleepers have got to go?"

Nancy apologised for me being put on the spot as we walked ahead of Helen and Stan.

"It's my own fault," I said, "they could have been lost forever in that field. You always seem to manage to follow these things up whereas I....well, sometimes I just don't."

"You've come to help us out today and we are very grateful.

Don't beat yourself up about it."

We gathered on one edge of the ditch that was to be bridged. I felt that I needed to redeem myself and it was the least I could do to lend my experience to the task in hand. It was a fairly simple job and I extended my tape measure to see where the sleeper lengths would reach.

"All railway sleepers are eight feet six inches in length," I said, "no matter where they come from."

Nancy shot me a glance to ensure that I was not going to elaborate on the possible origin of these particular railway sleepers.

"That's fine," I said, as I retracted the tape measure with the metal tape whirring back across the ditch, "let's move the sleepers down here then shall we?"

As we walked back up the path I lowered my voice to advise Nancy that Helen and Stan should really keep out of the way as neither had protective footwear on and to be frank they weren't going to contribute anything to the lifting process.

"Don't worry, I'll have a quiet word," said Nancy.

As we gathered back around the sleepers I lamented that it was not a situation where I could utilise the winch on the front on my vehicle.

"I thought that we could roll them," said Nancy, "I've brought some short round posts that we can put under the sleepers and move them along like that. We could put the rope on one end to guide it. What do you think?"

"They must have had a resourceful woman around when they built Stonehenge," said Helen.

"Well you showed me how to do it once Victor, don't you remember?" said Nancy.

"Did I?"

"Welcome to the forgetful club," said Stan, "we meet every..er.. um."

"Stanley, that isn't funny any more," said Helen.

"But you're right Nancy, sound advice, even if I can't remember giving it in the first place. I'll put on my back support as we'll have to lift the sleeper up a bit to get it on the roller."

To preserve a bit of modesty I retreated back to the van to strap on the back support and then decided just to put it on out outside my clothing.

"Oh, he's just like a Victorian strong man," said Helen as I returned.

"Are you sure about this?"

I held up my hand to silence Nancy's protestations.

"Just get ready to slip the round post under the thing once I've raised it up."

Nancy readied herself with the post that was going to act as a roller.

I put my gloves on and braced myself, crouching down at one end of the sleeper. Focussing on my breathing and activating the all important core muscles I prised my fingers under the solid oak railway sleeper.

"I've got a bad feeling about this," said Nancy, "wait, I'll lever it up with bar."

"Thanks for the encouragement, it'll be fine." I said.

There was a further moment of crouched poise as I attempted to grip the creosote impregnated timber and I silently counted to three before lifting.

"Get the blessed roller under it," I said through clenched teeth.

"You'll have to lift it another inch. There, well done," said Nancy.

I remained in my lifting position.

"What was that noise, or shouldn't I be asking?"

"No, that's a fair question," I said, "it was the sound of my trousers splitting and judging by the sudden cold exposure I should say that it's from front to back."

"Ooh it's just like a Carry On film," said Nancy.

"You can laugh," I said, slowly raising myself up, "it's these wretched moleskin trousers, I think they've shrunk in the wash."

"I've got a needle and thread in our car," said Helen, "I could put a few stitches in them, you'd have to take them off of course."

"That's very kind but..." I said.

"I emptied all that gubbins out of the glove box when I cleaned the car on Saturday, there was all sorts of rubbish in there," said Stan.

"Oh Stanley, trust you," said Helen.

"Have you got your chainsaw trousers in the van?" suggested Nancy.

I explained that I had washed them at the weekend and they were still hanging up at home to dry.

"No, I'll just have to soldier on," I said.

Whilst I was very conscious of my predicament we managed to manhandle and roll the sleepers individually down the footpath to the ditch, retrieving the short round lengths of post from behind the load and placing them underneath at the front. I then trundled the two kerb stones down the footpath in the wheelbarrow that Nancy had brought. One kerb was dug into position on the nearside of the ditch in preparation for the short bridge to rest on.

"It prevents the damp from rotting the ends of the sleepers where they rest on the ground," I explained to the on looking Helen and Stan.

We now needed to work on the opposite bank and on trying to leap the ditch my foot slipped and a boot disappeared into the dark still water.

"Lovely," I said to myself as I felt the cold water soak through my sock.

"You are in the wars today Mr Wayland," said Helen.

Having marked where the sleepers were going to sit I now had to bend over to dig out a section of the bank in preparation to positioning the second kerb stone.

"Please avert your gaze," I said, "there's no dignified way of doing this."

Having completed this task, with the rope still attached to one end of a sleeper I managed to lift and drag it at the same time so that it was now wedged lower down on the opposite bank, thereby crudely bridging the ditch next to where it would eventually sit. Nancy then balanced on the uneven sleeper to cross the ditch and between us we managed to lift our end up higher to make it level. Having a means to cross the ditch now meant that we could drag the kerb stone across to the other side along the railway sleeper and wrestle it into the hole that I had prepared. With one railway sleeper in place we then shunted and levered the second railway sleeper across until it settled level on the two kerbstones

"Stop excusing yourself every time you bend over," said Nancy, "it probably feels worse than it looks, not that I am looking, well trying not to but it's a bit difficult when it's staring you straight in the face."

The unwelcome ventilation and the wet foot at least had the effect of making me forget about my dodgy back and I felt galvanised to the task.

Whilst Helen and Stan fetched and carried tools and smaller pieces of timber, Nancy and I assembled the sleeper bridge. We added a single hand rail and nailed a board across the end of the sleepers to join them together. A drill was required as it was impossible to nail into this solid oak without first making a pilot hole. Stan was given the final task of nailing on a footpath waymark to indicate the continuing direction of the footpath beyond the bridge.

We all gathered together on the bridge which felt firm and solid.

"It's a very good use for these old railway sleepers," said Stan, "it gives them a second life. Thank you very much."

"Yes, thank you," said Nancy and I together.

Nancy took out a handkerchief and blew her nose.

"I'm sorry about your trousers Mr Wayland, but it is nice to put a face to a name," said Helen.

We made our way back along the footpath and I said goodbye to Helen and Stan and promised to be more receptive in the future should they send any further correspondence. Nancy and I watched as they walked away towards their small car parked in a gateway.

"Don't get me wrong," I said, "they are lovely and dedicated but there has to be some young blood out there somewhere?"

"We managed though. We always get it done somehow.. eventually. What about your young man, Harrison?"

"He's only been with me for one week so it's a bit early to say whether he's going to be the saviour of public rights of way. I somehow doubt it."

We finished packing up and putting away our tools and I went over to say goodbye to Nancy.

"I am really grateful Victor, thank you. I'd like to come down and say goodbye to Michael on Friday if you let me know where you are going to be. I can meet young Harrison too. At least you and he have one thing in common."

"What's that?" I asked, as I could not readily think of anything that we did have in common.

"Your pants are showing."

I drove directly back to the office and took off my left boot and sock to dry them out on the radiator and then realised that the heating was not on.

An hour or so later Harrison was dropped off in the yard and I walked around to let him in the front door.

"It's late, they normally knock off at three," I said.

Harrison nodded and looked at the clock.

"That's ok. We finished what we was doing."

There were any number of tasks that I hoped Michael would finish before he left on Friday but I soon realised that Harrison was not about to elaborate.

"You might be wondering why I have got one bare foot and a huge rip up the back of my trousers?" I said.

Harrison shook his head so I told him anyway.

"So you was the hero then?" said Harrison.

"Well, I don't know about that but I do actually feel as though I have done something useful for a change."

A man that I did not recognise then walked passed my office window and pressed the buzzer on the front door.

"I don't think that there's anyone in reception today so would you mind answering the door please to see what he wants?" I said to Harrison, "call me old fashioned but I don't want to flash my underpants to a complete stranger."

Harrison soon returned with the man following behind him.

"He wants to see you."

"Thank you," said the man to Harrison, "is it Mr?..."

"Wayland."

"That's it, I knew it was something appropriate. I kept thinking waymark but those are the little discs that you put up to stop people getting lost on footpaths. Bill Benson, I'm an independent television producer."

We shook hands.

"Please sit down Mr Benson," I said whilst Harrison leant against the wall by the door.

"Thanks for seeing me so late in the day. Well, I'll get straight to the point. We want to recreate a sight not witnessed in this country for a good number of years but that was once a very common occurrence. Sheep."

"Oh? The last time I looked there were plenty of sheep out there," I said.

"Ah yes, in the fields, but not on the move. I anticipate that there will be upwards of two thousand sheep coming from all directions," said the television producer.

"Where will they be going?"

"To market of course, we're going to recreate the old sheep fair at Hagbury Ring. The place will be teaming with sheep, shepherds with smocks and crooks, gentlemen farmers and squires in their carriages. We are even going to revive the king of the shepherds contest."

"What's that?"

"It's a fight between shepherds to establish the toughest shepherd, you know a crude boxing match."

"Bare knuckles?"

"Well, I don't know about that."

"What about auctioning some wives?"

"Very good, I see that you're well read but no, probably not."

"When is all this happening?"

"Mid September, the traditional sheep fair season. There are a couple of other film crews who are interested as well as it will be a fantastic opportunity to capture the authentic and traditional movement of livestock through the landscape. Very Hardy-esque as you suggest."

"Sounds interesting, but how do I fit into all this?"

"The old drove roads are key to the whole thing and I'm told that you look after them. I've just been out today having a look around."

I admired the chap's enthusiasm and it all sounded very appealing and an opportunity to dust off my old camera gear and take some proper black and white photographs. I suddenly realised that in my reverie I had stretched out both legs in front of me and I caught the television producer glancing down at the great rip in my trousers. I hastily drew my knees together and sat up straight.

"There's quite a bit of organising to do with the various agencies who will all want their sixpenny worth. Nothing's ever as straight forward as it seems," I said.

"I like this guy," said the television producer turning to Harrison, "he even talks in old money. Don't worry, my team are onto that already, it'll be fine. So, are you on board Mr Waymark?"

"Very much so and I'll do what I can to help. I like nothing better than day dreaming about how things used to be. They were probably awful, truth be told but.."

"This is no daydream My Waymark, I can assure you of that. Great, I'll be in touch over the next few weeks about which droves we'd like to use and perhaps we can meet up then. Thank you for your time, I'll see myself out."

"Better not or you'll end up in the boiler room with the others," I said.

"Pardon?"

"Never mind," I said, looking at Harrison, "would you mind showing Mr Benson out please?"

After showing out the television producer Harrison returned and I sensed for a moment that he wanted to tell me something. The moment passed and he raised a hand before leaving the office.

7
JOKE

THERE WERE A number of birds that could be killed with one stone today but first things first I had to find Harrison some safety boots. Last night I experienced a rather unsettling dream where a great weight had fallen on Harrison's foot whilst he was working with me. In the dream it had not seemed to bother him but this morning I got to work early and rummaged in my old tin shed for a couple of pairs of safety boots that I found under some perishing sand bags. Having chased out the spiders I even wiped them over with a wet cloth before presenting them to Harrison when he arrived.

"I'm not sure what size you are," I said, "but here's a pair of sevens and a pair of nines. What size are you?"

"I ain't any of them sizes man, they is mingin'."

I finally established that Harrison was a size eight.

"Listen, you have got to wear the right PPE," I said, "personnel protective equipment. If anything happened to you then I would be liable. I simply can't take you out without them so you'll have to wear one pair or the other."

An hour later and we were back in the yard with Harrison testing out his new Dr Marten safety boots that we had purchased from the agricultural suppliers in town.

"That's sixty pounds of public money, I really do not understand why those other boots wouldn't do. You'd better be worth it and why do you need to bounce up and down anyway?"

"Cool," said Harrison, bouncing up and down.

"Ok, now we can load up the stile timber and perhaps we can get on and do some work," I said.

As I have mentioned, there were a few things that could be achieved by today's task which in horrid modern work parlance would "tick all the right boxes". I'll explain as we go on.

Before Christmas I had received a charming hand written letter from a resident in a care home. He was in his nineties and it stated that his bridge partner, who lived in a village ten minutes drive away, had lost his driving licence recently but there was apparently a public footpath that linked the village to the nursing home. As the crow flies it was only three quarters of a mile to this village across a couple of fields. My correspondent claimed only second hand knowledge of this path and had no desire to use it himself but his bridge partner, who was a mere stripling of seventy five, would make the journey if only it were negotiable. There were three barbed wire fences and a tied up gate across the footpath which made the whole exercise impossible. Having written back to the gentleman stating that it was a pleasant surprise to receive a proper letter and I would have a look at the problem when I got a chance, I placed no timescale on my intervention. Sensing that I had obviously not appreciated the urgency of the situation he rang me up.

"Ah, Mr Wayland, good. Yes, any progress?"

"No I am afraid not, what with all the other..."

"Never mind about that, how much? What will it cost?"

"Pardon? Well it won't cost you anything.."

"Well it must cost somebody something, how much? Look, I'll send you a cheque for one hundred pounds. Thank you, goodbye."

A cheque for one hundred pounds duly arrived within two days and I was going to return it immediately but then mislaid it somewhere in my office. After some fruitless searching for the missing cheque the least I could do now was go and have a look at the problem on the ground. I rang the farmer who begrudgingly agreed to meet me on site to discuss it.

"No bugger's used that path for.."

"Twenty five years?" I interrupted, as this was the commonly quoted figure that all farmers used in these situations.

"..twenty five year," he said, with no acknowledgement of my uncanny anticipation.

We then looked at his field gate at the start of the path.

"I turned 'ee upsides down after the bull went over 'un."

What now remained, effectively blocking up a hole in the fence, was the rust eaten skeletal remains of a gate ensnared in a great web of orange nylon baler twine.

"Don't want to spend money making it good if there ain't no need," explained the farmer.

It was perfectly obvious from the outset that there was no prospect of him providing four serviceable stiles on this public footpath without our recourse to legal action. To expedite the meeting I agreed to erect four stiles along the path and he went off grumbling that it was all a complete waste of money. I just wanted the job done.

We arrived on site a bit later than I had hoped and this was largely due to going shoe shopping for Harrison. The back of my van was laden with timber and we pulled up next to the tied up gate.

It was not even remotely cold and I felt over dressed for physical work but I decided that I would shed some layers after I had warmed up. My back was holding up well and had been tested yesterday after my exertions working with Nancy so I felt confident about today's task.

There is a safety procedure which must always be followed when working in different locations and I questioned Harrison about what would happen in the case of an emergency.

"If I get taken badly ill let's say, or you knock me unconscious, hopefully by accident, what would you do? Do you know where we are for instance?"

Harrison declined to accept the Ordnance Survey map that I offered him and instead took out his mobile phone. After fiddling with it for a moment he held up the screen for me to view.

"We is 'ere."

I shook my head at this perfect demonstration of sleepwalking into ignorance by our dependence on such devices but I couldn't be bothered to labour the point.

"Let's just get started shall we?" I said, copying down the grid reference from Harrison's phone onto a piece of paper and I also added the name of the nearest hospital and placed it on the dashboard.

"If I die, there it is."

Harrison nodded.

I dragged out the large hand tools that we would need from underneath the timber in the back of the van and threw them down onto the grass next to where we were going to start. The fence was in a shocking state and our new stile would look ridiculous supporting the string woven gate, the slack barbed wire and the swaying fence posts. I had recently bought a stock of posts and rails from a traditional sweet chestnut coppice in the neighbouring county and had yet to try them out myself and here was to be the first opportunity. Sweet chestnut has good lasting properties when it is in the ground and I liked the smell and the irregularity of timber split lengthways along the grain. The points were all cut by hand and there was something refreshingly un-mechanised about this consignment of wood.

"It is how posts used to look," I said, standing up one post and looking at it admiringly.

"Old is good and new is bad, is that what you always fink Mr Wayland?"

As far as Harrison knew, he was just giving me a hand but there was another bird to be killed today, or if you prefer, another box to be ticked. I saw little point in explaining the minutiae of public rights of way legislation or even the difference between a restricted byway and a bridleway to Harrison, if he was only going to be with me for a short time. It would be more beneficial for him to learn some practical skills and tool techniques as somebody once showed me, many years ago. I thought that I would try to be subtle about it as he might resist the straightforward "you do it like this" approach.

Having chosen the position for the stile I began to make a pilot hole with the long metal bar for the wooden post to fit into so that it could be knocked into the ground successfully. I made an exaggerated point of letting go of the bar as I flung it repeatedly down into the deepening hole and then dragged the inserted bar around in a circle to widen it before presenting the point of the wooden post into the hole.

"Can you pass me the maul please?"

Harrison cautiously surveyed the selection of tools on the ground and guessing correctly he picked out the maul, which is essentially a very large hammer with a big cast metal head for knocking in posts.

"Hold the post upright," I said to Harrison, "and when you nod your head I'll hit it."

This old joke has been around for as long as people have been knocking in fence posts and it drew the blankest of blank expressions from Harrison.

"Don't worry, I won't miss," I said to reassure him.

The smack of the maul square upon the top of a post is a very loud and satisfying sound. Hydraulic post rammers that fit on the back of tractors have been around for many years and are used to erect long sections of fencing but occasionally you will hear the experienced fencer at his work from some distance away when he is carrying out a repair by hand.

For this first stile I decided just to get on with it myself and Harrison could then see what was involved and as the day went on I would let him have a go. A basic but functional stile can be erected around an existing fence line so there is no requirement to cut the fence. In most cases to cut a wire fence would be to compromise its tautness but here, if it were cut, the fence would simply fall apart altogether. Once the cattle come outside in the spring then these stiles will be the only solid things around for them to scratch against so they must be done properly.

"There," I said, once the stile was erected, "now, there's nothing wrong with that is there?"

Harrison made a face and a gesture with his hand to suggest that it was all a bit wonky.

"Beauty is in the eye of the beholder," I said, "I love it that the wood is not all neatly sawn and straight, it's got character. There was a crooked man and he walked a crooked mile, he found a crooked sixpence upon a crooked stile.. never mind."

I urged Harrison to try out the new stile and he crossed over and back again, springing down from the top step onto the soft ground after which he inspected his new boots to make sure that they were not getting muddy.

We loaded up the tools and drove around on a farm track to a point where it bisected the footpath and I parked the van next to where two further stiles were to go.

"I'll move it if the farmer wants to get by," I said.

There is a slow rhythm to knocking in posts with a maul, knocking in a nail with a hammer or sawing a piece of wood. There should be no jerky movement or forcing, no jarring of the body and no tension in the wrist. It takes an awful lot of practice to make it look easy and to begin with Harrison struggled. For a start he is too short to knock in a longer post with a maul and so after I knocked these in and added the three cross rails I let him knock in the posts for the steps which are only four feet long. After a tentative few taps he tried with a bit more force and split the post.

"You're not hitting it square," I said, "and you are forcing it with your right hand which makes the maul come across at an angle."

I was not sure what Harrison's threshold was for learning or for a fear of failure but he persisted with another post.

"That loud smack tells you that you've got it right," I said, "you also need to stop and straighten the post once it gets started, I'll push against it with the spade to make sure it stays straight."

With the first pair of posts in for the higher step he knocked in two more for the lower step.

"Can you hear the echo when you hit it right?" I said, "that's a good sign. Now we have to nail on the step boards and these go diagonally through the stile. I have bought a couple more hammers from home since that..idiot..kicked my other one in the river. You stay on this side and I'll pop over and do the other side."

The boards sat reasonably well on top of the short posts and I started off by nailing my end but did not drive the nails home. Harrison bent the first two nails and I told him to prise them out again with the claw on the hammer.

"You need a limp wrist to hammer in a nail," I said.

"Is that anuver of your old jokes?"

"Not at all," I said, "again when it is hit squarely you get a good ringing sound."

Harrison had more success with the third and forth nail and I told him to drive them right in and now I did the same on my side.

"You can drill these holes first if the wood splits but I think we should be ok as the wood is pretty green. Now I just want to saw a couple of inches from the end of the step on this side as it doesn't need to overhang quite so much and the farmer will probably clout it with the tractor."

I was just demonstrating how to saw with an easy rhythm when Harrison must have felt his mobile phone vibrate in his pocket as he took it out to answer it. To be fair for someone of his age he was not constantly fiddling with his phone which was a great relief as there seems to be a whole generation physically crippled by this activity. I waited with the saw standing upright in the cut that I had started and Harrison wandered a few paces away apparently listening rather than talking and he then suddenly burst out laughing which surprised me as I had never heard him laugh or express any kind of emotion before. It did not last long and he slipped his phone back into his pocket.

"Good joke?" I said, not really expecting any clarification.

"New joke," said Harrison, "and funny."

I finished off the sawing without labouring the point and with a few more nails and staples to hold the fence up we had now completed two stiles.

"A spot of lunch?" I said.

Harrison nodded and we sat in the van, blocking the track but as the farmer had not appeared all morning and he would now be having his own lunch it was not a problem.

In between mouthfuls of sandwich Harrison questioned why the farmer was not putting in his own stiles and it was interesting to note that at least this aspect of rights of way knowledge had sunk in.

"That's a good question," I said, pausing to take another bite of sandwich whilst I thought about the best way to answer Harrison.

"Have you ever wondered what it would be like to view things as other people see them? Just suppose, for the sake of argument, that you could put on a pair of old farmer vision glasses. You know at the start of the path where we put up the first stile and there was a heap of corroded scrap metal bound up with orange nylon string next to it? Well with these special glasses you would see a field gate that with a bit of tinkering would be perfectly usable again. On our way into the farmyard you might have noticed the past generations of decaying farm implements, dumped tyres, heaps of plastic and general crap that makes the place a complete eyesore? With these special farmer vision glasses then it becomes a treasure trove and a rich store of opportunity born out of years of prudence. Farmers, like our friend here, will not spend a penny unless he absolutely has to. Nor will he ever understand the concept of recreational walking and in his world if you do have to cross a barbed wire fence then you lift up the top strand and clamber through snagging the odd testicle on the way."

I punctuated my explanation with the finishing off of my sandwich.

"Never in a month of Sundays is he ever going to erect four serviceable stiles on this path. As an authority we could eventually make him do it if we served a legal notice and it would take successive visits on my part and a couple of months down the road, if you are lucky, you will have some sub standard stiles made out of scrap wood. It just is not worth the effort or the expense of my time so for the sake of the cost of the timber then at least I know it is done properly and we can move on. Sometimes we might want to replace a stile with a kissing gate where there is a well used path, say in the centre of a village. The farmer does not have to agree to this improvement and if you have already pissed him off in the past by serving notice on him they have long memories so he probably won't consent to it. Does that answer your question?"

Harrison shrugged which I took to mean yes.

"Whilst I am explaining stuff, this wood that we are using is sweet chestnut that survives for a long time in the ground without rotting so by doing these stiles properly with the timber of our choice, I know that it stays done for a few years. Modern commercially produced softwood for fencing has had all the nasty chemicals legislated out of the preserving process so it is no longer an effective option. Hence I am going back to one of the woods that was traditionally used for fencing. Another fine goal for Old United, we must be leading by about four nil.

Ok, four one at half time."

Harrison was not to be drawn into any easy to please football banter and ate a banana instead.

After lunch we began on the next stile and I could see Harrison looking at the nascent blisters forming on the palms of his hands. You cannot use gloves when swinging tools as the glove could come off and the tool disappear with it. It was just a question of toughening the skin.

No real problems occurred with this stile and I now explained to Harrison about the practical skills that I had learnt when I was young.

"I was taught by an old countryman many years ago when I worked for a summer on a farm and I am just passing on his skills."

"And 'is jokes," said Harrison, massaging his hands.

The final stile was on the roadside just down from the nursing home and after a long drive around I pulled up on the wide verge to ensure that we were well away from the traffic.

Harping back to killing birds and ticking boxes for a minute, there was one final facet to our work today. There is a bus stop outside the nursing home which must be very useful for visitors who have no car but it also presents another opportunity. I have been harangued of late by a new and keen chap who keeps mentioning something called sustainable transport and health promotion. Apparently there are targets to meet and boxes to tick so to get him off my back I promised some time ago to consider some "bus walks". Nancy seems to have done quite a few so, in an effort to catch up, it occurred to me that this path would fit the bill nicely. It is a walk of about five miles back to the town but it is perhaps a bit naïve to assume that the presence of a bus stop also means that there is an active bus service. Nancy would have certainly checked such minor details and rather worryingly I had not noticed any buses whilst we were working beside the main road. I had decided against trying to broach the concept of bus walks with the aged farmer when we had talked about the footpath. He was incredulous enough about the idea of walking for pleasure, let alone getting off a bus in the middle of nowhere and trudging five miles back to town.

"Did 'un break down? Did 'un gist thee money back?"

Hopefully he would remain blissfully ignorant about the whole affair.

I cautioned Harrison about the potential for roadside services placed in the ground such as electricity cables, water pipes, gas pipes or fibre optic cables.

"You don't want to stick your metal bar into an electricity cable if you can help it.

We have a scanner that can detect such things but I had forgotten to bring it so I exercised caution in making the holes for the posts. Harrison was getting better at knocking in the step posts whilst his sawing was still a bit jerky. He then pouted his lips at me whilst he exercised a limp wrist to knock in a nail with the hammer.

"Very funny," I said.

After a few final nails and staples I let Harrison attach the footpath waymark to indicate the direction of the path and we were finished for the day. There will be a footpath sign post erected at this point but I would return to do that as soon as I could.

"Shall we go and break the good news to the frustrated bridge player that his footpath is open?" I said to Harrison.

I drove into the nursing home car park and decided that Harrison could do the deed as he had probably never set foot in a nursing home before and it would be a new experience. There was also another aspect to this which would do him good and that was liaising with the public. I wrote a short note to the original correspondent and folded it before handing it to Harrison.

"I have a couple of calls to make now so I thought you could do it. His name's on the front. You haven't got any identification but just explain that you are a volunteer with the rights of way section. If they get funny then come and get me."

The nursing home was an old converted farm house which had been massively extended with ancillary buildings behind it. The footpath once served the farm and now it served the nursing home so here was a good demonstration of how purposeful public rights of way can be.

I had just finished my third telephone call when Harrison reappeared.

"That took a while, everything ok?" I said.

"He's dead," said Harrison.

"What?"

"That man what wrote to you, he's dead."

"Oh Christ. Oh no. I wish I'd sorted out that path straight away. He would have at least had a few games of bridge before he went. You idiot Victor will you never learn, always procrastinating. Oh sod it."

Harrison sat in the passenger seat and waited for a moment before taking a folded piece of paper from his pocket and passing it to me. I opened and read it and I now copy it out in full:

Dear Mr Wayland,

I am not dead after all. Sorry that was my little joke and please do not blame your young lad Harrison. I am instead very grateful and our little game of bridge shall resume tomorrow. It is not only my bridge partner that your path will convey as there are staff here who have said that they will use it to walk to the village shop or perhaps the pub on a fine day. It is in fact a lifeline if you can refer to such things when in God's waiting room.

Many thanks again to you and to Harrison.

P.D.L.

I shook my head with an overwhelming sense of relief.

"So you get the last laugh then?" I said, "you... so and so..I'd better not say what I was thinking or I would get reported again."

"Can I show you somefink?" said Harrison as he got out of the van, "you 'as to get out as well Mr Wayland."

I did as I was told and Harrison pointed towards a large and brightly lit full length upstairs window where a crowd of ancient people were waving and laughing to the point where their old frames were convulsing. I waved back and started laughing myself at this ridiculous sight and at the joke.

8
THE MISSISSIPPI BOWEAVIL BLUES

"I CANNOT ABIDE those eucalyptus trees. Nasty Australian imports that should never have been allowed into the country," I said to Harrison without really considering the implications of this remark.

"Then you is a tree racist."

"No I am not," I protested.

"Yes you is," said Harrison who then raised his voice and shook a fist at the eucalyptus tree as we passed by, "go back 'ome to Oz, we don't want your kind round 'ere no more."

"What are you implying? It is entirely different matter not wanting a type of tree to not wanting..well, an Australian in your country, for instance."

"Why is that?"

"It just is," I said, trying to think of a straightforward answer, "I'll have you know I am definitely not a racist, I've got a good friend who's an Australian. I just do not like eucalyptus trees when there are plenty of fine native trees to plant instead."

I looked around at Harrison and having raised the issue he had now gone reticent on the subject and I decided to ignore it rather than fall into the trap of protesting my innocence.

We had a drive of another ten minutes or so and I put on the radio to expunge the unsavoury undertones of Harrison's observation. After a short while it became apparent that it was a phone in about monkey chants made by the crowds at football matches so I hastily turned it off again.

"I hate phone ins," I explained to Harrison, "it is just a cheap way of making radio programmes."

"Yes boss," said Harrison.

We then got stuck behind a herd of cows with their full udders swinging beneath them as they were driven a short distance along the road to the dairy. Whilst we waited I leant across and riffled in the glove box for a Charley Patton compilation compact disc and slipped it into the player on the dashboard.

"I like a bit of early blues. He was a songster really if you want to be pedantic about it," I explained to Harrison.

Harrison picked up the case and studied the photograph on the front.

"That's the only known photo of Charley Patton," I said.

"Sounds old..," said Harrison.

"Of course it sounds old, it is old. This is the Mississippi Boweavil Blues recorded in 1929."

"And 'ee's black and that's why you is playin' it now."

"Of course he's black. Look, I do not have to prove to you that I am not a racist. I listen to a lot of old blues and I don't like eucalyptus trees and whilst we are about it I don't like Japanese knot weed either so you can stick that in your pipe and smoke it."

Harrison looked at me askance but said nothing.

The cows had now spattered their way into the entrance to the dairy and we were able to continue on our way.

After a couple of minutes I turned down Charley Patton's hollering voice.

"Ok, I would admit to being a bit intolerant at times," I said, "it's probably an age thing. I'm very intolerant about wheelie bins for example but that is because they are the scourge of modern society. There's nowhere to put the bloody things and any photograph taken today of any street just shows wheelie bins everywhere. When you look at old photographs of streets you see the people who lived there going about their business and now it's wretched road signs, wheelie bins and of course cars, there's far too many cars cluttering up the place. It wouldn't be so bad if they looked nice but they are all the same colour and the same horrible bulbous shape. It's as if our cars are now growing in girth to accommodate an obese population whereas old cars are slender because we were slender back then. If you see an old Mini or an old Ford Anglia on the road today they look tiny.

So, yes I am intolerant about foreign trees and some inanimate objects but I am hopefully not too intolerant about people, unless I am driving of course but driving makes everyone intolerant. Do you drive?"

"Yes and no," said Harrison.

Charley Patton continued to holler faintly and I couldn't be bothered to turn him up again or turn him off.

I haven't mentioned it to Harrison but I felt very stiff today. Installing four stiles yesterday was pushing it even though the ground was soft and the posts were easy to knock in. I notice that Harrison's hands are half closed up and claw like and this is a consequence of not wanting to open them up and stretch the blisters. He hasn't complained and I pretended that all was well even though I did not feel like doing very much at all today. A long slow drive to the edge of my area was just the ticket with plenty of cows in the way or other interruptions to slow us down. Harrison has informed me that he has a dentist appointment around lunchtime so that should disrupt the day nicely as I will have to bring him all the way back again. I also think that I have a cold brewing and this can occur when you use up all your reserve energy. I woke up this morning as stiff as a post and last evening I could barely stay awake after eating my dinner.

"We 'as bin this way before," said Harrison.

"Lushington," I said, reading the road sign, "yes, well spotted, we have been this way before. I have to go back down and talk to that wretched developer again who won't take no for an answer and it's bound to be a waste of time but he keeps pestering me."

It then dawned on me that Harrison must have read the village name sign as we passed by as I could see no other significant feature on this stretch of straight road until we entered the village itself. I could not bring myself to ask outright whether he could actually read as it seemed such a personal and sensitive an issue. I now wondered about how he had supposedly read about me in a magazine at the dentist and even yesterday when I wrote the name of the elderly chap on the front of the note that Harrison had taken in to the nursing home. Had he read it himself or would he have shown it to someone in reception?

"Will you be going to the dentist on your own?" I said.

I turned to look at him briefly and he frowned before answering.

"What like with my mum when I was a kid?"

"Well no, maybe Dolores, or, I don't know, someone else?"

"Why is that?"

"Just wondering," I said, trying to make it sound like an innocent enquiry.

"Does you take someone wiv you when you goes to the dentist?"

"Well no. Actually I haven't been for a couple of years now and I really ought to make an appointment," I said.

This was just another example of a conversational cul de sac that seems to occur whenever I ask Harrison even the simplest of questions and now I am left fretting about making a dentist appointment.

Peter Knowles crossed his yard with hand outstretched.

"Mr Wayland, I seem to remember that we got off a bit on the wrong foot last time. Can I offer you a cup of tea or coffee?"

"No fanks," said Harrison._

"Well, actually I wouldn't mind a cup of tea," I said.

Harrison turned to glower at me. There was no doubt that my resolve had weakened from our initial meeting with Peter Knowles and today I could not summon up the energy to be overly bureaucratic. More than anything I just wanted a cup of tea even if Harrison behaved as though I had committed some form of heinous treachery.

"Come into the kitchen," said Peter Knowles, "my wife's not here and I just hope I that can find the tea bags. Are you sure you won't have anything..."

"No fanks," said Harrison, confirming his position.

"Now Mr Wayland, Victor isn't it? Can I call you Vic?"

I winced at the mention of my christian name and doubly so at the abbreviation. I could sense Harrison's vigilance of my behaviour intensify.

We settled upon stools at what I believe is called a breakfast bar whilst Peter Knowles hunted for tea bags and I asked him how the work was going.

"Nothing's ever straight forward is it? I now find that there is a wretched tree preservation order on a long line of yew trees and we've got to hand dig the trench for the services and drainage pipes. The contractor wants to charge me a fortune for the manual labour so I think I'll put the feelers out and get some desperate illegals in to do it for peanuts. Don't worry, I'm obviously joking, but wouldn't it be worth it just to get the local tongues wagging and there has to be some benefit from all these plucky migrants turning up on our doorstep? "Opportunity knocks" as old Hughie Green used to say, now you must remember him Vic? Where does she keep those blasted tea bags?"

Harrison's eyes narrowed as if I were somehow partisan to the views being aired around the breakfast bar but before I could say anything to the contrary or state that I never liked Hughie Green, Peter Knowles changed tack.

"And another thing, your bloody planning department, I have never known such incompetence and maladministration, not that I've had a lot of dealings with other planning authorities you understand. We are definitely not property developers and I would like to make that clear."

"Perfectly," I said.

"No, it's just from my own limited experience, they really are an absolute shower."

I was pleased to be able to banish Hughie Green's face from my thoughts and replace him with an image of Terry Thomas and his gap toothed bounderish smile.

"An absolute shaah," I said, without intending to give voice to this delightful phrase.

"What was that?" said Peter Knowles, peering into yet another kitchen cupboard.

"Immense pressure," I said hastily, "the planning department are under immense pressure, as we all are on the front line."

"Ah ha, here's the tea bags. Milk, sugar?"

"Just milk, thank you," I said.

We sat in silence until I was presented with a cup of tea.

"Thanks," I said.

"The thing is Vic, we simply cannot have the footpath running across the yard and I'm looking for your help here," said Peter Knowles.

"But you knew it was there when you bought the place, you can't ignore these things," I said.

"I know all that, but you know what women are like? Once my wife drove in through the gate then that was it, it was love at first sight. Since we became grandparents it just seems to make so much sense for our daughter to live in one of the cottages here and then we can all be together with no traipsing back and forwards to London to babysit and what have you. It is simply perfect apart from your wretched footpath."

"It isn't my footpath," I said, "I am simply entrusted to look after it in my tenure. It is everyone's footpath and anyone can use it at any time of night and day."

"Now Vic, I'm not the type who will simply roll over and accept something just because rules are rules. There's always a way and I'll get it closed or shifted or I'll simply make it so that nobody can use the bloody path at all and then the great unwashed will be crying out for an alternative way around our property. Have you met our dogs?"

Peter Knowles slid off his stool and left the kitchen by another door and returned shortly afterwards escorted by two large Alsatian dogs.

"This is King and Kong, they have proper pedigree names obviously."

"That's nice," I said, stiffening at the sight of these two slinking beasts as they encircled the breakfast bar.

"Make no mistake about it, these aren't pets, these are guard dogs and guess what? They will be out in the yard once I've sorted out the fencing."

Harrison spun around on his stool and looked across at Peter Knowles as he extended a hand towards the two dogs.

"Don't even think about it Sunny Jim," said Peter Knowles, shaking his head slowly.

King and Kong, although I have no idea which was which, took it in turns to sniff and then lick Harrison's hand.

"Obviously, it's a bit different when they're inside the house and when I am present."

"'Ave you got a ball or somefink?" asked Harrison.

"No, they don't chase balls, it's not in their nature, I can assure you of that. The only things they chase are people."

"Ok," said Harrison, "come on boys."

Before their owner could intervene Harrison had opened the front door, beckoning the two dogs with a click of his tongue. Peter Knowles followed to the open doorway to observe his two Alsatian guard dogs scampering about the yard chasing an old broken surveyor's peg and returning with it in their mouths before dropping it at Harrison's feet.

I finished my tea and left the breakfast bar.

"Well, if there's nothing else Mr Knowles, I think we'll be on our way. Thank you for the tea," I said.

"King, Kong. Come here at once," shouted Peter Knowles, to no avail.

Harrison casually tossed the broken surveyor's peg onto the roof of one of the outbuildings and the two dogs barked furiously at their unexpected and now unobtainable new toy.

"Bloody dogs," yelled Peter Knowles, "King, Kong...Kong, King. Come here now."

"See you later," said Harrison.

The puzzled and infuriated owner scowled at Harrison before crossing the yard to wrestle the barking dogs back into the house.

"Jolly good show," I said as we approached the van.

We drove away in silence and on the outskirts of the village Harrison spoke.

"There's that stink again. What is that smell?"

My nose was a bit bunged up but I could confirm to Harrison that there was a large sewage treatment plant nearby. It then occurred to me that it was surely this smell that had triggered his earlier remark about having been this way before and not after all the name sign for the village. I was still no nearer to resolving the question as to whether Harrison could actually read or not.

I wanted to explain about my weakened resolve back at the Mr Knowles' house and also what action we would be able to take if the public were intimidated by King and Kong when using the footpath across the yard. If all the public were like Harrison then there would be no issue. What is it with him and dogs? I settled for keeping quiet and he could make his own mind up about my spineless display and inconsistency. At this time I simply did not have the energy to care whilst Charlie Patton resumed hollering faintly in the background.

I dropped Harrison off at the dentists and returned to the office, not really expecting to see him again today.

Back at my desk I ate my lunch without a great deal of pleasure as I could not taste what I was eating. After brushing a few stray crumbs onto the floor and winkling a couple more from the computer keyboard I settled down to feed the insatiable e mail monster for the rest of the afternoon.

After half an hour or so I was startled by a voice from behind me that I did not recognise.

"Hi, it won't take long."

A young overweight man entered the office with what I can only describe as a discourteous air and with no sense that he had entered my domain. I now recalled that earlier this morning the chap from the other end of the building had popped his head around the door with an exasperated look on his face.

"Expect disruption," he said, "there's a couple of blokes from IT coming down today to do something or other to everyone's computer. If it's anything like last time it will be a right pain in the arse and they'll take ages about it. I should go out for the day if I were you."

The IT man loomed over me peering at my computer with his hand on the back of my chair making it perfectly clear that I should now vacate my position and let him sit down.

"I'll just send this e mail, if you don't mind?" I said.

"No probs," said the IT man without moving, "do you ever clean your screen?"

Rather than be irritated by the situation I decided that I would demonstrate tolerance and accept that whatever this chap was about to do was necessary and that any disruption was entirely justified.

"Ok, it's all yours. Would you like a cup of tea?" I said.

"Yeah, great, white two sugars," said the IT man slipping into my chair, "Jeez, look at the crud, it should have a health warning. Do you want to know what I am doing or shall I just get on with it?"

"I should just get on with it, I don't suppose I'd understand even if you could be bothered to tell me. I'll get the tea."

The chap from the other end of the building was just leaving the kitchen when I entered.

"Throttled him yet?" he said.

"No, I am exercising great restraint, he's got a job to do after all," I said.

"Hmm, interesting approach, good luck."

I returned with the tea and tried to busy myself with something else but soon realised that unless I was on the telephone, all I ever did in my office was sit in front of the computer.

"How's it going?" I said.

"It won't take too much longer and I'll be out of your hair."

"I didn't mean.."

I began tidying up the piles of waymarks on a shelf in the corner which is something that I had never done before. I decided that there was an awful lot of rubbish in my office and I probably would not miss ninety percent of it truth be told.

"How long have you worked for the Authority?" I asked.

"Don't feel that you have to make small talk," said the IT man.

"Is that what happens?"

"Yeah, it's just another way of saying get out of my office and let me back on the computer. People don't get it that this is my place of work, whoever's desk I am working at."

"Sorry."

"That's ok."

A few minutes later Harrison walked passed the window and pressed the buzzer on the front door. I was pleased with the opportunity to do something other than shuffling waymarks and resisting small talk and I walked around to let him in.

"Hi," said Harrison to the IT man, as he entered the office.

"Hi, don't mind me," said the IT man.

"How was the dentist?" I asked Harrison.

Harrison shrugged.

"It's the injections I can't stand," I said.

"I don't 'ave no injections," said Harrison.

"Hey, brave dude," said the IT man, "my uncle was like that. Pain is for pussies he'd always say."

I now felt rather miffed that the IT man was joining in our conversation having earlier snubbed my own attempt to be sociable.

"Are you nearly finished?" I said.

"Is 'e on your case?" said Harrison to the IT man.

"I have been perfectly civil," I said, "and I even made him..I'm sorry I don't know your name..a cup of tea, which is more than you would ever do for me Harrison."

"It's Brett," said the IT man.

"Brett," I said, belatedly completing my sentence.

"What?" asked Brett.

"Nothing, I don't want anything, I was just saying your name."

Harrison leant against the far wall, observing me and shaking his head.

"There, all done," said Brett, "nobody wants the IT guy around but you'd all be screwed without us. We get used to it."

With that Brett left the office and opened the door to the boiler room.

"Please show him the way out," I said to Harrison.

On Harrison's return the telephone rang and it was the manager from the Gilbert Trust to inform me that they were not going to replace Michael and in fact were now stopping the outside gang altogether to concentrate on their core work with the homeless in the town. Apparently a stream of funding had now dried up which made it no longer viable to employ another supervisor or run the van.

After receiving this information and ending the call I slumped back in my chair.

"Guess what?" I said to Harrison, "the Gilbert Trust are not going to replace Michael or run an outside gang at all."

"I know," said Harrison.

"What? How come you knew and I didn't?"

"Mikey told me."

"Great, who manages this place me or you?"

" 'E told me not to say nuffink, so I didn't."

"I thought you looked shifty on Monday afternoon. Did you know then?"

Harrison nodded.

"Now we're really in the soup," I said, "there's no way that I can afford to pay a proper contractor."

I jabbed at the computer keyboard in frustration and soon established that I could not log on.

"Great, now my bloody computer's not working after that bloody oaf has been playing with it."

I looked out of the window just in time to see Brett and his colleague driving out of the car park.

"Marvellous, I tried to be tolerant, and where does that get you? This day is going from bad to worse. Let's go out and clear up the yard then at least something useful will have happened today."

When we got out into the yard I noticed that something was amiss.

"Where are your safety boots? The new boots that I bought you yesterday? You can't lift stuff without protective footwear."

"Clean," said Harrison.

"What do you mean, clean?"

"I is lookin' after them."

I took out my handkerchief just in time to capture a jolting sneeze that made my eye balls ache.

"That's it," I said turning towards my van, "I have had enough. I am going home to soak in a hot bath with a glass of whisky."

"Ok boss," said Harrison.

9
ZOMBIE KIDS

"I AM FEELING a little hoarse," I said to Harrison and Dolores outside the village hall.

"Isn't that a pony?" said Harrison.

"No, my voice is a bit weak, can't you tell? Oh, I see a joke."

Harrison nodded.

"Very good, an old joke even," I said, "but I don't see why you two want to turn out in the evening and listen to me, surely you've got better things to do?"

Dolores held up a small video camera.

"I'm going to film you, if that's ok? It's for a project."

"No pressure then," I said.

"I'm thinking about doing a film making course and I want to get some practice in different situations. I won't just be filming you," said Dolores.

"Come on, we should go inside," I croaked, "once more unto the breach, dear friends, once more."

Earlier in the day I had considered cancelling my engagement as guest speaker at Posford parish council AGM. Everything had been an effort and for the second day running not a lot had got accomplished. My computer is working again after Brett reappeared and was defensively aggressive in the way he attacked the keyboard as if it had all been somebody else's fault. I did not offer to make him a cup of tea. As Brett was tutting and drumming his fingers on the desk whilst he waited impatiently for something or other to load, the chap from the other end of the building popped his head around the door.

"Um, when you've finished in here there are one or two other glitches that need sorting out."

"Yeah, whatever," said Brett without turning around.

The chap from the other end of the building mimed a strangling action with his hands before departing.

Harrison had gone out again with the Gilbert Trust this morning and I had spoken to Michael briefly about the Trust stopping the outside gang.

"I'm really sorry," said Michael.

"Don't be silly, it's not you fault. I ought to go down to their office and have a chat with them to see if the situation is completely irredeemable."

"I think it was on the cards to be honest and I have just speeded up the process by leaving now. They simply can't afford to do it."

"What with my maintenance budget shrinking and taking another hit in April, I'll be lucky if I'm still here next year at this rate. The whole thing's going to rack and ruin and we could be witnessing the death of rights of way. What are you going to do now?"

"I've got a job in a cling film factory, no not really, I don't know is the real answer but for my own sanity I feel ok about it. You don't look so good though, are you ok?"

"I've got this cold thing, the trouble is I think it's going to my chest. Where are you going to be working tomorrow?"

"Finishing a clearance job in Stopp, well hopefully finishing it, if Harrison can come out today then we'll make better progress. He seems to get the lads working, I don't know how he does it. Perhaps he's bribing them when I'm not looking. There's something about Harrison, god knows what it is. I'd better go, see you tomorrow. Look after that chest."

I then spent an hour or so scribbling notes for this evening's talk and I wrote out a few prompt cards. Actually when you consider it the "origins of our public rights of way" is a bit of a nebulous subject. I don't know why I suggested it as it's much easier to talk about the recording process of rights of way and the successive legislation that protects them. The crooked wanderings of a horse and rider in the dark ages is all a bit vague even if that was part of the formative process. I thought that I would take the village that I visited last week with Harrison as an example where the path network connects the older facilities in the community. Services that are now extinct like the school, the post office, the blacksmiths forge, the pub, the mill and so on. The connecting paths still exist but the former properties have now all been developed as second homes by people who can afford second homes. It was a too depressing avenue to go down so I had to find another angle.

I decided to leave work a bit earlier and have something to eat before I went out to the meeting even though I did not feel remotely hungry but I had to do something to keep my strength up.

It was certainly a surprise to meet Harrison and Dolores in the village hall car park as I had no idea that they were intending to come or even how they got there. I guess Dolores must have a car as Harrison's answer of "yes and no" when I asked him if he could drive was typically ambiguous and I didn't wish to know any more after that.

So, returning to where I began, we entered the village hall which was only half full.

"I'm hoping there's going to be a few old farmers here that I can film," said Dolores.

"You'll be lucky, more like the friggin' brigadiers," I said, "I'm really struggling here with my voice. You'll have to find yourselves somewhere to sit, I'm going up onto the stage with the parish council officials."

"Good luck," said Dolores.

The chairman spotted me and we shook hands but before I got a chance to explain that my voice was a bit ropey his attention was diverted elsewhere. I took a seat at the end of the long table on the stage and poured myself a glass of water from the jug on the table. Harrison and Dolores had managed to seat themselves in the front row and Dolores gave me a little wave.

I sifted through my prompt cards and wondered if I were a member of the audience then would I really want to listen to me. I probably wouldn't be here in the first place but I would rather listen to someone talk about the history of brewing, the introduction of the 35mm camera, the folk blues revival and how Big Bill Broonzy once came to England in fact anything but the subject written down on the agenda sheet in front of me.

I took another sip of water and leant back in my chair to attempt a surreptitious gargle and as nobody seemed to notice I tried it again.

This time I was accosted from behind by the parish clerk who in passing slapped me on the back.

"Not too long this time Victor," said the parish clerk, "there's something on telly at nine thirty that I want to watch."

He continued on his way to take his seat as I involuntarily projected myself back into an upright position whilst somehow gulping and spluttering simultaneously. In an attempt to restore some composure I wiped away a few trickles of escaped water from my chin and had a crack at clearing my throat but even this forced cough came out silently. Another parish councillor sat down next to me and stared morosely at the evening's agenda. I lent across to say that I think that I had lost my voice but he did not even notice that I was attempting to speak as not a sound came out.

For a guest speaker to lose one's voice was a hopeless situation and I signalled further up the table towards the chairman of the parish council and eventually managed to attract his attention. Inexplicably he somehow misconstrued my throat gripping gestures as an indication that I was keen to get on with it and so proceeded to silence the audience to enable him to make his introductions. Whilst he made his preamble I hastily guzzled more water hoping that it might help.

"So, with the housekeeping out of the way I am very pleased to announce that our guest speaker for this year's parish annual general meeting is, I believe for the third time now, Mr Victor Wayland. Well known to us as our long suffering footpaths man the subject of tonight's talk is the origin of our public rights of way. Mr Wayland."

I could see Dolores levelling her video camera at me and amidst a slow and lacklustre clapping of hands I rose from my chair to look out upon the rows of largely indifferent faces. I hastily took another gulp of water and hoped blindly that when the moment came my voice would pull itself together.

"......."

I took another sip of water but still I could not emit even a squeak. The audience began shuffling in their seats followed by a growing murmur.

"Mr Wayland," the chairman announced again as if this was somehow going to restore my voice.

"........"

I shook my head and looked across in panic towards the perplexed chairman causing him to rise from his seat and come round to whisper in my ear.

"What's going on?"

"........"

"What, not at all?"

"........"

"I see. Well that's put the kibosh on that."

After returning to his position he clapped his hands to silence the impatient and bemused audience.

"Thank you. It appears as though our guest speaker has .. ahem.. lost the power of speech which is unfortunate for him and of course for us but.."

At that moment Harrison rose from his seat and skipped up the short flight of steps to the stage and positioned himself in front of the long table facing the audience. I leant across to try to claw at him with my hands but he was just beyond my reach. What an earth did he think he was playing at and I gestured towards Dolores to do something but she was now videoing Harrison.

The chairman had stopped speaking mid sentence to look at me and then at Harrison and the audience hushed themselves.

"You knows when you gets to a festival," said Harrison addressing the hall, "the place is buzzin' right and the kids is coming in fast?"

It must have been the surprise that caused the Chairman to slump back helplessly into his chair whilst everyone else seemed to be open mouthed and frozen to the spot.

"First fing you gotta do is put up your tent before you even finks of gettin' wasted," continued Harrison, "so all these kids.. in a field.. sticking up tents all over the place, you know what I mean? Maybe you ain't been to no festival, but your own kids 'ave or... lookin' at you, maybe your grandkids? No matter.. anyway.. they comes back all filfy and don't say nuffin' about what they 'as bin doin' when you asks 'em. Well this is what they does, 'ere we go."

Harrison clenched a fist before raising it slightly to begin a small up and down pulsing movement, generating a subtle rhythm to his delivery.

"Boom, boom, boom and the music is pushin' out down on the site.. and the kids is 'appy you know? They is pretty crap at puttin' up a tent.. but they does it.. and maybe someone 'elps 'em.. wiv the poles and that. More kids comin'..more random tents. Boom, boom, boom and the music fumps out. So your kiddies 'ave to get to where the music is appenin' right? They 'as got to find a tap for some water... and they needs a pi..they 'as to find a toilet somewhere. Nobody wants to put their tent next to the toilets.. cos it stinks of shit.. but they does in the end cos there ain't no.. more..room. So the kids is walkin' all ways.. makin'them little paths."

Harrison demonstrated walking back and forth along the front of the stage in his short urgent paces before continuing with the pulse of his monologue.

"Some of these paths is the main ways to the site.. where everyone is goin'.. and that's a big path.. boom, boom, boom ..and wow..the whole fing takes over and these kids.. your kids.. is lost to it.. right in the fick of it.. givin' it all this."

Harrison started dancing on the spot, well I presumed it was dancing but it looked more like a robot frantically stacking boxes and then waving its arms in the air.

It was now too late to stop him with the audience and the parish council members struck dumb by this bizarre account of what their children or grandchildren got up to at a pop festival. I buried my face in my hands and peered out at Harrison between my fingers.

With a single loud clap of his hands, Harrison briefly froze to the spot before slowly raising an arm to cast a wide arc above his head.

"When the sun is well up.. the kids gotta go back ..along all them paths to find their tents cos they 'as to sleep.. and it's reeeeeeal hot in them tents.. in the sunshine. This is a sunny festival.. not a mud festival, you understand? So these worn trails in the grass go this way.. and that way.. around a tent 'ere and a tent there.. right across the site. These are the paths.. for the weekend.. and they is followed by eeeveryone. Boom, boom, boom and the music fumps out. This goes on for free days wiv lots of comings.. and goin's.. and wivout realising it they is walkin' furver than they ever walks. Like when you says to your kids.. come on.. stop watchin' that crap on telly or playin' on some game.. and come for a nice walk.. and they can't be bovvered. Kids don't 'ave no energy for nuffin' most of the time.. but they 'as plenty for doin' fings when they wants to.

Very sad.. at the end of the festival.. cos these kids 'ave to go home.. to their mums and dads.. and don't tell 'em nuffink.. about what they 'as bin doin'."

There was a murmur of recognition as this description rang true with a few members of the audience. I lowered my hands from my eyes to look about at the mesmerised faces in the hall.

Harrison began to walk up and down in front of the long table as he considered what happened next.

"All these tents 'ave to come down and they gets put away.. by the zombie kids.. still 'aving a good time but man they is tired. The grass 'as turned like yellow where the tents 'as bin.. and that load of paths that I was tellin' you about?.. ain't important no more.. as you can walk anywhere.. but right across this field.. is the bare ways in the grass where your kids 'ave walked and stumbled about. This load of paths was made by the random kids.. as they was 'aving a gooood time and the grass will grow again.. and ..maybe.. the kids 'as picked up all their crap.. and left the field good.. but kids bein' kids.. they probably 'as not 'n people will 'ave to clear up after 'em."

Spontaneous laughter then broke out in the room and any earlier bafflement was being replaced by smiles and nods of recognition and approval.

"Now you 'as an empty field. No more boom, boom, boom."

Harrison stood motionless for a moment, the accompanying pulse of his clenched fist had now ceased.

"The grass grows and soon the cows is back and that's it.. 'til next year when the kids is trying to blag some money from the 'rents for anuvva ticket. Your rights of way ain't no different from those paths that your kids 'as made at a festival. Maybe the taps and toilets is like your places in the village where people 'as to go, you knows, the pub and shops and fings? Yeah, it's people doin' stuff and goin' places, not just for the weekend but for years and years, makin' them little paths and it all gets stuck on a map and becomes a legal fing...but only in England man..."

I had no idea that Harrison had registered that England, and of course Wales, are the only two countries in the world where public rights of way are recorded on a definitive map. I leant forward and tried to say "And Wales" but no sound came out and Harrison was unaware of my gasping prompt from behind.

"..oh yeah, 'n Wales as well, I fink, but I ain't never bin to Wales," said Harrison, who then shrugged, "and I don't know nuffin' about those legal fings so you better get Mr Wayland back when 'e 'as a voice again."

Harrison then raised a hand and left the stage to instantaneous applause at which he frowned as he sat back down beside Dolores.

The chairman rose from his seat and scratched his head.

"Well young man, that certainly wasn't on the agenda, um, we don't even know your name."

"Harrison," said Harrison.

"Well thank you Harrison, that was most enlightening and in your own way and through your own observations you have brought us to think about the living origins of our own paths. We certainly should not forget that they began simply as a matter of utility and an unconscious process devoid of planning, committees or consultation. They were paths worn into existence by the passage of peoples feet and of course horses hooves and it has been most refreshing to be reminded of that fact. I for one have never attended a pop festival and I can't imagine that I ever will but you have also brought some insight into that most beguiling world for the parents and grandparents amongst us. I hope that Mr Wayland soon recovers his voice but I hope that he won't think me overly callous if I say that tonight his loss was our gain. Mr Wayland you will no doubt be relieved to leave us before we embark on the more prosaic business of parish affairs but thank you for coming. Please let us show our appreciation for Mr Wayland and of course for Harrison."

Amidst the applause I left the stage and went up to Harrison and Dolores. I wanted to say thank you but of course I could say nothing. Harrison shrugged and Dolores said that they were staying on for a bit so that she could do a bit more filming.

I was very glad to return home and dose myself up before going to bed.

Sad to say things only went from bad to worse as a visit to the doctor on the following Monday confirmed that I had contracted bronchitis which in turn led to pneumonia and a stint in hospital on an antibiotic drip. Fortunately my neighbour looked after my cat and I had to stay at my sisters for a few weeks as I slowly recovered. Work was the farthest thing from my mind, whatever it was, it could wait. I knew that Nancy would cover for me if there were any serious issues and of course I never got to say goodbye to Michael properly or the work gang. Truth be told I was at a low ebb and when I did eventually return home from hospital, amongst all the accumulated junk mail was a brown envelope with "Mr Wayland" hand written on the front. Inside was a compact disc and a short note.

"Very sorry to hear that you have not been well. Here's a copy of the videoing that I did at the village hall. Thought it might cheer you up. Get well soon, Dolores."

PART 2 HARRISON AND THE PUBLIC RIGHTS OF WAY REVOLUTION

10
SCUM

IT WAS MY aim to slip unnoticed into the office and gently ease my way back to work. The doctor advised me to start with half days at first and only to undertake light duties as I still felt very weak. I was under no illusions that it would take a long time to check and respond to e mails and phone messages and sort out some kind of priority as eight weeks is a long time to just drop everything.

A few years ago there might have been some admin cover sent down from the big house to keep things ticking over but those days were long gone. First things first I needed a cup of tea and as we now have no cleaner in our offices my unwashed mug was where I had left it and it now had a thick blotchy pale green scum at the bottom that took some shifting. As I put it under the tap the first flush of water disturbed the culture growing within and a powdery smoke rose up out of the mug and the discharged skin of mould then blocked up the plug hole until I prodded it through with a tea spoon. I left the mug steeped in boiling water and washing up liquid and used somebody else's mug instead.

After half an hour I had been rumbled as the chap from the other end of the building popped his head around the door.

"You really were ill then, did you get our card?"

I thanked him for the card and said that it was very thoughtful of everyone.

"It was the least we could do, anyway, glad to see that you're on the mend." He then lingered at the door for a moment. "Um, I can't help noticing that you're using my tea mug."

"Oh, very sorry," I said, "I've nearly finished, I'll wash it up in a sec."

"No rush but I've got to go out shortly."

I suppose that is one thing to be thankful for as it is always reassuringly petty at work. I was equally culpable in this regard as somebody had obviously taken a fancy to my sacred parking space but I would soon be sorting that out.

The act of scrolling down the unopened e mails seemed to go on forever and when I eventually got to the bottom I already felt exhausted and decided to ring Nancy.

"Hey Victor, great that you're back, you had everyone worried for a while there. Pneumonia is a serious business after all."

"Who's everyone?"

"You know, the team, well there isn't really a team is there? You had me worried anyway. I had a few things directed over whilst you were away, nothing too serious. Most people have been quite understanding. There was one really annoying bugger, somebody called Peter Knowles? I never used to swear did I? Do you remember when I started? I never swore at all and now listen to me."

"We're driven to it Nancy, simply driven to it. Don't worry I won't report you. What did my old mate Knowlesy want?"

"Oh, I don't know, he wants to divert a footpath that crosses his yard and he says he's fed up with dealing with you as you were unhelpful and overly bureaucratic. I thought aye aye he's getting the old property developer treatment from Victor so I told him rules is rules."

"Good girl."

"He also said that he didn't want that street urchin coming back onto his property and I'm assuming he meant Harrison. I haven't heard anything from young Harrison whilst you were off."

"No, well I don't really expect to see him again, he'll have moved on to something else or who knows even got himself a real job. I bought him a pair of safety boots for sixty pounds. He saw me coming didn't he?"

"We'll have to find you another young helper, there has to be another Harrison out there somewhere. What happened about the swearing complaint against you by the way? It seemed like a perfectly reasonable bit of Anglo Saxon to me under the circumstances."

"Well there's a funny thing, a letter arrived at home shortly after I came out of hospital. I hate it when they write to your home address don't you? It's like saying "we know where you live", well of course they know where I live but I wish they wouldn't do it. Anyway, it said that the matter had been satisfactorily concluded now that an apology had been accepted. I certainly hadn't apologised so I don't know what happened there. They concluded by saying that it would not go down on my record. I should think not, I'm very proud of my hitherto unblemished record."

"Ok, that is bit odd but I shouldn't worry about it. Anyway how are you feeling in yourself Victor?"

"A bit listless since you ask. I think I've had enough."

"What, end it all?"

"No, I've had enough of work."

"Really? That's not what I want to hear."

"I don't think I've got the energy for it all anymore and I have definitely lost what little control I had of the situation. When I was lying in hospital I had this bizarre thought that each problem at work was a helium filled balloon on a bit of string and I had hundreds of these ends of lengths of string in my hands. I imagined that I was outside somewhere and I started to let go of the bits of string and one by one the balloons all floated away. I must have been a bit delirious but I recall it being very pleasant and satisfying watching them all go up and up and eventually disappear altogether. Now I find that they all ended up in my office."

"Oh dear oh dear, you are feeling sorry for yourself aren't you? Listen I'll come down and give you a hand one day a week for a bit. Look, I've got to go. Keep your pecker up."

"With your help Nancy I'm sure I will."

"Don't be filthy or I'll report you and spoil your unblemished record."

"Thank you for coming to see me those few times in hospital and I mean that. It helped me a lot."

"Of course I wanted to come and see you, you silly old...I'd better not keep swearing had I?"

"I don't mind but please don't say "old", the other word's fine."

"Sorry to disappoint you but I was going to say "sod" actually. Ring me tomorrow."

Very slowly I began to pick up the threads of long standing issues and other accumulated stuff. There were a number of successive e-mails and telephone calls on the same subjects as situations either developed or in some cases went away altogether. There were updates from the sheep droving television producer as more and more obstacles seemed to be thrown in his way. Neither highways or the police were happy about the proposed crossings of busy roads and were suggesting different and more expensive forms of traffic management. The owner of Hagsbury Ring, where the sheep fair was to have taken place, was now getting cold feet about it all which the television producer thought was a ruse to extract more money from the arrangement. Some of the owners of the sheep were now suggesting that the television company actually purchased the livestock rather than borrow them.

"Everyone seems to think this is an epic Hollywood production," complained the television producer, "it's only regional television for chrissakes and what the hell would we do with two thousand sheep afterwards?"

There was a call from a county councillor to say that the "little shits" were at it again in the wood on the edge of town and surely we could do something about it. They had chopped down another tree that had fallen across the footpath and narrowly missed a bungalow.

A half finished bridleway clearance at Featherbed was frustrating horse riders who kept riding down it thinking it might now be open and accessible. It was a task that Michael and the Gilbert Trust had not managed to complete before he left.

"It has now been four weeks Mr Wayland, four weeks of wasting my time riding up there only to find that I cannot get through. It really is not good enough. Please call me back to explain this unacceptable delay."

When you are feeling weak anyway, each phone message like this is another jab in the solar plexus especially as I now had no means by which to resolve these problems.

As I continued to jot down dates, names and numbers in my telephone call book I was made to replay one message to make sure that my ears were not deceiving me.

"Thank you, thank you, thank you. Finally we can get through and the bridleway is clear throughout. We are all so pleased and it makes such a difference to our riding circuit. Thank you again Mr Wayland."

I was rather bemused by this and under the circumstances was more than happy to take any credit going but I could not imagine who had cleared the rest of the bridleway. Perhaps some other equestrians had got so frustrated that they decided to clear it for themselves which was very unusual in my area. Either way it was the first piece of good news since I had returned to work.

Right at the end of the recorded messages was a description of something far more mystifying. It was the county councillor again who had earlier been complaining about the "little shits".

"I gather that you've not been well Victor but I just wondered whether you knew anything about this? I've only heard the story second hand but you know the wood near town where the kids have been wreaking havoc? Apparently one night after dark just after the little buggers had turned up again, a few yards away a figure all in black switched on a head torch and just stood there saying nothing. Then another light went on close by and then another and another until there was eight or ten of these sinister silent figures surrounding the little shits in amongst the trees all with these head torches on. They started to walk towards the gang of kids when suddenly all at once the head torches went off. One of the kids shines a light around from his mobile phone but there is nobody there, nothing but the trees. The little shits, who were really shitting themselves by now, legged it and haven't been back since. I heard all this from one of the locals who said that it was something to do with rights of way so I thought you ..."

At this point the machine had reached its recording capacity and cut short the rest of the message. I listened to the message again and it still made no sense but sounded vaguely encouraging nevertheless.

I then started to open up my e mails working my way up from the bottom when I had first become ill eight weeks ago. There was an initial flurry regarding the swearing complaint against me but these then ceased abruptly without explanation.

Lucian Poole's PA had sent a message in bold font in response to a thank you letter that they had received at the big house from the nursing home where rights of way had acted to "assist the plight of some ancients". This referred to the stiles that Harrison and I had erected in the week before my long absence. The director had been sufficiently moved to tell his PA to thank Harrison personally with no mention of me at all. The director will be disappointed once he finds out that the only name he knows from any of the front line services in the west of the county had now vanished into thin air and never actually worked for the authority in the first place.

Internal e mails between departments were usually pretty dull and uninformative and I was about to delete another one when I got lured in by a reference to volunteers. Apparently an incident somewhere in the west of the county had resulted in a review of the behavioural code for volunteers in the event that they should come into direct contact with the public. It did not specify the details of the incident but there was now a protocol to follow for any employee who worked with volunteers and as it was all predictably bureaucratic I soon lost interest. There are not many departments that engaged with volunteers in the first place so I was left to wonder what had occurred to prompt this review and then deleted the e mail anyway.

There were many individual complaints of varying importance and I began to scan through them with a growing sense of helplessness. On the first morning I did not even make it until lunchtime before I left the office and went home to fall asleep in a chair.

The pattern for the rest of the week followed a similar course until the Friday when it was decidedly spring like and I ventured out for some fresh air. Without too much conscious thought I found myself parking near the end of a path that passed through a long and narrow wood. The deciduous trees were not yet in leaf and only the dark clumps of holly broke up the early season sparseness of the wood. Beyond the wood the path entered some unkempt paddocks where the grass was always lush with patches of sedge and the only animals that you were likely to encounter were grazing deer. It was a good place for a peaceful and uninterrupted stroll which at the moment was just what the doctor ordered.

There was a lot of badger activity in the wood with the casting out of the old winter bedding from their sets and in places the freshly heaved heaps of red soil now encroached upon the footpath. I could smell traces of young wild garlic crushed under my feet and I inhaled deeply as I followed the path. A new and unpleasant smell soon imposed itself and I could hear voices approaching as the flanking holly bushes brushed against my coat. I did not really want to meet anyone today and this was the first time that I had encountered another soul on this path. Walking alone with no obvious purpose sometimes make you behave oddly as if you have to somehow account for your presence. If you have a dog then that explains everything and people can say hello to each other quite normally as long as the opposing dogs don't start fighting or having sex. Blackberrying with a bowl or a bag is ok or standing holding a small pair of binoculars is good as people do not want to disturb your birds or butterflies and they mouth a silent hello as they scurry by. A clipboard will do as that means you are monitoring something or other but a man just walking on his own can be tricky. These were female voices approaching and I backed in between the thick holly to make myself disappear altogether and the unpleasant smell grew stronger as I found myself standing in a badger latrine. I could clearly hear a portion of their conversation as the two ladies passed by.

"I can't say I've ever noticed that about donkeys, so what's hanging exactly? I must be really unobservant."

"Haven't you? It's an old expression. I saw some donkeys yesterday beside the road."

"That's a bit distracting."

"No, well Don usually drives, he's a hopeless passenger so it's easier to let him drive. I've lost my thread now. What time is it?"

"What's that awful smell? We should wait for the other two but let's stop at the end of the wood."

Fortunately these two walkers had no dog with them but I could not stay where I was and once they had passed by I pushed my way out of the holly bush before anyone else appeared.

The badger shit was very adhesive and I tried to shake it off as I walked and then paused to bend down to scrape the sole of my boot with a stick as two elderly male walkers confronted me on the narrow path.

"Hello Victor, what are you up to?"

"Oh, hi Don," I said, unable to conceal the surprise in my voice. I recognised Don as he used to work for the authority in development control and our paths used to cross on a regular basis but he had retired over ten years ago.

"So you're still at it then? Victor looks after the public rights of way."

"We haven't encountered any problems so far," said the other man blandly.

"No, that's true, what are you inspecting?" asked Don.

This was all I needed, some bright spark questioning what I was up to when all I wanted was some peace and quiet and fresh air.

"Badgers," I said, in a moment of inspiration, "you'll see up ahead. The spoil from their set is right across the path and I'll have to apply for a licence from the badger man before I can do anything. Don't want to cop a five thousand pound fine."

"What's that dreadful smell?" asked the other man.

"I trod in some badger crap when I was having a look around."

"All in the line of duty hey Victor? Yuck, we'll leave you to it or our better halves will be fretting, you must have passed them on the way? Keep up the good work."

I dodged any reference to meeting their wives and said goodbye before continuing along the path until they were out of sight.

It was a sham. I was not doing any good work at all and I would not be troubling the badger man or the badgers. I had now lost interest in my attempt to get a bit of fresh air and I waited five minutes until the coast was clear before heading home to fall asleep in a chair.

The next week was spent answering e mails and although I began to feel as though I had a bit more energy I continued with my half day routine. With all her best intentions Nancy had not managed to venture over from the East but that was fair enough as she has got more than enough to do without bothering herself with my problems. The reality of the situation is that I am on my own and I will just have to cope. Harrison it seems had disappeared and if I knew where he lived I would call by and retrieve those safety boots that had cost the taxpayer sixty pounds.

11
THE WILDERNESS EXPERIENCE

THE CHAP FROM the other end of the building wandered into my office with a newspaper cutting in his hand.

"I wondered whether you'd seen this?"

"What is it?"

"It was in the weekend paper, says they enjoyed getting lost on your paths."

"What?"

"You can keep it," he said as he wandered off back to the other end of the building.

There was a large photo of a couple of confused walkers at a junction of paths and a headline that read; "Lost in space."

As I began to read it I was not sure whether the journalist was being sarcastic or genuine but the initial thrust of the article implied that is was easy to get lost in our county, well to be specific, the west of our county which is the half that I look after. An early observation stated that there was a distinct lack of signage once you started out along the paths and you were left consulting your map on a regular basis.

I hackled at this accusation as I am always dishing out waymarks to parish councils, landowners and user groups though heaven knows what they do with them, perhaps they are used as drinks coasters.

Rather than ram home this obvious neglect by those responsible for the maintenance of public rights of way the tone of the piece then changed as if the writer had experienced some kind of epiphany whilst on his adventure in my patch. The author actually seemed to enjoy the act of getting lost or at least being challenged by his interaction with the landscape; "The wonderful vagueness of it all was distinctly liberating." He also wanted to refer to his map to work out where in the landscape he was; "To ignore the map is to lose another dimension and a wealth of contextual information."

The journalist then grumbled about branded paths and trails elsewhere in the country with names and logos and lamented that the user was often "dealt with" in the same manner as a visitor to a large airport or a vast shopping precinct; "Don't think for yourself, just follow the arrows."

He signed off by saying how refreshing his visit had been and how it had; "..provided an opportunity to engage with the world around you and make your own decisions. I even had a whiff of that elusive wilderness experience which is quite something for this densely populated and intensively farmed island."

Before I had time to digest the implications of this unexpected publicity the telephone rang.

"Hi it's Dave Barlow in comms.. you know, the old press office, we've now been rebranded the communications office, were you aware? No? That's typical, nobody's told anybody. Anyway it's about an article in the Sunday paper where we've come in for a bit of heavy criticism, no reflection on you Victor or anything. We've got to send out a pretty robust message rebutting these allegations about how we neglect our public rights of way, well it's specifically in the west of the county, that's your bit isn't it?"

"I think I agree with it?" I said.

"I'm sorry?"

"I said I think I agree with the journalist. Have you read it all the way through?"

"Yes, well no, not exactly. But it's the wrong sort of publicity. We want people to enjoy easy access to the countryside and come back and tell their friends about it."

"Do we?"

"Of course we do. Now, the leader of the council is going to make a response in next weekend's press. You know how these things work, he'll put his name to it once someone else has written it and we thought you could do it? Send it up to us first of course."

"I haven't got time for that sort of thing."

"When it comes to the leader of the council we've all got to find the time. End of play Tuesday?"

I sat and read the article again and found myself agreeing with it even more the second time around.

I decided to ring Nancy to see whether she had seen the article.

"Hi Victor, I was going to ring. I'm really sorry that I haven't managed to get across to see you, typical isn't it? Idle promises."

"It's all right, relax, I'm not a member of the public, I know what promises mean."

"Thanks, but how are you?"

"I'm ok, I can tap feebly on a computer keyboard and cough down the telephone."

"Well that's a start. It's nice and warm and sunny today and that makes everybody feel better doesn't it? I've seen the article by the way."

"I've had comms on to me."

"Who?"

"Comms, you know, oh never mind. I've got to write a rebuttal for the leader to use. I hate being the object of scrutiny, or having my name bandied around."

"I don't think they used your name."

"I know but people have suddenly woken up to the fact that I exist, I've got people I've never heard of ringing me up saying that they don't blame me. I like to be invisible, working in plain sight or an approximation of working anyway. I prefer to be a reassuring presence in the rural environment, you know, more of a PR exercise than a real person."

"Are you sure that you're alright Victor?"

"Oh, I don't know. The trouble is I'm quite sympathetic to this journalist's viewpoint. The other trouble is; I'm the last person who should be quite sympathetic to his viewpoint. I ought to be out there banging up waymark arrows all around the place from dawn to dusk like you do."

"I don't, well it helps people to find their way around. We are not trying to keep our rights of way the best kept secret or anything are we?"

"Aren't we? I'd sooner not meet anyone when I'm out and about."

"Oh, you're just saying that," said Nancy.

"Let's face it, you're just better at being a rights of way officer than I am."

"I am not. You taught me all I know."

"Not quite all."

"Don't start that again, you're good at your job Victor. I don't like to think of you fretting over there in the wild west."

"Don't be cruel."

"I've always called it the wild west, didn't you know?"

I found it hard to concentrate on anything else this morning with this wilderness business hanging in the air. There was also Nancy's "wild west" comment that kept popping into my head. Perhaps that was the answer though. The pages of the weekend broadsheets are full of middle class parents wishing that their kids could experience a good old fashioned childhood; climbing trees, damming streams, lighting fires and all the stuff that childhood memories should be gilded with. People always remember the good bits rather than the time when you fell out of a tree or burnt down your neighbour's shed. Anyway, the "wild west" could be the place for all those concerned parents to bring their kids. Not saloons and steer wrestling but a map and some pioneering spirit. Get lost and enjoy it. I could feel the twinge of an idea and fired off an e mail to comms with a few thoughts. Dave Barlow was quick to respond;

"Victor, I'm not sure if you've grasped the seriousness of the situation. There are enough pyromaniacs out there already burning down barns and setting fire to abandoned vehicles and I can just see the headlines when a bunch of kids successfully divert a river to flood half the town. No, you'll have to do better than that. Dave."

Nancy was right, it was warm and sunny and I went out to see if it would make me feel better, or at least give me a bit of inspiration. I inspected some outstanding stuff which looked just like it had when I last inspected it eight weeks ago. I even nailed up a couple of bridleway waymarks but by the time that I got back to the office a message had been left on my answering machine from an irate landowner saying that some idiot had nailed some blue markers to his gate post and he had removed them.

I went home and fell asleep in a chair which now seems to have become a habit.

The next morning I still had no idea what I should send up to comms and there was a scattering of screwed up balls of A4 paper around the waste paper bin where each abortive idea had been cast away in frustration. In my cricketing days I was a bit of a demon in the field and would frequently hit the stumps to run a batsmen out and now I could not even dispatch a ball of paper into a medium sized bin from across the office. I missed cricket and the camaraderie of cricket and during my recent enforced break from work I have mused with the idea of re-establishing a social life by taking up the game of lawn bowls in the summer. To my mind planet bowls has got to be a better destination than planet golf and more of a team ethic amongst its albeit aged inhabitants.

I was shaken from my semi retirement reverie by a tap at the window and I looked up to see Dolores, who gave me a little wave whilst Harrison yawned expansively standing behind her. I walked around to let them in and they followed me back into my office.

"Well," I said, "there's a surprise."

"Hello," said Dolores.

Harrison raised a hand slightly and yawned again.

"How are you Mr Wayland?" asked Dolores, "are you ok now?"

I told them that I had not long returned to work and was easing my way back into it.

I studied Harrison to try to establish why his appearance had changed.

"Is that a man of the road suntan?" I said, "I can't believe it is a golf tan and anyway there hasn't been enough sunshine to get a tan."

"It's sickening," said Dolores, "he's been to Cuba and just got back and that's why he's not quite his usual chatty self today."

"Cuba?" I said, "I've always wanted to go to Cuba. I agree that is sickening."

"Yeah," said Harrison, "I got invited."

"You got invited to Cuba?"

"Yeah, it was a cultural fing. It was cool, well it was hot man. You should go before it all gets fucked up."

"He didn't take any photos or film anything," said Dolores.

"I brought you this," said Harrison, handing me a green cap with a red star on the front, "it was the biggest one they had."

"Thank you," I said.

"Try it on," said Dolores.

"Me and hats don't really work."

Dolores produced a small camera and before I knew it she had taken a photo of me wearing a Fidel cap.

At that moment the telephone rang and I was going to let it ring and wait for the answer machine to cut in but Harrison frowned and gestured for me to attend to it.

"We'll come back," said Dolores, "are you going to be here for a minute? We've got something to show you."

I nodded and reluctantly picked up the telephone as they left the office and let themselves out.

It was Dave Barlow from comms who was wondering how I was getting on with my response.

"I don't want to hassle you Victor but today's the deadline and I need to know that you're on the case."

My eyes rested on the screwed up balls of A4 paper surrounding the bin and I assured him that I was on the case alright.

"Solid," he said, "just ping it across."

I wondered what Dolores and Harrison were up to and what they wanted to show me. It was typical that after weeks and weeks of no contact they had popped in briefly and then just disappeared again. After an hour of throwing more balls of paper at the bin and glancing out of the window I lost patience with coming up with some kind of slippery response for the leader of the council to send to the press. It was all down to resources. You cannot make a silk purse out of a sow's ear and I would just have to spell it out to them. I was beyond caring now as I hammered out an e mail and even gave it the subject title of "silk purse.." Dave at comms was not going to be happy and I was just about to press send when I heard the sound of an old but very familiar diesel engine entering the yard and the vehicle then clattered over the speed ramp before it came into view. Unmistakably it was the old Gilbert Trust van but I could not see who was driving and it parked up at the far end of the yard with the engine running. Curiosity got the better of me and I went to investigate.

Before I reached the van there was a very strong aroma that could only be the smell of fried food.

The passenger door opened and Harrison got out.

"Cool hat," he said.

I had forgotten that I was still wearing it and instinctively took it off.

"What's going on and why does it smell of fish and chips?" I said.

"It runs on oil from the Chinese in town."

The driver's door opened and Dolores jumped out.

"Sorry it took us a while but there must have been a bit of batter in the system and it wouldn't start. I don't really want to turn the engine off for a minute."

"It's making me hungry," I said, "but why are you driving the old Gilbert Trust van?"

"I went to see the guy at the Trust fingy and asked if we could 'ave it," said Harrison, "he said yeah and he gave us some old tools as well. They 'as anuvver van now and don't need no footpath tools."

Harrison stretched and yawned again.

"You'd better give us some more work," said Dolores.

"Yeah we've done all that other stuff that Mikey didn't finish," said Harrison.

"Have you been working on the rights of way whilst I had been off?" I asked.

Harrison then nodded or shrugged in answer to my various questions.

"Did you finish that bridleway over at Featherbed? What about the little shits? Was that you and what was all that about head torches?"

Dolores laughed.

"You didn't apologise for my swearing at that idiot who kicked my hammer into the river?"

Harrison nodded.

"But you didn't swear at him, it was me."

"I don't care what people fink," said Harrison.

"We've got a sponsor." Dolores pointed to some new writing on the van that read "Be wise, come to Confucius Chinese restaurant."

There had been some other changes to the wording on the side of the van. The "Gilbert" from the Gilbert Trust had been painted over and the handwritten word "Harrison" had been added afterwards.

"Trust Harrison?" I said.

"I fink Ollie did that," said Harrison.

"The lads are not still coming out in the van?"

"Yeah, two days a week most weeks," said Harrison.

"But who pays?"

"No money man, they wants to come out. They is volunteers. We is volunteers. Dolores can only do it for two days a week so that's it."

"It's a two day week revolution," said Dolores.

"Vive la revolution," said Harrison and they both put on their Fidel caps. I felt obliged to do the same and self-consciously replaced mine on my head.

The chap from the other end of the building strolled across the yard and paused to look across at the three of us in our green caps before getting into his car.

"It's all fine with me," said Dolores, "I'm going to make a documentary about it. We'll see you in the morning Mr Wayland, if that's ok?"

"Of course, yes, thank you," I said.

They both returned to the van and Dolores tooted the horn as she drove off.

I was left thinking of fish and chips and all the questions that I wanted to ask Harrison. Returning to my desk I deleted "silk purse.."

and began a new e mail to comms with "vive la volunteer revolution.." as the subject title.

I was in the office early the following morning and it was with some trepidation that I fired up the computer and checked my inbox. No news was good news as far as I was concerned regarding my response to comms. Either they had used my script or given me up as a lost cause and cobbled up something themselves for the leader of the council. Having promoted the idea of a volunteer revolution what happens next? Certainly Dolores and Harrison going out twice a week in a van with the lads is a huge help and it has meant that something has been happening out there when I thought that it had all ground to a complete halt. I would hate to rain on their parade and raise the uncomfortable issues of insurance, health and safety, first aid, risk assessments and the actual cost of keeping a van on the road even if it runs on old cooking oil. As an enterprise it needed to be encouraged and nurtured and not immediately crushed under a weight of bureaucracy. There was no money involved so therefore it was not a business and all it really amounted to was a group of people choosing to go out and do something useful. I would try to establish that there was some kind of insurance cover for the actual working on the rights of way but it would require prior knowledge of when and where they were working. I decided that in the first instance I had to keep the mechanics and details of the volunteer revolution a bit vague as far as the grown ups at the big house were concerned. It was all about feeding comms with success stories and perhaps by convincing people that something is happening then it may actually make it happen for real. Spin and PR are the tools of the modern world and with a bit of help from smoke and mirrors success will breed success.

As I was contemplating this new morning and the birth of a remarkable era in the maintenance of public rights of way the Trust Harrison van rattled into the yard. I watched as Dolores, Harrison, Ollie, Nigel, Council Peter and Knocker emerged from the old van and gathered together in a conspiratorial huddle. It was a sight to make any isolated householder in the countryside ring up the police instantly and inform them that there was a criminal gang operating in the area.

Rather than have them all troupe into my office I went out into the yard to say hello to the lads. Harrison's natural reticence seemed to have rubbed off on everyone and they scuffed around without meeting my eye or saying very much each wearing their own green cap from Cuba. I told them that it was great that they still wanted to come out and get involved and that I really appreciated it and the general public would to.

"It could be the start of something big," I said encouragingly.

"Need more tankin' tools," said Knocker gruffly.

Nigel's enormous frame swayed gently as he stood with his eyes closed whilst Council Peter used his steel hook to pick up a wet plastic bag that had been lying in the corner of the yard for months and he let it hang from his hook and drip. Ollie had the beginnings of a beard and he produced an enormous unlit cigar and put it in his mouth, gripping the end with his teeth.

"It's just like Kelly's Heroes," I said, "I expect you'll be needing dynamite and a sherman tank? Are there any other tools that you are desperate for?"

"Harrison's in charge now," said Ollie defiantly.

"We'll make a list of what we've got," said Dolores, "and then see what we need if that's ok?"

"And Dolores is in charge as well," said Ollie.

"I'll do my best but I've got no budget for this," I said.

We established what task they were going to do today and as they got back in the van I asked Harrison what he was up to on the other days when the van was not going out.

"I got loads of fings to do, why is that?"

"Well if you find yourself with a spare few hours one day you can always give me a hand, you know, if you want to that is. Like you did when you first started."

Harrison nodded and slammed the van door and Dolores gave me a beep on the horn when they pulled away.

I wondered whether I would ever find out how and why Harrison got invited to Cuba and what exactly happened in the woods with the head torches and the "little shits"? More importantly Harrison had returned and a new revolution was underway.

12
STRIKE

THE CHAP FROM the other end of the building was loitering outside the gate when I arrived at work this morning.

"What are you up to?" I asked on my way into the yard.

"I'm on strike."

"Oh, for a minute I thought you'd taken up smoking again."

"No, just the strike."

"How long are you staying there?"

"I'll be in for a coffee in a minute."

"Ok, I'll put the kettle on," I said.

Someone that I had never heard of then rang as I entered my office and asked me whether I was on strike today.

"If I was on strike I would not be answering the phone," I said, "I would be outside the gate with the others standing around the brazier."

"How many others?"

"Well, one in total and he's just making himself a cup of coffee."

"And no brazier?"

"No," I said, "who am I talking to anyway?"

"Oh, it's Terry Bromilow, I suppose technically I am your boss."

"Ok, hello," I said.

"Yes, hello, there's been a bit of a reshuffle of departments and it seems as though I am now your boss and as such I have been asked to establish who is on strike today from the new department. So..er Victor isn't it? I'll put a big fat tick in the register beside your name?"

Suddenly inheriting a boss from nowhere was enough to make me consider my position on the matter.

"Well, actually no, don't do that..um Terry isn't it?" I said, "I think that I might show a bit of solidarity after all so I will not be answering my phone again today. We must catch up sometime, goodbye."

Having put the telephone down on my boss I checked yesterday's county cricket results on the computer before making my appearance on the front line.

"What are you doing here?" asked the chap from the other end of the building who had returned to stand by the gate with mug in hand.

"I'm on strike," I said.

"Oh."

"Now what happens?"

"I don't know, I've never done it before. I promised the wife that I would. She's a northerner. She said that she would look out for me on the local news and if she couldn't see my face in the crowd outside the gate I wouldn't get any..you know..not that we..and actually there's been a bit of a.."

"So you're expecting the local TV to turn up?" I said, interrupting my brother in the struggle before he started telling me all about his sex life.

A works van pulled into the yard and beeped at us to get out of the way as we had inadvertently wandered out into the middle of the gateway.

"Scab," I called out as the vehicle entered the yard.

The van stopped and reversed back towards us.

"What did you say mate?" asked the driver through the open window.

"Er..I said "it's bad". It's bad ...enough to..."

"To take industrial action," said the chap from the other end of the building.

"Yes, thank you," I said, "it's bad enough to take industrial action."

The driver paused to scowl at us both in turn before accelerating back into the yard.

"Who was he?" I asked, quietly relieved that my fellow striker was prepared to watch my back before things turned ugly.

"I think he might have something to do with gully emptying."

"I don't think he was very sympathetic to the cause."

"No."

"What is the cause by the way?" I asked.

"I'm not entirely sure to be honest."

Excusing myself from the front line for a moment I popped back into the office as the test match was starting today and I wanted to make sure that play was going to get underway on time as it had been raining in Yorkshire apparently. There was also a recent telephone message left on my machine and I checked that the chap from the other end of the building was not peering in through the window to witness my lack of resolve.

"Oh..er..Victor, it's Terry Bromilow here again. I've just established that I am not your boss after all. There's been a bit of a misunderstanding at this end but no doubt somebody will be in touch."

When I returned to stand vigil outside the yard I mentioned that for almost an hour and a half this morning I actually did have a boss.

"That was a close shave then," said my colleague.

"What's it like?" I asked.

"I had a boss once. He wanted to go on a bike ride with me, some sort of bonding thing."

"Did you go?"

"No, he took the hump and I never heard from him again. Have you been in the office checking your messages?"

"Well...Yes... I couldn't help myself."

"Don't let it happen again. That is just the kind of weakness that the management prey upon. We are public servants and we just want to do our jobs..but today I'm afraid it's "no, we've had enough.""

"Are you what they call the shop steward then?"

"No but I was here first before you arrived and my missus has been banging on about it all week."

A smoker appeared from the office and stood on the opposite side of the gateway.

"All right?" said the smoker.

"All right?" we said in unison.

The smoker hurried his cigarette and I thought back to that old magazine advert of a rugged looking American out on the prairie somewhere sitting on a rock and obviously enjoying the smoking experience. After pacing up and down impatiently the smoker then rammed the unfinished third of the cigarette into the special box that had appeared on the gatepost when smoking was banned from all public buildings and premises.

With the departure of the smoker all conversation had now dried up.

"I've just got to pop into the gents," said my fellow striker, "and you're in charge until I get back."

I took the opportunity of ringing Nancy on my mobile phone to tell her about the strike.

"Yes, I've got things pretty much under control here on the front line," I said, "I guess you're out by the front gates as well?"

"No I'm not as a matter a fact, I booked the day off before it became fashionable and I'm on a walking and kayaking holiday, I did tell you about it remember?"

"Ok, well I won't keep you but by the way, I've told comms and the leader of the council that the volunteer revolution is now well underway in the west."

"That's amazing," said Nancy.

"Well it isn't really is it? It's just a bit of hype to get them off my back."

I let her know about the return of Harrison and the reappearance of the old Gilbert Trust van.

"Did you say Cuba? You are joking?" said Nancy.

"And...with souvenirs. I've no idea how he managed it and knowing him, which I don't, I'll probably never find out. So they are volunteering for two days a week and Dolores is taking out Harrison and the old gang in the van to work on public rights of way. It's a revolution sponsored by a Chinese restaurant."

"That's the best thing I've heard for ages," said Nancy, "listen Victor, I'm getting left behind and a bit cold and so.."

"Bye, I've got to go," I said hastily shoving my mobile phone back into my pocket.

"Ok?" said the chap from the other end of the building returning to his position.

"Nothing to report," I said.

We obviously did not want to talk about work so a stoic silence ensued on the front line. It occurred to me that it was not necessary to punish ourselves as we stood vigil on this special day. We, the workers, had done nothing wrong and we were actually the victims after all.

"Do you follow the cricket?" I asked cautiously.

"It starts today doesn't it?"

"Certainly does," I said, "I'll pop inside and get an update."

"I've got a little tranny radio in the office," said the chap from the other end of the building with a wink, "we can listen to it on that."

Once the radio was tuned in we were now in the timeless world of uninterrupted test match cricket commentary and there were no more awkward silences.

After a while the smoker reappeared.

"All right?" he said.

"All right?" we said in unison.

"What's the score?"

"We're twenty six for two," we said.

The smoker now appeared to savour his cigarette amidst reports of pigeons, buses, cranes, sticks of rhubarb, lowering cloud, corridors of uncertainty and dogged cricket from Yorkshire.

"Cheers," said the smoker as he departed.

"Cheers," we said.

More vehicles came and went and I resisted any glib remarks such as "scab" or "blackleg", whatever that meant.

Before we knew it the smoker was back for an update on the cricket and this time my fellow striker asked whether he could have a cigarette. They both gathered on the opposite side of the entrance and I felt a curious feeling of isolation.

"What if your wife catches you smoking on TV?" I said, resorting to some divisive tactics to make my fellow striker return to his post.

The two smokers wandered out to look up and down the road.

"Not much chance of that is there?" said the chap from the other end of the building.

"You know the trouble with this strike action?" I said boldly, "it lacks purpose and profile. If we want to draw attention to our plight we need placards and I for one am going to do something about it. Oh bugger there goes another wicket."

At the very bottom of the yard is a small compound where illegal signs are kept after they have been removed from the highway verges. Event organisers spend hours making up large signs to promote their local event and drive miles around the lanes placing them in prominent places. The next day council workmen remove them all and bring them back to the depot until the disillusioned event organisers eventually track them down and sulkily collect them. They question why all their hard work has been undone and that their event failed dismally due to a lack of publicity.

"Not our fault," they are told helpfully, "you can't place signs willy nilly on the highway verges. It's illegal."

I rummaged through the signs still attached to their posts that had yet to be retrieved by the event organisers until I found three that were blank on the reverse. I then unearthed a large black marker pen from the passenger foot well in my van and returned to the gate.

I wrote on the back of one sign "what do we want..?".

"What do we want?" I asked.

The chap from the other end of the building shrugged and looked blank.

"I'll just write that for now," I said and handed the sign to my fellow striker.

"Thank you," he said.

I prepared a sign for the smoker who had taken a short break to return to the office and propped it up next to the metal box on the gate post where you stubbed out your cigarette.

The smoker returned to his position with an unlit cigarette already in his mouth having left the packet back in the office as a precaution to dishing out any more cigarettes on the front line.

"Oriental carpet sale?" said the smoker.

"Sorry, I've got it back to front," I said.

"What do we want?"

"Yes we couldn't decide," I said, "I thought about writing "we could do with not losing any more wickets before lunch" but that wouldn't fit. There's a placard for you as well."

"Oh, cheers," said the smoker.

A small car pulled up outside the entrance to the yard and the lady driver wound down her window.

"Are you on strike?"

"We certainly are."

"Oh good, I have been doing the rounds of council establishments and you're the first ones that I have found. Let me take your picture. Could you all stand closer together."

"I'm not on strike," said the smoker, "I'm just having a fag."

The lady took our photograph and before we could enquire as to the extent or the purpose of the strike she drove away.

"I suppose that photo could be shown on local TV," I said.

"Doubtful," said the chap from the other end of the building who was beginning to look a bit morose at the prospect of not getting his face on television.

Another small van turned in from the road and raced towards the gateway. The driver wound down his window after skidding to a halt.

"Hey, classic supercar show. Great."

"Sorry," said the chap from the other end of the building turning his sign around causing the van to accelerate away into the yard.

Lunch came and went and we ate our sandwiches in silence. The situation in the cricket was not helping to keep our spirits up and I could sense some deterioration in our resolve.

The chap from the other end of the building wandered out to look up and down the road.

"Aye aye," he said, "here comes trouble."

The familiar diesel rattle, loud modern Cuban music and the accompanying smell of fried food heralded the arrival of the Trust

Harrison van.

As it turned into the entrance the van slowed down and spluttered to a halt in the gateway.

"I know that I've just had my lunch but suddenly I feel hungry again," said the chap from the other end of the building.

Dolores got out and opened up the bonnet of the van.

"Hi Mr Wayland. There's too much batter getting through into the system again."

Harrison wound down his window and I walked around to the passenger side of the van.

"Hi man, what's goin' on?" asked Harrison, turning down the music.

"Strike," I said casually as if it was a regular occurrence.

"Safe," said Harrison.

The side door of the van was hauled open from within and Ollie, Nigel, Council Peter and Knocker emerged to wander about the entrance to the yard. The green Fidel caps were still being worn by one and all and I noticed a greater presence of army camouflage clothing amongst the gang. The two Cuban flags were still attached to either side of the roof rack.

I asked Harrison where they had been working today and he informed me that they had just called in to pick up some more timber to replace a broken stile.

"The farmer shot 'imself earlier in the week," said Harrison, "so we fort we'd just get on wiv it."

"Dead?"

"Yeah."

"That's awful," I said, "nothing's that serious is it?"

"I dunno. Why is you on strike?"

"Solidarity," I said, "you know, one out all out, well me and him anyway. To be honest I'm not really sure but it seemed like a good idea this morning."

The smoker returned to his own vigil beside the mounted metal box of now smouldering cigarette ends.

"You is getting' squeezed right?" said Harrison, "no money for nothin'. We needs new stuff, strimmers and fings. All the tools we 'as is shit."

"But I haven't got a budget anymore for things like that," I said.

"Well, there you go man, that is why you is on strike," said Harrison slapping the flat of his hand on the outside of the van door, "you can't do fings wiv nuffin.'"

"You should write that on your placard," suggested the smoker, listening to our conversation, "here, gimme the marker pen. There you go. "You can't do fings wiv nuffin.""

"Ok," I said, "at least we have a cause now that the flying pickets have arrived."

"You've got to shout it out," said Harrison, getting out of the van with some urgency and pumping his arm. "YOU CAN'T DO FINGS WIV NUFFIN. YOU CAN'T DO FINGS WIV NUFFIN"

Ollie was soon in on the act following Harrison's example.

"YOU CAN'T DO NUFFIN' WIV FINGS," shouted Ollie.

"No man, it's fings wiv nuffin'," said Harrison,"YOU CAN'T DO FINGS WIV NUFFIN. YOU CAN'T DO FINGS WIV NUFFIN. YOU CAN'T DO FINGS WIV NUFFIN ..."

In no time at all we were all shouting it with the smoker holding nothing in reserve as he gave full vent to the mantra. Dolores attempted to start the engine with our voices rising to the challenge and as the exhaust coughed out a large black cloud of floating fat and as we all beat upon the side of the van a TV crew appeared at the gate.

A very young reporter and cameraman quickly gathered up their equipment from the back of their small van and approached us choking through the miasma with microphone and camera at the ready.

"We have just encountered the blockade of a local authority premises by industrial action," shouted the reporter into his microphone, "this is obviously a very volatile situation and with no visible police presence."

Smoke was now billowing out of the metal box mounted on the gate post where an un-extinguished cigarette had ignited the contents.

"I am going to try to talk to the ringleaders to establish the cause of their discontent but I .I..can barely make anything out through the smoke ..is that a Cuban flag? There seems to be a distinctly paramilitary look about this picket line and it's deafening."

"What has brought about your action here today?" asked the reporter pressing his microphone towards Council Peter.

"Farmer shot 'isself," said Council Peter without hearing the original question.

"Somebody has been shot?"

"Ah."

Ollie nudged the journalist from behind to propel him forward in Harrison's general direction.

"Somebody has been shot and I..I am being jostled in the melee and my eyes are streaming. Are you in charge?" said the white faced reporter to Harrison.

"The people is in charge," said Harrison.

"Are we witnessing a Communist uprising here in the sleepy shires?"

Dolores tried the ignition to again raise the noise and smoke levels whilst Knocker seized the opportunity to make a point and forced his whiskered face before the camera.

"Need more tankin' tools see," he shouted at the microphone.

"Tanks?" said the alarmed reporter.

"You 'eard," shouted Knocker menacingly.

"There is obviously military hardware and a militaristic intent linked to these protests..have you got enough?" said the young reporter anxiously to the equally young cameraman who was already retreating to their vehicle as the Trust Harrison van backfired gloriously and spluttered into life. The burning rubber from the tyres of the small TV van added to the complex fusion of aromas outside the council gateway and having successfully flushed away the obstructing batter Dolores drove on into the yard. Harrison gestured for the gang to help to load up the stile posts, steps and rails whilst the smoker returned briefly with a kettleful of cold water to douse the flaming metal box on the gatepost.

"Good," said the chap from the other end of the building as he handed me his placard, "I'm taking my radio."

"Is that it?" I said.

"Yep, job done. I'll check the local TV news later," he said rubbing his hands together.

"Don't you fancy one last cup of tea on the front line?" I said.

"Actually Victor, I've been meaning to say, as you haven't paid your tea money for the last three weeks you have now been excluded from the tea club, under the new rules."

"What new rules?"

"I sent you an e mail about it remember? So you'll have to provide your own tea and milk from now on."

"So all this counts for nothing?" I said.

"You won't tell the missus about me smoking will you? She sometimes comes into the yard to give me a lift home...so don't.. you know..let it slip if you happen to bump into her?"

I made a mental note to strike up a conversation with his wife at the first opportunity just to reminisce about our trenchant day on the front line and I might even mention her husband's heroic incendiary contribution.

The Harrison Trust van beeped as it departed from the yard and I was left on my own for about five minutes on the picket line before the smoker reappeared.

"Alright?" he said.

"Alright?" I said.

"Jumbo car boot sale?"

"Sorry," I said, turning the sign around, "any idea what's happening in the cricket?"

"All out."

13

A SUMMER WALKING STICK

"LET ME GET this straight Mr Wayland. I ring you to inform you that I cannot ride a bridleway as it is too overgrown and you tell me that I am now part of some sort of solution?"

"Well, do you have any friends that ride this route?"

"What have my friends got to do with it?"

"I thought that there might be some like minded riders who would be prepared to come out and help to keep the bridleways open."

"Mr Wayland, somewhere in the small print it will say that it is in fact your job to keep the bridleways open and it is not down to me ..or my friends."

"Mrs Coundley.."

"Now that we have established who does what, please can you tell me when you are going to clear our bridleway?"

"We no longer have the resources to do everything that people request, it is not as simple as you are suggesting."

"Well, I will talk to my MP who happens to be a friend of mine, as you appear to be so interested in my social life and I can assure you that it will be very simple. He will tell you to do it and you will get on and do it as a matter of priority. Thank you and goodbye."

This inclusive public engagement approach does not always work. Whether Mrs Coundley likes it or not things have changed and folk will have to help themselves more and, as I tried to explain, become part of the solution. When the e mail from the local MP starts bouncing around then it will be an opportunity to test how robustly the grown ups at the big house are supportive of the new rights of way self help revolution.

Experience tells me that they will cave in at the first whiff of trouble and so thought I'd better have a plan B up my sleeve.

Plan B is to get Trust Harrison to help and I texted Dolores asking her to give me a call. I was pleasantly surprised that she rang back immediately and when I explained the problem she offered to meet me on site.

"Give us an hour and a half to get sorted," said Dolores, "I've got to pick up whatshisface first."

An hour and a half later and I had pulled up on the verge at the start of the overgrown bridleway. It was a warm and windless day and I stood in the middle of the minor road and concentrated on the sounds around me. A woodpecker drummed on a tree some way into the woodland whilst small birds foraged in the undergrowth not ten feet away. A herd of deer stared at me from a clearing in the wood, held in stasis awaiting my next move but I kept as still as I could. Eventually and with no alarm they shirked away deeper into the wood and I lost sight of them. Ten minutes into my stationary vigil a bicycle came into view along the narrow road and I eventually realised that it was a tandem with Dolores at the front and Harrison at the rear.

Dolores was breathing heavily when they stopped beside me.

"Where did you get this old thing?" I said.

"Someone was giving it away. It would be ok ...but he's not putting any effort into it ...and so I'm doing all the work," said Dolores turning around to glower at Harrison, "I'm going behind on the way back so I can keep an eye on you."

Harrison shrugged and they both dismounted and lay the tandem down in the long grass.

"Thanks for coming out," I said.

"Phew," said Dolores.

"Yeah, phew," said Harrison.

"Well, this is the path. Do you want to get your breath back or shall we take a walk?"

"Have you hurt your leg Mr Wayland?" said Dolores.

"No, it's just my very useful stick that I use in the summer for knocking back nettles and brambles. It's what country people used to do to ensure that essential paths remained passable. This one's just about had it and I really ought to cut another one. We'll need a stick to fight our way down the path to take a look. I should have done it whilst I was waiting for you. There's some hazel bushes over there if you don't mind waiting for a mo?"

"Can I video you doing it? I am looking for traditional crafty sort of things to film for a project."

Harrison stood with his legs crossed looking bored whilst Dolores got her video camera out of her rucksack. I returned from my van with a small clasp saw and inspected the hazel bush for the right sized straight rod to cut.

"Ok, here we go," said Dolores, "can you explain what you are going to do first?"

"I'll try," I said, "right, er hem, this is a hazel bush. Hazel grows everywhere but it once played such a vital role in country life. It should be cut back or coppiced every few years to regenerate new growth. Sheep hurdles were made from it, spars for thatching to pin down the reed or straw, they made charcoal from hazel and it was laid as living fences. Hazel nuts were collected by roving bands of itinerant nutters and formed an essential part of the diet of the labouring poor. Ten thousand years ago the first hunter gatherers knew the worth of hazel and hazel nuts and it is sad that we have lost touch with this wonderful resource today."

Dolores gave me a thumbs up sign from behind her small video camera whilst Harrison yawned beside her.

"So," I said, approaching the chosen bush, "hazel can also provide the perfect walking tool. Traditionally a straight rod of growing hazel would be trimmed out and it was essential that it had a v at the top, where two smaller branches separated higher up the straight stick. When it was trimmed up this v was where the walker would place their thumb and it would be called a thumbstick. So the thinner, top end of the stick would be held in the hand and the thicker base of the hazel rod would be down on the ground. Having cut myself many hazel sticks over the years I do it differently. I cut the rod from the base of the trunk of the bush, where there is a slight curve to it and that will form my handle so my finished stick is thicker at the handle and thinner at the tip. In this way you have a whippy stick that can be used to flick off nettles and brambles and whilst it is fresh, green and bendy it works best. It has to be sturdy enough to support you as well so it is a fine line as to the thickness of the best stick. Once it dries out it is not so effective so it is very much a working tool. It is not meant to be a coveted heirloom that will be varnished and plonked in the hallway to be handed down through the generations. It's just a very useful stick to smash the undergrowth back and once it breaks you just cut yourself another one."

I now cut my chosen straight hazel rod with my clasp saw, trimmed it to the desired length and brandished it like a rapier before the camera.

"This is my summer walking stick, a stick for summer walking. The sad fact is that if hazel is not cut back regularly then it will grow too large and the branches will fall and the main stump will rot. Somehow we need to bring hazel back into our lives or it will be lost through neglect. A managed hazel coppice is a wonderful thing, cut right back to the stumps the fresh growth will flourish and it is a haven for butterflies. It has always been a dream of mine to reclaim a hazel coppice and manage it properly but like most of my day dreams they do not seem to materialise. It is a lot of work and a real long term commitment."

"Is this bush part of an old hazel coppice?" asked Dolores.

"Not really, this is just the fringe of the wood. Hazel coppices can cover quite large areas. The trouble today, if people are trying to manage a coppice, is the amount of deer that are around. Deer will browse all the fresh young growth from the cut stumps so it is essential to keep them out somehow."

"That's it," said Dolores, putting her video camera away, "thanks that's really interesting."

"I hope so," I said, "I could have done with a bit of hair and make up but we professionals must soldier on in adversity."

Harrison stared at me blankly.

The summer growth had already taken a grip on the bridleway choking it with brambles and nettles. As we forced our way further along we met a tunnel of vegetation that engulfed the route and these lower overhanging branches would need removing to enable horse riders to pass unhindered.

"We could do with one of those chainsaws on a stick," said Dolores.

"A pole saw?" I said, "yes, that's exactly what you need. My heroic day of industrial action does not seem to have altered anything and we still don't have the right tools for the job."

It was a hopeless mismatch beating a trail with my freshly cut hazel stick and we soon gave up and returned to the road.

"Well I'm sorry but that wasn't much fun," I said as we brushed ourselves down to remove all the twigs, brambles and insects from our hair and clothing.

"Well at least we know the extent of the job," said Dolores, "we'll stick it on the list of clearance jobs but it's getting quite a long list now."

"I know, I'm sorry. I am very grateful," I said.

"And we know we can get about on this thing," said Dolores struggling to raise up the tandem from where it had been dropped in the long grass on the verge. I went to her aid and pushed it onto the road, holding the back saddle as she climbed into the frame at the front.

"Oh, I was going to go at the back wasn't I so I could keep an eye on him. You'd better do your share of the work on the way back matey boy."

Harrison returned to his position at the rear of the machine.

I thanked them again for coming out and as the old tandem creaked into motion I could not resist singing a portion of Daisy Bell.

"Peddling away down the road of life, do you know that old song?"

Harrison turned and scowled which only encouraged me to sing out the chorus.

"Daisy, Daisy give me your answer do. I'm half crazy all for the love of you. It won't be a stylish marriage. I can't afford the carriage but you'll look sweet on the seat of a bicycle built for two.. well, you would look sweet if your trousers weren't falling down."

Harrison lifted up an arm and gave a one fingered salute as they gathered speed.

As I had predicted the response from the local MP caused the grown ups at the big house to scurry about and an e mail was swiftly dispatched from the director's office. The director's PA requested confirmation that the bridleway would be cleared as soon as possible and I reminded her about our newly adopted self help approach. After another exchange of e mails she rang me up.

"It's Julia here from the director's office, look I don't want to bother Lucian with any of this. I just need some clarity about when this bridleway will be cleared. From what you're telling me it all sounds a bit open ended, I mean how long is this piece of string that you keep referring to?"

I wish I had not mentioned the piece of string as it was only confusing matters.

"Sorry, forget the string," I said, "the facts are these; I have no work force. I have no budget. I have no prospect of clearing the bridleway in the short term. I have some volunteers who come out twice a week and I am entirely beholden to their good will and there is already a long list of paths to clear."

"Well, they must give this path priority."

"Why should they? They are unpaid volunteers and we do not even have the proper tools for the job, do you now understand the predicament we are in as a front line service? And anyway, the whole point of our new rights of way self help revolution was that those who use the paths should be prepared to come out and help to keep them clear. I did explain all this to Mrs Coundley. All I am asking for is a bit of back up here."

There was a pause at the other end of the line.

"I am going to inform the MP that the bridleway will be cleared in the next two weeks," said Julia, "politicians need to be able to respond with positive reassurances to demonstrate that they take each matter from their constituents very seriously. I'm not going to mention pieces of string and from where I am sitting two weeks is an acceptable time scale."

As Julia gave me a businesslike goodbye on the telephone, Harrison's expressionless face appeared at the window to provide a welcome distraction.

"There's two ways of doin' it," said Harrison, when I explained the predicament that I was in, "either we does it and that MP can still go for drinks wiv the horsey bird or we does not do it and fings get interesting."

"Like a sort of strike, to demonstrate the plight that the council is in?"

"Yeah."

"Hmm, the problem is that it is just me," I said, "one employee not arranging to do something can't really be called a strike."

Harrison obviously had other things on his mind and changed the subject.

"We wants to do a coppice, can you fix that?"

I was taken aback as yesterday he did not seem very interested in hazel or coppicing. I explained that it was a question of finding a landowner who would agree to it and I emphasized the long term commitment that would be required.

"We as bin looking at the stuff you can make wiv it and I fink it's cool."

"Do you know anything about the conservation aspects, the butterflies or the dormice management?"

Harrison shrugged.

"We was finking that we would make plenty of your sticks and give them to everyone out walking in the summer."

"Summer walking sticks," I said cautiously but with a growing enthusiasm for the idea, "they could be used as a symbol of the self help rights of way revolution and from a renewable source."

My eyes misted over as I imagined an army of walkers armed with nice whippy sticks of hazel thrashing away on the footpaths in the west of the county.

"So you just has to get us a coppice. Fanks," said Harrison on his way out.

By the end of the day I had settled upon the names of a couple of the more relaxed landowners who might just consider some coppice management and I made one or two phone calls. One pleasantly eccentric landowner kept an open mind when I suggested it.

"Well I don't know, I suppose it might bump up my annual subsidy, get a few green brownie points if you see what I mean."

He agreed to meet up the following week and I texted Dolores with the details and a grid reference.

When we met up Dolores had obviously walked to the agreed site and there was no sign of Harrison.

I introduced the landowner to Dolores and realised that I did not know her surname either. I had given up on finding out what Harrison's surname was.

"Not what I was expecting," said the landowner, "I thought you'd be a wizened old countryman who'd already chopped off a few of his fingers in some grizzly woodland accident."

"No, I've got all my fingers," said Dolores holding up her hands in front of her.

"Yes, I can see that," said the landowner keenly.

Dolores explained that she and some like minded souls wanted to rejuvenate a small coppice and she would keep a video log of the process. They would be committed to keeping it going in the longer term, encourage butterfly and dormice conservation and arrange school visits. She went on to make a very persuasive case and as we walked about the neglected woodland the owner consented to give it a try.

"Well, as you can see it's a mess. Deer will be a huge problem though. Actually there's a great heap of high fencing from an old pheasant pen just over there that we'll probably never use again now that we're not running the larger shoot. You'll have to get yourself some long posts but you're welcome to that old fencing. Nothing formal and if you run into difficulties we can review the situation I mean have you got any experience of this sort of thing?"

I explained that they had formed a group of volunteers and were helping to maintain the public rights of way in the West of the county.

"And you can sort of keep an eye on all this can you Victor?" said the landowner nodding towards the overgrown coppice.

"Well, yes I imagine I can," I said.

"Splendid, so that's that then."

Dolores was really excited when we parted and I just hoped that it was a sensible decision.

As a consequence of this new project any Trust Harrison rights of way work seemed to have been put on hold as I saw no sign of either Harrison or Dolores for the next week. The deadline for the clearance of Mrs Coundley's bridleway was fast approaching and I was bracing myself for a terse e mail from Julia the director's PA.

Julia rang instead and evidently there was an additional problem to deal with.

"We've received an e mail from Harrison of rights of way stating that as of today he's going on strike until further notice and the director has taken this all very badly. He says.. and these are Lucian's words not mine.. that he feels stabbed through the heart by his trusted people person Harrison of rights of way. He wants to know how things could have gone so badly wrong and he's beating himself up for not being approachable. Who is this Harrison of rights of way anyway? I've tried to find him on our global address book."

"He's a volunteer," I said.

"So he doesn't even work for the authority?"

"No."

There was a pause whilst we both considered the implications of a volunteer going on strike.

"Oh crap, this is even worse than I thought," said Julia, before ringing off abruptly.

I tried texting Dolores but got no response. At least this volunteer strike had distracted attention from Mrs Coundley's bridleway and I tried to keep my head down.

Arriving at work one morning I found a large bundle of hazel sticks resting up against my shed door. There was also a note from Dolores.

"We have been leaving the sticks at the beginnings and ends of paths and they keep disappearing. Hope you like them. D."

The sticks were ideal and a good assortment of lengths as well. I left one in the tea room and that disappeared so I put the rest in my van to distribute them wherever I could.

As the owner of the coppice thought that I was some sort of guarantor or a trustee of the Trust Harrison coppice trust that was not actually a trust, I thought that I ought to go and see what was going on. With no formal invitation forthcoming I drove down to the estate and walked a half mile or so along a footpath to the coppice. I was amazed by its transformation from a neglected woodland to a fortified conservation area. The high fence had been erected and a handwritten sign on the padlocked six feet high wire gate read "Conservation Area-Keep out."

The most striking feature was the closely cropped hazel stumps around the perimeter of the site inside the fence with the fresh cuts gleaming in the sun. Heaps of branches were stacked up towards the centre of the coppice so from outside you could not see beyond the stumps and the fading green bio mass.

They had obviously been very busy but all was quiet today and I could not see or hear any activity within the coppice compound.

When I got back to the office the chap from the other end of the building popped his head around the door.

"I found a stick in the tea room, I've been asking around," he said, "I don't know what it was doing there so I thought that it would be safer if I put it in the cupboard in the gents toilet."

"Why?" I said.

"I see that Harrison of rights of way has called off his strike," he said, "there's a thing in the Examiner. I'll fetch it."

Whilst he was doing that I retrieved the stick from the toilet cupboard and leant it up against the wall in my office.

The chap from the other end of the building returned with the newspaper and handed it to me.

"There you go Victor, aha, there's another one of those sticks," he said, picking it up as he left and I heard the gent's toilet door open shortly afterwards.

I was too curious about the newspaper article to explain about the stick. The headline read "Volunteer calls off his strike" but my eyes rested on a photograph with Harrison standing amidst a group comprising of the director, the local MP and a few other unknowns. Harrison had a stick in each hand and he was presenting these simultaneously to the director and the local MP, both of whom appeared delighted with their respective gifts. The sticks were not the summer walking sticks that I had been advocating but were instead conventional stout thumbsticks with a large V at the top. The text explained that Mr Harrison, the co director of Trust Harrison, had now called off his strike after a successful dialogue between all parties. As the local MP was present it was also an opportunity to launch a new initiative dubbed "the thumbstick project" which had been the brainchild of the director, Mr Lucian Poole, to reintroduce that old icon of the countryside, the traditional countryman's thumbstick. The council would be giving some away as prizes in a forthcoming competition with details to be announced shortly.

The director and the MP both said that they would treasure their thumbsticks and keep them in the hallway to pass them down through the generations.

"It symbolises everything that we're about and I might even give it a coat of varnish," said Mr Lucian Poole.

I cast the paper aside in disgust and went out in the van without considering my destination. How could Harrison have done this? Everything about it was wrong and it was a lost opportunity to get the right sort of publicity for the summer walking sticks.

After a while I drove on a minor road that bisected a wood and at the far end of the wood I was surprised to see the Trust Harrison van parked upon the verge. I stopped and the van was locked but I could hear the rise and fall of a two stroke engine. It was Mrs Coundley's bridleway and the first one hundred yards or so were now clear. I could see figures moving further ahead and a pole saw was cutting off the higher branches and Harrison and the Trust Harrison lads were hauling the fallen branches to the sides of the track. I realised that it was Dolores operating the chain saw on a stick wearing some new protective clothing. She looked back and pressed the off switch.

I must have looked bewildered as Dolores asked me whether I

was ok.

"Where did that come from?" I said pointing at the pole saw.

"The director found some money from somewhere," said Dolores, "and I've had some training to use it."

"So they met your demands and the strike was called off?"

"Yep, that's about it," said Dolores.

"And this "thumbstick project" nonsense, the supposed brainchild of the director?" I said, looking across at Harrison in the hope of receiving an explanation, "he can keep his varnished thumbstick in the hallway to pass down through the generations for all I care but my big plan was for very useful summer walking sticks if you remember?"

"You can't do fings wiv nuffin'," said Harrison gesturing towards the shiny new pole saw, "how many sticks does you want boss?"

14
SLAVES

"I GOT SIX for you today," said a husky voice on the telephone.

"Who is this? Six what exactly?"

"Slaves."

"Slaves?"

"I guess you call 'em...volunteers in your game, just to keep it all... respectable," said the voice.

"What are they supposed to be volunteering for and why the phoney gangster accent whoever you are?" I said.

"Oh it's just a bit of fun, it's Phil Smailes here, I'm not really a human trafficker. I was given your number and they told me that you'd know what to do with them, I'm just the driver. They call me ..the slave driver."

Thinking on the hoof I did have a task that required a few bodies and I asked Phil Smailes the slave driver to meet me at a convenient lay-by and I gave him the location details.

"Is it near a library?" he asked.

"No, it's not near anywhere," I said.

"Oh well, I suppose that's ok," said Phil Smailes who then remembered what fun he was having with his generic gangster accent, "dis is how it's goin' down see. Half past ten in the lay-by wid the used twenty pound notes and no funny business see. You understand punk?"

"Is this all absolutely necessary?" I asked but the line had gone dead.

I sent Dolores a text with the agreed code word which was now the only means of communication with Harrison and the gang. Since they had assumed their clandestine and covert modus operandi I had lost all control of what they were doing or where they were working. I could only imagine that there was some kind of jungle telegraph out there relaying breaking news of each developing rights of way crisis and Trust Harrison would then swoop down to sort it all out.

"I'm not quite sure what's been going on but it all seems to have gone strangely quiet now," I would be informed by a bewildered parish clerk after some mysterious intervention in their village, "we thought that you might know something about it Mr Wayland as you are the rights of way officer?"

"I expect it's something of nothing," I would say vaguely, "sometimes things just sort themselves out."

Harrison had gone to ground for a few days but was evidentially back in circulation as I received a swift response from Dolores requesting details for the agreed rendezvous. Due to Knocker's acquisitive nature all my hand tools were now in the Trust Harrison van so it was essential to meet up if I wanted these new volunteers to undertake some path clearance work. Everywhere was hopelessly overgrown and I was getting complaints of blocked paths from all quarters so a few willing volunteers helping to clear the paths had come just at the right time.

Now that the so called "volunteer revolution" had been embraced by the politicians up at the big house I needed a few obvious successes to show that progress was being made. It seemed as though volunteers had suddenly become a valuable commodity and everywhere I went I would encounter retired folk already involved in this or that. At the community shop in my village I found myself being served by my next door neighbour.

"What are you doing here?" I said, "I thought that you were an aeronautical engineer."

"I've retired," said my neighbour, "I now volunteer here for two mornings a week."

"I don't suppose you fancy doing a bit of work on the rights of way?" I asked quietly so as not to attract the attention of the rather bossy volunteer manageress.

"Well..I'm not sure..but there is a bit of an opportunity on the occasional Friday.."

"Don't you come in here trying to poach our volunteers," exclaimed the bossy manageress popping out from behind the crisp carousel, "Keith's going to be on stand by in the café on Fridays from now on."

The museum in the town was similarly replete with volunteers working on the desk, guiding the public around exhibitions or organising the storeroom. The library was another hotbed of volunteering and then there were the various charity shops. I photocopied a small poster that Nancy helped me cobble up promoting the health and wellbeing benefits of volunteering on public rights of way and pinned them about the town. I also folded them into four and slipped them to any volunteers that I encountered when the overseers were not watching.

"What's this Victor?" said my next door neighbour at the till in the community shop separating the folded poster from a five pound note and holding it up.

""Try volunteering on the rights of way, it's fun?""

Despite my winking and shushing at him it was too late and the volunteer manageress bounded over from tidying the greeting cards to confiscate the poster.

"I'm watching you rights of way..hands off."

Finding volunteers was not as simple as I first thought so I was pleased to be offered some out of the blue.

It was a warm day and I hoped that the volunteers had brought some water, sunhats and sun cream with them.

When I arrived the slave driver was standing in the layby smoking a cigarette with six elderly people sat inside the minibus apparently wondering why they were waiting in the middle of nowhere.

"They keep telling me that this isn't the way to the library," said the slave driver.

"It's probably a walk of three miles back into town along the footpath so I suppose it is a way to the library of sorts," I said.

I popped my head inside the minibus and attempted to introduce myself.

"Have we broken down? Have you informed the library?" interrupted one elderly man.

"Which library are we going to?" said a small wiry lady.

"You know I think I might have forgotten my medication this

morning," said a very tall man vaguely.

Just at that minute the Trust Harrison van swooped into the lay-by and coughed to a halt.

"I'm looking forward to lunchtime already," said a large smiling lady.

I withdrew from the minibus.

"Have you got any younger ones?" I asked the slave driver quietly, "younger ones who aren't obsessed with going to the library?"

"Nah, dat's it fella, take it or leave it," said the slave driver.

It seemed that the six people in the minibus belonged to a pool of peripatetic volunteers who were shipped out to help in any of the various libraries in the west of the county. A few weeks ago I had also put our section forward as a potential recipient for volunteers but had heard nothing back until today. I quietly suspected that somebody had got their wires crossed but desperate times called for desperate measures.

"I'll take them," I said.

The slave driver took a final drag of his cigarette before smearing the butt under his heel.

"Ok buddy, a word of advice, you gotta watch these wise guys like a hawk."

Phil Smailes then politely asked the elderly volunteers to disembark from the minibus and they watched forlornly as he pulled out and drove away promising to return at three o clock.

"So it's a bit of a change from your normal routine," I said, ushering them towards the Trust Harrison van where Knocker, the self appointed quartermaster, was preparing to distribute a selection of tools.

"We usually work in the book store," said an elderly couple as they cradled a pair of long handled loppers and a bow saw.

"And don't cut yer hand off..," scowled Knocker gesturing towards Council Peter who displayed his steel hook. "..or you'll end up like 'im see? Now tankin' well ghed on wid it."

The public footpath began at the lay-by and now clutching their respective tools the volunteers gathered at the footpath signpost peering into the dense corridor of neglect that awaited them.

Harrison emerged from the front seat of the van and gave me a quizzical stare as he passed by the group and fought his way up the footpath and soon disappeared amidst the burgeoning summer growth.

"If you'd care to follow young Harrison and then everyone can spread out a bit," I said cheerily.

The volunteers took one last look behind them and met the stony glare of the Trust Harrison gang lined up at the rear to discourage any thoughts of a break out. As the last of the peripatetic library volunteers became enveloped by the summer wilderness Dolores slammed shut the bonnet of the old Trust Harrison van.

"Do you think they'll be ok Mr Wayland, they didn't look very keen?"

"Well I hope so," I said, "nice for them to get a bit of fresh air though for a change."

"Not exactly what they were expecting I imagine?"

Dolores collected her video camera from the front of the van and followed the trail to catch up with the others.

My mobile telephone rang and I spent an hour or so in the lay-by receiving and making calls.

I then rang Nancy to see how she was getting on and mentioned in passing that I had kidnapped six elderly people and set them to work in the heat clearing dense undergrowth.

"Oh Victor, have you no scruples?"

"I've never really understood what scruples are, funny word. Yes I am obviously feeling guilty about it that's why I rang you up to confess. I just need to show the grown ups at the big house that the volunteer revolution is actually underway."

"But you have got to match the volunteer resource to the right task and get people doing what they want to do. They would be much happier in a library."

"Yes, you're right, I'd better go and sort this mess out before..."

"Yes quite, before something happens then you'll really be up paddle creek without a shit or whatever it is. Oh listen to me again, I've got to stop swearing. I'm not even any good at it. You'll find some younger volunteers in time, there's Harrison for start, I could do with a Harrison. Go and be nice to your volunteers, buy them an ice cream or something."

Nancy was right, these were elderly folk who had intended to give up their time with the intention of supporting the library service and enough was enough.

"I'm very sorry," I called out following their beaten trail from the footpath signpost, "I think that there has been some kind of mistake."

At first I could see no sign of the volunteers or the Trust Harrison gang as I picked my way carefully further up the path. After fifty yards or so I came to a clearing where I found the entire group standing around in a circle. In the centre was the short wiry lady addressing this curious assembly whilst pointing to a tall plant beside her with Dolores videoing the scene.

"So this is conium maculatum. A very common road and path side plant and a member of the umbelliferae family. Can anyone tell me its common name?"

"Thas cow parsley," said Council Peter, "every countryman do know that."

Ollie stepped forward and tugged at the plant with his bare hands, ripping away the top third and holding it up.

"Interesting that you should do that..er Ollie isn't it?" said the short wiry lady, "if it were cow parsley then fine but this is not cow parsley, it is hemlock and as such it is extremely poisonous. The symptoms are these, if ingested you effectively die from the outside in. Firstly the failure of the peripheral nervous system makes your extremities feel numb.."

Dolores now closed in on Ollie with the video camera.

"..then it attacks the central nervous system and death is the result of respiratory failure as the chest and muscles become paralysed. They say that the brain is perfectly lucid throughout this process until the end of course when death is inevitable."

Ollie dropped the severed foliage.

"I would advise you to wash your hands thoroughly young man," said the short wiry lady.

Looking distinctly pale Ollie thrust his hands out to the sides and emitted a loud wailing noise that could be heard until he reached the lay-by with Harrison following behind with the van keys.

"As I was saying, hemlock is a killer but it is easily indentified as there are distinct long purple flecks on the stem and it has a rank and unpleasant smell. This smell could be described as "mousey" and if you are familiar with the smell of mouse urine then it smells like that."

Dolores now videoed an adjacent hemlock plant to assist with future identification.

"And whilst we are about it," said the very tall man holding out his hand, "you might care to have a look at this. You will have to get a lot closer as it is very small. This little spec is a tick and quite fortuitously I have just noticed it on my skin."

The very tall man offered up the back of his large and liver spotted hand to the lens of the video camera.

"This is a deer tick and it is after my blood. It is the parasite ixodes ricinus. The six legged larvae climb onto tall grass to wait for a suitable host which more often than not will be a passing deer but they are partial to humans as well. Once they take their blood meal, which could take three to five days, the engorged tick will then drop off. The taking of your blood is not the problem, it is the bacterial infection that could occur from infected blood from a previous host. This potential infection is called lyme disease and if left untreated by antibiotics can cause real problems and could even be fatal in some cases. So it is very important to check yourselves thoroughly when you have been out amongst tall or dense undergrowth as we have today. Check the skin folds in and around the genitals as that is a favoured area, nice and warm."

Knocker pulled up the collar of his gabardine coat and began to scratch his groin with his hands thrust deep into his coat pockets.

"To extract the deer tick it is best to use tweezers and just pull it all out. Do not use the tip of a lit cigarette or try and drown it in vaseline as that could be dangerous in the former, particularly in the areas that I have described and would be ineffective in the latter. If the bite area does get infected then you will notice a red and inflamed ring around it. "

"Thanks guys," said Dolores lowering her video camera, "that's really useful stuff."

"Let's do a bit more clearing before lunch shall we?" said the large smiling lady, "I am working up quite an appetite."

As the working party resumed their task I noticed that Knocker had disappeared and I met Harrison on my way back up the footpath.

"That was very interesting," I said, "there's obviously some very learned experts amongst our volunteers and they seem to have got used to the idea that they are not going to the library today."

"Yeah," said Harrison as he passed me on the path, "and we is now two men down."

The side door of the Trust Harrison van was open and peering inside I saw Ollie in self imposed paralysis with his arms outstretched in an attempt to keep his hands as far away from his mouth as possible. Beside the van there was a large pool of water where the washing of Ollie's hands had taken place presumably with Harrison's help. Knocker sat huddled in his gabardine coat, scratching and scowling and viewing the outside world with newly informed suspicion.

I left both groups to it and went off to attend to a few bits and pieces and looked at some stuff whilst I was in the area. Remembering Nancy's earlier suggestion on my way back to the lay-by I called in at a newsagent's to buy ice creams for the volunteers. I had not bought an ice cream for a number of years and I was astonished by the size, variety and cost of it all. I counted on my fingers the number of ice creams I required. I could not very well produce ice creams just for the peripatetic librarians so I had to buy them for the Trust Harrison gang as well. I did not have enough fingers for this calculation. Did Harrison eat ice cream? Did I want an ice cream? The newsagent walked around from behind the counter to slide the lid of the freezer closed and he pointed to the illustrations on the lid.

"You're letting all the cold air out and putting a strain on the unit," he said, "make your choice then open the lid."

"You don't get a sense of scale or bulk from the illustrations," I said, "it might be a good idea to have measurements on the drawings if you don't want people to handle the goods?"

I eventually chose thirteen small ice cream lollies and asked if the newsagent could wrap them up in newspaper to prevent them from melting.

"I haven't got any newspaper," he said.

I looked at all the unsold newspapers on the shelf beside me.

"Tomorrow's chip wrappers," I said, "come to think of it, what's happened to yesterday's tomorrow's chip wrappers today, have you got any of those?"

I left the newsagents with the lollies bulging out of a thin paper bag. When I reached the van I wrapped an old fluorescent yellow vest around the bag and put my foot down to get back to the lay-by before they melted.

Knocker and Ollie were still in the van and neither seemed willing to accept an ice cream lolly. Ollie remained in a position of self imposed paralysis whilst Knocker was preoccupied with peering down his trousers and scratching his groin.

I caught up with the volunteers further down the path and another of the elderly volunteers was addressing the video camera. Evidently Council Peter had dropped the tool he was using into a ditch that contained stagnant water and the dangers of this scenario were now being explained. Council Peter was slowly wiping his right hand on the back of his trousers.

"So, Peter here has placed himself in danger by coming into contact with still water when he already has a scratch on his hand from a bramble thorn. What we are talking about is leptospirosis. Historically it had names such as "rat catcher's yellows" and "sewerman's flu". No surprise then that it is through infected rat's urine that we catch this potentially fatal "weil's disease" which is what we call it today. As rats are perpetually urinating there is a good chance that a rat has urinated in Peter's ditch and therefore as the water is not flowing the urine will not disperse. Jaundice appears first after five to nine days followed by vomiting and diarrhoea. A severe bleeding from the lungs will precede the onset of kidney failure and it kills two or three people each year. So, it is imperative that Peter has his hand washed thoroughly and any cut is given a jolly good scrub with disinfectant."

Dolores finished her videoing and escorted an anxious Council Peter back to the van to sort him out.

The peripatetic librarians stopped to enjoy their ice cream lollies. I handed Harrison the remaining ice creams after taking one for myself.

"There you go," I said, "a bit of a treat."

"Fanks," said Harrison,"what am I supposed to do wiv these?"

"Well, hand them out to the lads and one for Dolores and one for you. Where's Nigel incidentally?"

"Dunno, we is now four men down," said Harrison returning to the lay-by and leaving a faint trail of melted ice cream on the now cleared footpath.

Nigel's position was soon betrayed by his snoring and he was uncovered from a heap of recently cut vegetation. He arose slowly and plodded back towards the Trust Harrison van trailing a skein of bramble behind him that had become snagged to his clothing.

"Just like a large mammal after a long winter's hibernation," said the short wiry lady.

The volunteers collected up all the tools and placed them in the Trust Harrison van at Knocker's feet. The distracted quartermaster suspended his scratching for a moment and scowled back in acknowledgement of each returned item. The water container in the van was found to be empty after the washing of Ollie's hands.

"We have to get some water for Peter," said Dolores starting up the van and leaving hastily.

Phil Smailes arrived bang on time and stepped down from the minibus to welcome the elderly volunteers aboard.

"Hey, smiling faces," he said.

"It made a nice change," said one of the elderly volunteers.

"Consummatum est," said another.

"And we got an ice cream," said the large smiling lady.

As the peripatetic librarian volunteers eventually took their seats the slave driver muttered briefly under his breath before bursting into song.

"Always wid the fancy latin these wise guys, well we'll see about dat. Ok homeward bound it is. "Home where my thoughts escaping, home where my music's playing...'''

I was soon on my own in the lay-by.

I could now report back to the big house that an overgrown footpath has been cleared by the collective efforts of two groups of volunteers, coming together and working in partnership.

As I walked back to my van I noticed that the ice cream lollies that I had presented to Harrison were now squashed on top of an unemptied rubbish bin. A trail of ice cream flowed down the front of the bin and formed a small white pool on the kerbstone.

15
OLD ROPE

IT SEEMED TO be the season for ultimatums and a telephone call that completely disrupted any plans that I might have for the day.

"You do realise that today is national public rights of way enforcement day today don't you?" said Mr Wriggle on the telephone.

"Of course," I said peering at the calendar in my office which still displayed the previous month.

"So, what enforcement have you got ..planned..for today?" said Mr Wriggle with more than a hint of sarcasm in his voice.

"Well..there's a footpath that is obstructed by wheat that the farmer should clear," I said. The digital photograph of a pristine cornfield was currently displayed on my computer screen where I had just been glancing at a fresh complaint from a member of the public.

"OK, where's that?"

"Oh, it's at.." I squinted at the written details of the complaint, "it's down at Upfield, near the old railway, it goes across to the bypass."

"No, I don't think I know it. Well at least you're doing something I suppose."

"Er, yes," I said.

"I would be grateful if you could send me a plan of where the path is and I want to see before and after photographs. From my observations you lot have been letting the farmers get away with far too much and I'm not going to be fobbed off. If you don't provide proof of enforcement action by tomorrow morning at the latest then I shall be writing to the leader of the council, our local MP and the national press, how does that sound? I'll be sending you an e mail confirming all this just so there's no misunderstanding."

Mr Wriggle was a seasoned rights of way campaigner of national repute with many successfully contested public enquiries under his belt and was no stranger to the ombudsman. I had been forewarned by Nancy that Mr Wriggle had not long moved to the county and was obviously settling in by getting his teeth stuck into the local authority.

"Until tomorrow morning then," he said.

I worked out who the landowner was and called him on his mobile phone.

"No I don't want to meet you down there now," said the farmer, "what's the urgency all of a sudden? You've never contacted me before about it and now you want me to drop everything and rush down there to meet you. It will be harvested in a month or so for goodness sake. Tell you what, you lot sort out the atrocious roads around here and I'll deal with my footpaths, how about that?"

Before I could remind him of his rights of way compliancy agreement upon which his farm subsidy partially depended he rang off.

I printed off a copy of the photograph of the pristine cornfield that a member of the public had sent in along with the relevant section of the definitive map and stapled them together. When I returned to my desk from a trek to the printer my computer pinged and I knew without checking that it would be Mr Wriggle's e-mail outlining what was expected of me on national public rights of way enforcement day.

My immediate reaction was to ring Nancy but she would only say something like "Oh I thought you knew about it Victor, actually I've got one or two enforcement things lined up that should be resolved today." This of course would only make me feel worse so I resisted the temptation. Whilst I had paused to conduct my imaginary conversation with Nancy I realised that I had doodled a picture of a hanging man on a gibbet in the middle of the photo of the pristine cornfield. Underneath I had written "Victor Wayland RIP".

I went out to the shed and with difficulty trundled the old rotary flail mower out into the sunshine as I could see no resolution to this issue unless I cleared the path myself. After changing the spark plug and cleaning the air filter I poured in some fresh fuel and connected jump leads to the battery in my van but all to no avail. Having reached the limits of my expertise and patience I was about to hit the wretched thing with a large piece of wood when the Trust Harrison van entered the gateway and parked up in the yard. The side door slid open and Ollie was the first to appear followed by Council Peter, Knocker and finally Nigel blinking and yawning in the sunlight. One by one the gang slowly wandered over and gathered with graveside solemnity around the inanimate flail mower. Dolores and Harrison seemed to be having an animated discussion in the front of the van.

"Is it dead?" said Dolores when she and Harrison finally emerged.

"Very," I said. I told them about my phone call earlier this morning and that it was national public rights of way enforcement day apparently although it was the first I knew about it.

"I have to clear this footpath that runs through a field of wheat by the end of the day or all hell is going to break loose. What are you up to today?"

"We've got that last bit of bridleway to do," said Dolores, "then you can tell the MP that it's all cleared."

"Well that's some good news at least, I really appreciate you sorting out that one, thanks," I said.

"'Ave you got a long rope?" said Harrison.

"There's my old climbing rope hung up in the shed from when I was young and fit enough to undertake tree surgery. Why do you need a long rope?"

"We just needs one."

"Of course you do, how silly of me to ask but I want it back even if it's just to hang myself in the morning."

"Oh yes," said Dolores, "and can we borrow your Ordnance Survey maps of the area as there's stuff we need to organise? Is that ok?"

"By all means, I must try to get hold of a set for you to keep in the van," I said, holding up my oil and petrol soaked hands, "do you mind getting them? You know where they are in my office and someone will let you in."

Dolores and Harrison returned with the maps and I asked the lads to help me to push the dead flail back into the shed. I unhooked the old rope and handed it to Harrison before locking up.

"Good luck Mr Wayland," said Dolores, "I hope you find a way to sort out your path. Sorry we can't help you with that one."

I held up my oily hands and pretended to be philosophical about it.

"Que sera sera," I said.

"Whatever," said Harrison.

Once they had gone I collected up my tools and washed my hands in the mess room.

With no means to clear the path, the very least I could do was go to Upfield and inspect the blocked public right of way. I looked for the map and photograph that I had printed off earlier but was unable to find it. After making myself a cup of tea I decided that I did not really require the plan anyway and taking my camera I left the office.

Twenty minutes later I parked in a lay-by on the bypass next to "Josef's snack bar" caravan and a very bored looking proprietor watched me take a photograph of the field from the elevated bypass. The field of wheat looked as pristine and uninterrupted as it had in the photograph that I had been sent recently.

As I walked back to my van the man rose to his feet to stand expectantly behind the counter.

"Tea, coffee, burger yes?"

"Thanks but I'm ok," I said.

"Why you take a photo of that?" said the man in the snack bar pointing towards the field.

"It's my job," I said, not wishing to explain further.

"Come back when you want, I am Josef."

I said goodbye to Josef and drove around for a while before finding myself back in the office where I downloaded my own photograph of the public footpath that was obstructed by standing corn. I wrote a letter to the farmer requesting that he should cut out the public footpath. At the very least I could demonstrate that there was correspondence dated on public rights of way enforcement day requesting that the farmer should fulfil his responsibilities. I did not think for one minute that Mr Wriggle would be satisfied with my actions and was already preparing myself for our conversation in the morning. As it turned out the printer in the main office was broken and nothing could be printed until the engineer came out in the morning to fix it. I thought about a hand written letter but in the end I gave it all up as a bad job and would just have to face the music.

The next morning I was a bit late for work after experiencing a restless night with the luminescence of a brilliant moon blazing through my bedroom curtains. I made a cup of tea and slowly got on with things whilst awaiting Mr Wriggle's call and when the telephone rang it made me jump. It was not Mr Wriggle but the farmer who yesterday had refused to clear his crop from the public footpath near the bypass.

"What the bloody hell happened last night? One minute you're asking me to cut out some stupid useless footpath and the next day the whole bloody crop's been flattened."

"Sorry but I don't understand," I said, "how can it all be flattened? Has a heard of cows got in there overnight or something?"

"Never mind bloody cows, there's people wandering all over the field now, it's a mass bloody trespass. It's one of those crop circle thingys in my bloody field."

It took me a moment to digest this information.

"Well? Are you still there?" said the farmer.

"Yes, sorry I'm just surprised that's all."

"You're bloody surprised, imagine how I feel, my crop's ruined."

"Er, has the crop circle thingy actually cleared the line of the public footpath by any chance?" I asked tentatively, holding the phone slightly away from my ear as I anticipated the response.

"What? WHAT? I can't believe I'm hearing this, oh what's the bloody point."

The farmer rang off abruptly.

I was still stunned by this curious twist of fate but grabbed my camera and dashed out of the office.

When I attempted to pull off the bypass into the lay-by it was full of cars and I ended up parking on the grass verge. A cluster of people were standing around the snack bar but more still were wandering around the wheat field. From the elevated view of the bypass it was hard to establish the form of the crop circle but it seemed to occupy the full width of the field from the old railway line to the bypass. I took a few photographs before descending the embankment and climbing the stile into the field. I walked a short distance along a tram line into the field before entering the area of flattened corn. Standing at the same level as the crop circle it made even less visual sense and ahead of me it appeared as though people were randomly walking about the field. At my feet the wheat seemed to have been brushed flat and all in the same direction. This circular band of flattened crop was perhaps ten feet wide and the interior of the circle was unaffected. I set off in a clockwise direction and was impressed by the sheer and crisp distinction between the unaffected standing corn and the imprint of the crop circle.

A man approached me walking anti clockwise.

"Hi," said the man.

"Good morning," I said.

"Are you the farmer?"

"Do I look like a farmer?"

"Well, yes, a bit," said the man.

"No, I'm not the farmer," I said, "you'll be able to tell the farmer as he'll have a very angry face and it'll be quite unlike my own pleasant but slightly bewildered countenance. He will also be balling and yelling at everyone to get out of his field."

"Fair enough," said the man.

"I'm just here out of curiosity having never seen a crop circle before so I've no idea what I am actually looking at," I said.

"Ok," said the man, "well these days it's not often that you get a form that is tangible and straight forward. Someone's already photographed it from the air with a drone, we croppies don't hang around you know. I can tell you that this figure is a perfect figure eight, it's two adjoining rings, simple really."

I asked how it compared to others that he had seen.

"Oh it's pretty good actually, nice and neat, I would call it old school. To be honest it's a bit of a welcome return to the simpler figures as it has all got a bit outlandish over the last few years with really complex and bizarre designs where you have to ask yourself could a plasma vortex actually create that?"

At this time of the morning I had no desire to get drawn into a deeper discussion that contained the words "plasma" or "vortex".

"But why the figure eight?" I asked.

The croppie smiled.

"Yes, now I can tell that you're new to this game. Why anything? What's the message? Well that's the fun of it, there are some pretty extreme believers out there and then there are others like me who just enjoy the wonder of each new event. There's been so little activity this year and that's why they're all over this one like a rash. Take a walk around. See you later, I'm going for a cup of tea," said the croppie.

I continued on my circuit.

"Nonsense, who on earth told you that, of course it's not an eight?" said the next man that I encountered, "I've never heard such guff."

I explained that I had been informed by an actual croppie that it was a figure eight and he had seemed quite confident about it all.

"It's infinity and don't listen to those amateurs. I happen to be an experienced cereologist and a figure eight on its side is the symbol for infinity which is interesting for a number of reasons. Space?" The cereologist looked at me intently with his head leaning to one side.

"Sorry," I said, "I'm not very good at this sort of thing. Is that a question?"

"Yes, what is space?"

"The final frontier?" I said.

"No, let's be serious about this please. Space is infinite and that is what this is all about, just to remind you how insignificant you really are."

Having been told that I was insignificant I moved on.

Ahead of me a young couple who seemed to be wearing clothes made from the same bright patchwork quilt were facing each other and holding hands with their eyes closed. My mobile phone rang and the couple opened their eyes to frown at me whilst I answered it.

"Don't you just hate those wretched automated sales calls from banks?" I said as I passed by.

The couple raised their hands to cover each others ears and closed their eyes again.

An elderly man was pacing out measurements and making notes in a little black book whilst further on another man held up a camera on a long pole to achieve an elevated perspective of the crop mark.

There was a gathering of people at the union of the two circles and a fairly normal looking middle aged man with his head down made very slow progress with two dowsing rods held before him. The rods began to converge as he approached me and then crossed just before they poked me in the groin.

"Oh," said the dowser looking up.

"Is that a significant spot?" I said.

"Are you wearing steel toe capped boots?"

"Yes, I'm afraid it's the old personal protective equipment at work regulations, 1992."

The dowser grunted something and shuffled away.

The second circle seemed identical to the first circle and I found myself being drawn back towards the snack van in the lay-by. Before I left the field I met the croppie again.

"Fun isn't it?" he said.

"Yes quite an insight into a different world," I said.

"It's the pleasure of possibilities isn't it? The conundrum of coincidences. Everyone's got a theory, how about you now that you've had a look?"

"Well yes, sort of," I said.

The croppie looked surprised.

"Ok?" he said.

I explained that there was a public footpath that crossed the field that the farmer should have cleared through his crop. Each path has a number which is prefixed by the parish that the path is in.

"So," I said, " this is Upfield public footpath number..."

"Eight?" he said before I could finish.

"Exactly."

"Well that's a nice coincidence."

"Is it?" I said, "I'm not so sure that it is a complete coincidence."

"Well there you go," said the croppie, "you've made it work for you and that, my friend, is what it's all about."

I took a few more photographs before joining the queue at the snack bar for a cup of tea. Josef was looking much more cheerful this morning.

"You're busy today," I said when I finally reached the front of the queue and ordered a cup of tea.

"Yes, aha hello again," said Josef recognising me from yesterday as he swirled a large metal teapot around before pouring out my tea, "I like the corn cycle."

"Corn circle," I said correcting him.

"Yes it is a corn cycle, it is a bicycle with two wheels."

"Did you make it?" I said.

"Ha ha, no, no I did not do it. The farmer he is angry but for me it is good."

"Who do you think made the corn cycle?" I said receiving my change.

Josef shrugged and leaned forward to peer out of his serving hatch towards the heavens.

"I don't know, maybe it is the man from space, David Bowie. Or maybe it is you?"

As I walked away from the counter to drink my tea the farmer's land rover pulled into the lay-by and drew level with the snack bar. Although I had not met the farmer face to face for a few years I did not want to risk the chance of being recognised and positioned myself behind a young man with a tall pointed felt hat.

"You lot can keep out of my bloody field," shouted the farmer through the open land rover window.

"I beg your pardon," said an elderly man standing in the queue, "I'll have you know that I've got no intention of going in your field, I'm just driving back to Yorkshire and I have stopped off for a nice cup of tea."

"Ok not you then," said the farmer, "but the rest of you, I was down here earlier this morning and there was already people wandering about in my bloody field and smoking pot. The police are supposed to be here by now."

"That's the police for you," said the man on his way back to Yorkshire, "I waited two flippin' months for a policeman to come to my house after someone shot at my cat and do you know what?"

"I bet you're loving this," said the farmer to Josef, ignoring the man who was driving back to Yorkshire.

Josef nodded and smiled.

"Have you seen anything suspicious going on before today?" asked the farmer.

I drained my plastic cup of tea and slipped it in the bin before pacing away to my van.

"I saw a man," said Josef, "he take a photo of the field yesterday."

"I want some fresh tea bags in that pot son and I'll tell you that for nothing," interrupted the man who was driving back to Yorkshire. Josef peered over the counter at the queue, before pointing in my direction.

"I see him today. He is gone, no he is there."

I glanced back to see the collective of croppies and cereologists craning their necks to see who it was that had taken a photograph of the field the day before the event. I hastily got in to my van and started the engine just as the farmer clambered out of his land rover. I hastened away from the verge to join the traffic on the by-pass and turned off at the first opportunity to vanish into the maze of narrow lanes.

To bring some normality back to proceedings and before returning to my office to contact Mr Wriggle I inspected some outstanding stuff that I had been meaning to look at for some weeks. I took a photograph of eight bald tyres that had been dumped on a byway and in another parish I took a photograph of eight llamas in a field crossed by a public footpath that had been terrorising the local dog walkers.

I was back in the office before midday and I e-mailed Mr Wriggle the before and after photographs of the reinstatement of Upfield public footpath number eight. He rang up shortly afterwards.

"Is that the farmer's reinstatement? He's been rather generous hasn't he? Is it on the right line? It seems to be a very popular path as well with lots of people using it."

"Yes you could say that he's been creative with his reinstatement,"

I said, "but the public are happy as you can see."

"I've not long moved to this area and things were a bit more.... conventional where I come from," said Mr Wriggle, "this is all a bit baffling."

"We tend to do things differently down here," I said, "it's not to everyone's tastes."

Mr Wriggle thanked me for my positive contribution and still sounded rather unsure about it all as he said goodbye.

I rang Nancy shortly afterwards to explain how I had played my part in national public right of way enforcement day and I e mailed her the before and after photographs.

"Ooops, bugger, I'd completely forgotten about it," said Nancy, "and you satisfied Mr Wriggle, well done."

"Well, you've got to keep on top of these things," I said.

"That's a very unusual path reinstatement Victor?"

"Yes, it is rather."

I could not keep up my pretence for long and told Nancy the entire story.

"I think Harrison had something to do with it," I said.

"Harrison? Why?"

I explained about Harrison wanting to borrow a long rope and that I had been quietly informed by one chap, whilst I queued for a cup of tea this morning, that a long rope was apparently an essential item for creating crop circles.

"That and a few planks," I said, "and.. also.. a plan showing the location of the path disappeared from my desk yesterday when Harrison and Dolores popped into my office when I was out in the yard."

"Hardly compelling evidence though?"

"Oh yes and another thing, the path is Upfield footpath number eight."

"And it's the eighth day of the eighth month today," said Nancy.

"Is it?" I said.

"It's just numbers and coincidences, and anyway you couldn't do something on that scale in the dark with just two of you, you'd need a gang."

The chap in the queue who seemed to know a lot about the practicalities of these things had muttered in my ear that about eight people would probably be enough.

"What about the Trust Harrison gang and there was a bright moon last night?" I said.

"Come on Victor, they have enough trouble staying awake during the day, you don't honestly think...?"

"I don't know what to think. Hopefully Mr Wriggle might consider moving back to where he came from and the grumpy farmer's pissed off, so that's something I suppose."

After ensuring that Nancy congratulated me again I said goodbye.

I sat and mused over these strange events and decided that I ought to get on and do some work. After lifting up a large paper report of a pending footpath diversion that I had been meaning to flick through I realised that underneath was the map and the photograph of the pristine corn field with the drawing of me hanging from the gallows that I had doodled yesterday. I was just digesting the implications of this find when the chap from the other end of the building wandered in carrying my old climbing rope.

"The chip shop bandits called by yesterday afternoon and asked me to give you this. I'll dump it here."

He dropped the rope in a heap on the floor by the radiator.

"As you know Victor I arrive at work before you arrive and depart after you have departed and I was just locking up when they drove in the yard."

I got up from my chair to inspect the old rope. It was still tied up with my own particular knot and I could see no sign of rogue ears of wheat attached to it. It had obviously not been used and it had been returned before the crop circle appeared. I sat back down with the rope heaped up on my lap.

"It's a pretty musty old rope and I don't think I'll be borrowing it when I next attack the north face of the Eiger. Oh yes, and more importantly, pick any number between one and forty nine."

"Why?" I asked.

"That's a letter."

"No, why do you want me to pick a number?"

"Oh, I see, well out of sheer desperation we've resurrected the lottery syndicate. It'll be two pounds a week from now on, are you in?"

"Ok," I said, staring at the rope on my lap, "I'd hate it if you lot all won and I didn't, that would be too depressing."

"Good, so it's favourite number time. Pick a number between one and forty nine and try and chose a high number."

"Eight."

"Not you as well," said the chap from the other end of the building throwing up his arms in despair and wandering away shaking his head, "please think of another number, any bloody number other than eight, what's the matter with you all? Anyway, eight's my number and I'm organising it so tough titties."

"Actually, you might just have something there," I called out after him but he had finished ranting and was now out of earshot. That crop circle might not be a figure eight after all and I found a pen that worked to doodle again on the photo of the pristine corn field to test out this new theory.

16

THE HARRISON FILES

SOMETHING THAT HAD recently struck me about Harrison is that he is always on time, in fact he is often early. I tested out this theory and sure enough, on the few occasions when I now arranged to meet him, he was ten minutes early. There was very little that I knew about Harrison but the realisation that he was always ten minutes early I found very satisfying.

Busy people are often late as they are trying to cram in lots of things so arriving early may give the impression that you have time on your hands.

Harrison always gave the impression that he has plenty to do but lord knows what it is or where he does it.

I mentioned to Dolores when she popped in briefly to return my Ordnance Survey maps that it must be good to have a boyfriend that is always early.

"I haven't got a boyfriend," she said.

"But what about..you know..Harrison?"

"He's not my boyfriend, you are so funny Mr Wayland, why would you think that? Thanks for the maps and I'm sorry that I've had them so long, bye."

I blurted out some sort of apology and continued to go bright red even after Dolores had left the building. What began as a smart arsed observation had turned swiftly into an unhealthy interest in young people's private affairs and I kicked myself for it.

Shortly afterwards the chap from the other end of the building popped his head around the door and pointed to the cupboard in the corner of my room.

"We've had the fire officer round and strictly speaking ..that is a fire exit."

"But that's where we store all the old copies of the Examiner," I said.

"Exactly and I think that was his point. The two things are not really compatible, a fire exit blocked by stacks of old dry newspapers."

"But there's nowhere else to keep them."

"I don't think that will wash, he wants them gone pronto."

"Well I'm afraid that's a job for a rainy day," I said.

At that moment there was a great rushing sound from outside as the heavens opened.

The chap from the other end of the building smiled benignly before departing.

I took a few calls and watched the summer rain splatter down in the car park. A temporary lull raised some hope but I soon turned my back on the rain distorted view through the office window. Dolores sent me a text telling me that one of the maps she had brought back was not mine and could Harrison call around and collect it. I requested that he came at twelve noon and sure enough he appeared ten minutes early and I walked around to let him in.

"Oh, hi," I said, "I wasn't expecting you until midday."

"Is you busy?" said Harrison.

"No, it's fine, ten minutes won't make any difference, I expect you wanted to dodge the showers."

"Yeah, there's a map?"

Once we were in my office I picked up the small pile of maps that Dolores had brought back and an older map was sandwiched between them.

"Ah, here it is," I said, opening up the map fully on top of the clutter on my desk.

"Fanks boss," said Harrison, pulling at one corner of the map.

"Hang on a sec, oh look it's just started raining again, how are you on grid references?"

"I ain't got time for that now."

"Well, you see that fluorescent marker dot there on your map?"

Harrison rubbed his face with his hand.

"Don't worry I'm not going to test you, I was just going to show you an easy method. You follow the scale at the bottom of the map until you get directly beneath the dot," I wrote the three digit number down on a scrap of paper, "then you find the same scale running up the side of the map until you are level with the dot." I finished writing down the second half of the grid reference.

"So there it is, the grid reference for that fluorescent dot. If you just remember that it's along the landing at the bottom of the map and up the stairs at the side. Does that make sense?"

"Fanks, yeah, cool," said Harrison whisking the map from the desk. He then tried to take the scrap of paper on which I had scribbled the grid reference.

"You don't need that, that was just an example," I said throwing it back onto my scrap paper pile, "do you want me to show you how to fold up a map?"

"No fanks boss."

With the map awkwardly bunched up in his hands he left the office.

"Don't forget, it's along the landing and up the stairs and you're going to get wet," I called out after him. It was barely noon when he left.

Reluctantly I opened the cupboard that was a fire exit and there were the stacks of the Examiner that had accumulated over the years. The Examiner is the long running local weekly newspaper and it is where all the local authority public notices appear. The office has bought a weekly copy paid for out of the petty cash for as long as I can remember and as I was last on the office circulation list this is where they ended up. Very occasionally they have proved useful. In our modern paperless system this hoard is probably treasonable but now all of a sudden they also presented a major obstruction to a fire exit and they had to go. By unbolting the outside door I could take the heaps of newspapers directly out to the large recycling bin near the gate. I had never thought of using this door before and I left it propped open. It began to rain heavily again and as I waited for the shower to pass I noticed a picture on the front page of the newspaper at the top of the pile. Positioned at the bottom of the page was a photograph of fairly poor quality that had apparently been extracted from closed circuit TV footage. There was something about the face in the image that for a brief moment made me think it was Harrison. The head was turned to the side showing a partial profile and although there was some resemblance, the shoulders were too broad and I soon decided that this was a stockier person. The photograph was placed at the bottom of a column with the headline "Day Centre Cannabis Mystery". I stood and read the report of how the police were called to a day centre in the town when it was discovered that the elderly visitors were smoking cannabis in the garden. "Joints" were apparently being passed around and when questioned police were told that it was a "garden herb" and one elderly lady said that "it sorted out me lumbago a treat". The police confiscated a packet of the drug and it was established that one visitor had supplied the cannabis to her friends after she had been advised by her gardener that "a little of this special herb would help with my aches and pains". On searching this lady's garden three large cannabis plants were discovered but after making enquiries the police have been unable to identify or trace the gardener. The elderly lady, who has not been named by the police, said that she had joined a local "share your garden" scheme after being told about it by a friend. A nice young man had appeared and explained that he would tend the garden and plant vegetables that they could then share. It transpires that other elderly residents were also participating in this scheme and it had grown on a word of mouth basis. All the gardens involved were fairly large "presumably so the gardeners could secrete some cannabis plants about the place without raising suspicion" said PC Robert Hope who had made the initial visit to the day centre. "We think that this scheme has been going on for about three years but the residents involved have all been a bit tight lipped about it as they do not want to get the gardeners into trouble. We suspect that there were about eight different people involved in this scam and they only gave their first names which were probably false. Nothing has been stolen from the properties and the gardeners were apparently all very polite and helpful and they produced lovely vegetables."

The photograph at the bottom of the column had been provided by the accident and emergency CCTV camera as two days before the day centre raid one of the elderly residents had got stung by a wasp when in her own garden and had reacted badly. The quick thinking gardener had driven her to the hospital and had been caught on camera in the process.

"Basil was such a nice man," said the elderly patient who has made a full recovery, "I shall miss him and the vegetables and all my aches and pains have returned."

PC Robert Hope states; "This has been a brazen scam and the elderly residents have unwittingly been involved in substantial and organised cannabis production. If any person can identify the face in the photograph or can shed any light on the identity of this gang then please contact me directly."

I opened the paper and scanned a few more articles describing thefts or vandalism and they all ended with requests from the police for information. I decided that policing and crime detection is not what it used to be.

The rain had abated and I continued with disposing of all the remaining newspapers but tore out and kept the photograph and the "Day Centre Cannabis Mystery" report even though I had already decided that it was not Harrison.

Before I left the office for a scheduled meeting I caught up with a few outstanding e-mails and then found myself retrieving the scrap of paper with the grid reference that pinpointed the location of the fluorescent dot on Harrison's map. I wondered what those markings signified and there must have been seven or eight of them scattered about on the rights of way. After my uneventful meeting I drove back a different way and stopped off to check the location of the fluorescent dot. There was a walk of ten minutes or so from where I had parked and I crossed a field that had very recently been harvested with my boots crunching on the fresh stubbles. I entered a sunken lane where I disturbed a buzzard that flew along ahead of me beneath the overhanging hazel bushes before it broke free of this restrictive tunnel of foliage and disappeared. The narrow lane opened out as I reached the brow of a hill and I entered a broad clearing and checking my map again, this was the location of the fluorescent dot on Harrison's map.

I could see nothing exceptional but searching amongst the long grass I found the neat remains of an old fire now comprising of ash and a few remnants of charcoal. I am not sure what I expected to find but seeing the Harrison "lookalike" in the old newspaper combined with a complete lack of knowledge of his activities had caused my imagination to fill in the gaps. What was he up to and why had he marked this position on a map? When Harrison first introduced himself to me he had mentioned something about gardening and after reading about the "share your garden" scam perhaps I thought that I might stumble upon a cannabis plantation at the location of the fluorescent dot. There was also the fortified coppice that I had not managed to gain entry to despite me being some sort of quasi trustee. Was the old fire something to do with Harrison and why was I questioning my trust in this very reticent young man?

I was none the wiser after my investigation of the grid reference location and I bumbled about distractedly for the rest of the day feeling as though I was missing some vital link that would help to clarify the situation.

The next morning I had arranged to meet a couple on a popular footpath that connected two villages although until I arrived I was not really sure about the purpose of the meeting. I established that Mr Hartgrove was a recently bereaved husband and that Mrs Downs was the sister in law.

"Thank you for coming out to meet us Mr Wayland, we want to know where we can put Pat's bench," said Mrs Downs.

"What bench?" I asked.

"Pat's memorial bench, this was her favourite walk, we just want to know where it should go?"

"It's a very narrow path," I said.

"Yes, she loved this path," said Mr Hartgrove, "we would come here every day with Dilys. Dilys was our spaniel and she died a week after Pat died didn't she?"

"Yes, it's been awful Mr Wayland," said Mrs Downs, "such a terrible time."

"I'm sorry," I said.

We all shuffled up against the fence to let a dog walker pass by.

"This path is too narrow for a bench I'm afraid," I said.

"But this is where it has to go," said Mrs Downs, "Pat requested it before she...passed away."

"And we've already bought the bench," said Mr Hartgrove.

"And we've had a little inscription made," said Mrs Downs.

The couple stared at me waiting for me to say something.

"What can I say?" I said, "I'm sorry but the path is just too narrow. I had no idea that this was being proposed or I would have said so at the beginning to save you the trouble."

"But everyone's put towards the bench," said the couple in unison.

"What about planting a nice tree somewhere?" I said, "in your garden?"

"Pat didn't want a tree she wanted a bench," said Mr Hartgrove lowering his head, "and we can't ask her now because.. she's..gone."

"There, there Graham," said Mrs Downs comforting her brother in law.

"I'm very sorry," I said, "but it is just too narrow for a bench and another thing, if you had a bench then you'd have to have a litter bin next to it and who's going to pay for that and have it emptied? Then someone will ask for street lighting and by the time the local youths gather up on the bench everyone will be too intimidated to use the path anyway. Is that what you imagined happening?"

The couple huddled closer together and shook their heads. A chewed tennis ball fell out of Mr Hartgrove's coat pocket and bounced once onto the narrow grass verge.

"That's Dilys' ball. She loved that ball," said Mr Hartgrove.

I stooped to pick it up and handed it back to the bereaved husband and dog owner.

"Thank you," said Mr Hartgrove.

"Thank you," said Mrs Downs.

We stood in silence for a moment.

"Well...er goodbye, I have to go I'm afraid, I'm sorry that the footpath is too narrow for a bench," I said, departing slowly to leave the couple standing on the footpath.

Back in the van I rummaged for a Django Reinhardt cd and drove away listening to "I'll see you in my dreams".

As I was nearby I decided to see how the Trust Harrison gang were getting on with their latest bridleway clearance. I parked just off the road and as I walked down the track I followed the tyre marks of the Trust Harrison van. Before I caught sight of the van I could hear loud music but it was not the customary modern Cuban music with the robotic voices but a more traditional style and I could also hear outbursts of laughter. I approached cautiously to see what was going on before I announced my arrival. From behind a large ash tree and also obscured by some leafy hazel I peered towards the Trust Harrison van with the music blaring out of the open doors. Dolores and Harrison were dancing together to the music. Spinning and neatly choreographed they moved apart and drew back together with wonderful rhythmic style. Harrison was leading and Dolores followed with light flourishes of her hands to embellish the dance. Harrison seemed to be talking her through the routine and when the song ended they pulled apart and laughed together.

The lads stood around as an appreciative audience and as the next song started Harrison clapped out the slower tempo. Dolores grabbed Knocker and began to dance him around guiding her fiercely concentrating partner whilst Harrison demonstrated the steps to Nigel. This unlikely paring then joined hands and Nigel demonstrated a remarkable daintiness as they shuffled about on the bridleway surface. I then witnessed Dolores and Council Peter locked together and moving about in a slow embrace with Council Peter's raised stainless steel hook glinting in the sun. Ollie was equally willing to learn the rudiments of salsa from Harrison and then practiced with Dolores.

It was as if I had stumbled upon a magical event, a fairy dance or an elvish party that would vanish into thin air if I stepped out from behind the tree. I did not wish to be a voyeur and so I withdrew back to the van to eat my lunch.

I was startled by a knocking on the roof of the van and Harrison's face appeared at the window.

"Hi man," said Harrison.

I do not know whether I jumped visibly.

"I'm just eating my lunch," I said.

Harrison nodded.

"What is you writing in that book?"

"Oh, it's just a few notes..you know," I said, closing and casting my notebook onto the passenger seat.

"Let us see," said Harrison.

"What, see what I am writing?"

"Yeah, why not?"

"But..I.."

"It's ok, it's cool," said Harrison, "you is a private person I guess."

"What? Excuse me but if anyone around here is private then it is you," I said.

Harrison laughed briefly as he leant on the van door.

"What does you want to know?"

Put on the spot like this I could not think of any questions to ask Harrison.

"Well what about your name for a start?" I said after a moment's thought trying not to appear to be too interested.

"Harrison," said Harrison.

"No, your surname?"

"That is it."

"Harrison?"

"Yeah."

Harrison laughed and shook his head. He appeared to be in a good mood.

"Why is you 'ere boss? Gis us a lift to the village as I needs to buy Nige a cake."

"I was just passing and thought I'd call in to see how you were getting on, you know. Cake?"

"Yeah it's 'is birfday."

Without consenting to drive Harrison to the village I found myself clearing the passenger seat and leant over to unlock the passenger door.

Before he got in I buried my notebook behind the passenger seat and made a mental note to scribble out the words "The Harrison Files" that I had written on the front of the exercise book.

"Seat belt please," I said, "right, cake it is then."

I turned the vehicle around and headed back to the village which was a distance of no more than three quarters of a mile and we drove in silence. As we pulled up outside the village shop my eyes fell on the scrap of paper on which I had written the grid reference from Harrison's map and had left in full view on the dashboard.

"Let me give you a contribution towards the cake," I said hurriedly extracting a five pound note from my back pocket and thrusting it towards Harrison.

"That's enough for two cakes."

"Oh, is it? Well I don't know, get two cakes then."

Harrison took the money and once he had entered the shop I grabbed the scrap of paper with the grid reference and screwed it up into a ball before stuffing it behind the passenger seat. I also pulled out the exercise book that I had been using for a notebook and obliterated the words "the Harrison files" from the front cover with a biro and jammed it behind the passenger seat.

Harrison returned with two inexpensive cakes and we set off back to the bridleway.

He broke the silence.

"They is dark places."

"Pardon?" I said.

"Them places on that map, they is dark places."

I began to feign incomprehension but then realised how futile and dishonest that would be.

"Dark in what way," I said, "do you mean evil?"

"Not evil, just dark."

"Ok not evil, but mysterious in some way?"

"No, they is just dark places so as you can see the stars."

"Oh, you're into astronomy, do you take a telescope?"

"I ain't got no telescope."

"So, just with the naked eye? Can you identify things, you know the constellations and the individual stars?"

We had arrived back at the entrance to the bridleway.

"It is just a fing I does when I wants to see shooting stars. Them places 'as no lights, no farms or roads. That's it."

Harrison got out the van and I kept the engine running.

"Fanks boss," he said, holding up the cakes as he slammed the van door.

"Do you light a fire?" I called out after him but he did not hear. I did not wish to intrude upon Nigel's birthday celebrations and when Harrison was out of sight I pulled away and returned to the office.

A couple of days later the Harrison Trust van pulled into the yard and parked up next to my tin shed. I wandered out to see what they were up to and there was no sign of Harrison.

"Hi," said Dolores, "we're just getting some more bits and pieces, it's stiles today."

"Great," I said, "no Harrison?"

"He's late."

"Oh?"

Dolores and the lads continued sorting through my pile of pointed sweet chestnut posts looking for the straightest ones.

"I didn't know that he was a star gazer, an amateur astronomer?" I said.

"Ha, ha, I'll make him see stars when he gets here," said Dolores.

I left them to it and ten minutes later Harrison walked in through the gate.

17
THE FERRY

THE CHAP FROM the other end of the building wandered into my office looking reflective.

"I think I'll stick a flag pole up in the garden when I retire," he said.

"Why?" I asked.

"Well you could put up different flags to mark different occasions."

"Still why?"

"I like flags, there's something definite about a flag. When you put up a flag then you are tying your colours to the mast."

"I would have thought that you'd need pretty strong convictions if you were going to broadcast them by raising a flag."

"I have got strong convictions," he said defensively.

"Ok," I said looking up from my computer screen for a moment, "I didn't realise that it was possible to have strong convictions.. and work for the local authority?"

"I see your point. The trouble is my wife would probably haul down my national cheese day flag and raise the hammer and sickle or the Cuban flag and then I'd have your fast food revolutionaries turning up outside. Perhaps I won't put up a flag pole after all. I saw Barry Bishop in town the other day."

"Old Bazza?"

"Yes, he looked well. He must have retired about five years ago now."

"Flag pole?"

"He didn't say."

"We could all learn a thing or two from old Bazza," I said.

"Hmm," said the chap from the other end of the building

turning to leave, "you haven't coughed up for the lottery this month by the way."

"I thought I had?"

"Nope, you must be thinking of last month."

Barry Bishop was "old school" in modern parlance. He spent his entire working life with the local authority, speaking too fast and not opening his mouth properly so as to appear mildly incomprehensible. He also seemed to be slightly deaf from time to time and his teeth were always unkempt which was a bit off putting. Well meaning colleagues gave up trying to explain the intricacies of a new system of road inspection or anything else that they thought might be a bit too technical for him. Being left to get on with whatever it is that you do and to be able to do it in your own time is the ultimate objective for the old school local authority employee. Above all he had bumbling down to a fine art and so not a great deal was expected of old Bazza. If you bump into him now he is unrecognisable with his bleached teeth and a spring in his step. He will chatter away with animated clarity before excusing himself to dash off to sort out a glitch in someone's computer.

Retirement would be upon me before I knew it but there were still one or two long standing rights of way issues that I wanted to have a crack at before I contemplated erecting a flag pole or bleaching my teeth. There is a footpath in the centre of my area that has caused frustration to walkers and visitors to the area for years. On the map there appears to be a really useful connecting path but in small letters where it meets the broad River Adze is printed the word "ferry". The ferry has not existed for eighty years or more but the path still runs to either bank. On the western side of the river stands "the Old Ferry House" but there is no requirement for the owners to operate a ferry service and neither has there ever been a bridge at this location and as such the local authority are not obliged to provide one. If there had ever been a structure here then we would be required to replace it but it had always only ever been a ferry service and now there is nothing. I have erected notices at the beginnings of each approach to the river to advise that there is no means by which to cross the river with a small section of map and a brief explanation. As with all notices they fade, get torn down or ignored and then I get the phone call or e mail from a frustrated member of the public.

Recently the proposal to build a bridge has gathered a bit of momentum and despite the very considerable costs involved I have been approached to assess the viability of the scheme. Goodness knows where the money would come from but I agreed to take a look in the first instance. I had never met the occupant of the Old Ferry House, Dr Douglas Frazer, but I had spoken to Mrs Frazer a couple of times on the telephone. There had been rumours in the village about the misanthropic Dr Frazer indicating that he was either a bit mad, eccentric or at the very least unpredictable. I wrote to Dr Frazer a few weeks ago requesting a meeting and I had not received a reply until this morning when a card arrived in the post;

"Dear Mr Wayland,

I think a meeting would be fruitless. The best way forward would be to remove this public right of way altogether from the map to prevent any further confusion to the walking public.

Yours sincerely,

Dr Douglas Frazer."

I decided to take a look at the path and assess the obstacle of the broad river and hope to bump into Dr Douglas Frazer when I was down there. On the way I had to check out a recent flytipping report and taking my camera I left the office.

There are extremes of flytipping but it all amounts to the same thing which is a complete disregard for the countryside, not caring a stuff about how it affects other people and a presumption by the offender that as soon as it has been dumped then it will be somebody else's problem. I recall walking a path on a frosty day where small multicoloured plastic bags containing dog shit had been repeatedly cast into the leafless hedges on either side. These frozen baubles of packaged excrement hung like Christmas tree decorations and this vision still haunts me periodically. The latest report stated that a number of fridges had been dumped on a byway and with a heavy heart I turned off the road and the van bounced along the wide unsurfaced track for one hundred yards or so. The seventeen fridge freezers were a surprise.

It was not a surprise that somebody was brazen enough to deposit them here at this beauty spot after stripping out the compressors and presumably releasing the chlorofluorocarbons to further damage the ozone layer. The surprise was that somebody had arranged them into a partial Stonehenge formation and I suspected that it was not the original flytipper's that had gone to this trouble. These very large fridge freezers had been stood on end in a horseshoe formation with a row laid flat on top to form the lintels. A lone washing machine stood some twenty five yards away and I wondered whether that solitary piece of discarded white goods might have represented the Hele stone not that I know much about Stonehenge. The fridge freezer lintels were all attached with bolts to hold the structure together and for a load of flytipping it was extraordinary.

I took a few photographs as a police car appeared cautiously negotiating the potholed byway.

"Aye, aye," said the policeman, "the local youth's had a bit of a knees up here last night apparently according to the farmer who could hear the music over two miles away."

"A knees up? Is that what they call it these days?"

"Actually I think they call them "free parties" but it's the same difference."

"It seems very clean," I said, "I mean apart from the fridge freezers, there's no party debris. Do you think they constructed this... Stonehenge thing?"

"It's going to be a bugger to take down, I don't envy your lot that job," said the policeman.

"Ok," I said, "I'll put the wheels in motion when I get back to the office."

I continued on my rounds to the Old Ferry House. Having parked up the lane I walked down the footpath that in practise led to the bank of the river Adze and no further. I decided to ignore the house at first and stood gazing across the broad slow moving river. It was all very quiet until a voice from behind me gave me a start.

"You'll have to go back the way you came."

I turned around and a tall slim elderly man with a striking head of stiff white hair was pointing back up the driveway that served the property.

I was about to introduce myself when he started to explain why the ferry was no longer operational.

"Yes it was the old river navigation licensing act that did for it, a piece of legislation that was probably overshadowed by Beeching's swingeing railway closures. People forget that, no you'll just have to go back," the man paused for a moment and cocked his head to one side, " ...but something tells me that you're not just another disappointed walker?"

I introduced myself to the owner of the Old Ferry House.

"Is that true?" I said afterwards, "about the legislation?"

"Oh that? No I made it up. It gets boring just repeating yourself so they get all sorts of old flannel, my favourite for a while was old wartime mines that had been placed as over zealous internal defences along major rivers. Another one is that the punt got impounded by the police after a major robbery on a house down the river and when they forgot about it and it got woodworm they simply refused to replace it. What do you want anyway? You can't come into the house as the visiting chiropodist is in with my wife."

I explained that I just wanted to talk to him about the potential for this public footpath.

"That sounds ominous," said Dr Frazer.

"Well ultimately it could mean a footbridge across the river to link the severed paths, what do you think about that idea?" I said.

"Would you care to follow me please?" he said, hailing me with a long and bony finger.

We walked up the grass slopes towards the house and I was invited to sit down beside him on an old bench and we gazed together out across the extensive water meadows beyond the river.

I was waiting for him to speak but we sat in silence for some minutes.

"You see the snipe?" said Dr Frazer finally, "I've usually got my binoculars at the ready, there's a good many breeding pairs now. It's a glorious sanctuary from people and the wildlife has prospered. The punt is no longer serviceable but when the ferry was operational, for a period of two centuries or more, it served a very local community. People would cross to go to the market in the town and children crossed every day to attend school and it's a long walk on the other side. Damn bleak in the winter I should have thought for the poor mites but that is what you did back then. I know this because I have spoken to an old chap in the village whose father was one of the last school children to use the ferry. It was so much quieter then and nature was not so marginalised. I am not a romantic although I suspect you might be from that rather misty look in your eye when I mentioned the ferry and its purpose. Things can never be as they once were, I realised that some time ago Mr Wayland. People are now everywhere demanding access and recreation and it can be so destructive as they neither respect nor understand their environment. One loose dog in those water meadows charging about and flushing out the ground nesting birds would be catastrophic. I'm afraid if you intend to build a bridge then you will have to bury me in the foundations as I shall not go down without a fight. Does that answer your question?"

We sat in silence for a while and I tried to banish the image that had just popped into my head of dog shit hanging from the hedgerows.

Dr Frazer told me a bit more about the ferry and that it had been operated by generations of the same family until the first world war. He had bought the house twenty five years ago on his retirement from a pharmaceutical company where he had worked as a research chemist. I scanned the garden and despite his obvious convictions Dr Frazer did not seem the flagpole type.

I sat for a moment longer to watch the house martins skimming the river surface in the dark purple shadows of a large copper beech tree and had to force myself to leave this spot and continue with my working day. As I stood up the front door to the Old Ferry House slammed shut and a young man walked hastily up the path to a parked car and was soon driving away up the track. For all the world it looked like Harrison and I just stopped myself from calling out his name.

"Who was that?" I asked Dr Frazer.

"Oh that's the visiting chiropodist, a polite young man, why do you ask?"

"I thought I recognised him, that's all. What is his name?"

"Er..is it Duncan something? No not Duncan, is it important? You've got to like feet to be in that profession."

"I may have been mistaken," I said and I thanked Dr Frazer for his time.

Once back in the office I downloaded the photographs of the flytipping and looked again at the massive structure that had been created on the byway. I zoomed in to check something that now caught my eye although I had not noticed it at the time when I took the photographs. Something had been stencilled on the fridge-freezers in green paint and as I looked closer I could see that it was the figure eight. Perhaps the crop circle of a couple of weeks ago had spawned a cult interest in the figure eight. I attached the photographs to an email with a brief explanation and a location plan and sent them over to the section that had the thankless task of sorting out and disposing of flytipping.

A little while later the telephone rang.

"Hi it's Dave Barlow from comms, your fridgehenge has gone viral."

"I've no idea what you are talking about," I said.

"You know the stacked up fridges made to look like Stonehenge, the photo's are all over the internet."

"But I've only just sent them to Tony in flytipping," I said.

"And somebody wants to buy it."

"Buy our flytipping?"

"Yes, it's art now," said Dave Barlow, "it's an outside installation."

"Is it possible to have an outside installation?"

"Don't split hairs Victor, it's on the highway so therefore it's ours and that's what matters."

"You want us to keep the fridges?"

"We can sell fridgehenge."

"Is it not the property of the artist?"

"Who is the artist?"

"I don't know but it might have something to do with the

number eight."

There was a brief pause before Dave Barlow rung off saying that he was going to contact a sculpture park in the neighbouring county.

Fridgehenge was on the national news that evening with the arts correspondent in raptures about the significance of this extraordinary outside installation. Despite the ingenious transformation of a hideously irresponsible and criminal act of flytipping into a work of art my thoughts turned instead to Harrison the chiropodist. Was that really possible? It did look very like Harrison and there were similarities in the way he walked with those short urgent paces. To my knowledge Harrison could not legally drive and neither had I seen that car before.

Harrison had apparently dispensed with his own mobile phone some weeks ago and the only way to make contact with him was through Dolores so the following morning I texted Dolores requesting that he got in touch. She got back to me after an hour or so stating that Harrison would call into the office later that afternoon but gave no precise time.

I made a point of returning to the office by mid afternoon and busied myself until he gave a tap on the window and I walked around to let him in. I had already removed my socks and shoes and so sitting back down in the office I began to massage my feet.

"Ooh, my feet have been aching a lot lately and I don't know what to do about it."

Harrison frowned and then shrugged.

"I think one of the toenails might be in-growing," I said, displaying my left foot to Harrison, "I might have to see a chiropodist, what do you think?"

Harrison remained inscrutable but I pressed on.

"Feet are pretty essential but are largely ignored by their owners, well by men anyway, I suppose women paint their toenails," I said.

"You 'as got bunions boss and that is bad news," said Harrison.

"Is it, what these bits that rub on my boots? How do you know about bunions anyway?"

"Me mates nan had 'er bunions sawed off," said Harrison.

"Ouch, did she? Funny word bunion, sounds like onion and they look like onions as well. Do you think that has anything to do with it?"

"You says you wanted to ask me somefink?" said Harrison.

What I really wanted to ask him was whether he was masquerading as a chiropodist or was he really a chiropodist and could he actually drive after all?

"Yes," I said replacing my socks, "I just wondered whether you had any time to come out in the van and give me a hand sometime, you know like you used to?"

"I is busy boss, maybe in a couple of weeks?"

"That's fine, a couple of weeks is fine."

We settled on a day and I wrote it in my diary.

"Oh and another thing, have a look at this," I said.

I opened up the picture of fridgehenge on my computer screen and turned it towards Harrison so that he could view it properly. I watched his face for a reaction.

Harrison almost smiled.

"Fridges, cool," he said.

18
THE WRONG TEAPOT

I WAS A GOOD ten minutes late for work and Harrison had already arrived. He was standing motionless at the end the yard with his back to me and I felt a sense of déjà vu. I was not going to repeat my mistake of talking to him when he was listening to music with his ear pieces in and I was just about to tap him on the shoulder when he turned around.

"Hi man, what is you doin'?" said Harrison.

I withdrew my arm quickly.

"Oh, I was...I didn't think you'd hear me," I said, "you're not listening to your music or whatever it is?"

Harrison shook his head.

"Right, well thanks for coming," I said, "I've got one or two things to do quickly in the office before we go out and I shan't ask you to do the filing or make me a cup of tea."

Harrison followed me into my office and perched on the corner of a desk. After hammering on my computer keyboard for ten minutes or so I announced that we were now going out in the van. I had to clear out the front seat to make some space but we were soon heading out of the depot and it felt good to have some company for a change. Harrison remained silent and did not even enquire where we were going or ask what I had planned for the day.

I realised that after all this time I still had not explained to Harrison even the basics of public rights of way; the various status of rights of way and who is legally entitled to use which classification of path. Neither had I explained about the evolution of the definitive map, our legal document on which are recorded all the rights of way in the county. Somehow it did not seem like the right time and I put on a Jake Thackray compilation cd instead whilst Harrison stared out of the passenger window.

"Do you remember the property developer that we met when you first came out with me?" I asked, after turning down the beginning of "the Blacksmith and the Toffee-Maker."

"Cool dogs," said Harrison.

"That's right, nice cool wolf like guard dogs, well I have to call in on him again this morning."

I turned the cd player back up again and "the Castleford Ladies Magic Circle" just ended as we arrived.

I parked the van in a field gateway and as we entered the old farm yard Peter Knowles marched across the yard after breaking from his discussions with the contractors. He stopped a few yards short of us and pointed at Harrison.

"I thought I said I didn't want him on my property again, is he an employee of the council?"

I had forgotten about this and it was something Nancy had mentioned some months ago.

"No, Harrison is a volunteer working with me," I said.

"In that case he can stay off my property," said Peter Knowles.

"I is standin' on the footpath," said Harrison.

"Yes, he is standing on the public footpath where he or anybody else is entitled to be," I said.

"Look, I will let my German shepherds out if he does not leave."

"Sick," said Harrison.

"Oh for god's sake. Look Wayland, this footpath nonsense is going to give my wife a nervous breakdown if it is not closed or moved or something. I intend to develop the whole yard and under the town and country planning act the path will have to be moved for the development to take place. I've taken legal advice on the matter and it is as straightforward as that."

"Nuffink to do wiv footpaths is straightforward," said Harrison.

"I was not addressing you," said Peter Knowles.

"But he's right," I said, "nothing to do with public rights of way is straightforward." I was pleased to note that Harrison had worked this much out for himself.

"Who's in charge here, him or you?" said Peter Knowles, "I can assure you that I will get my way in the end and in the meantime I intend to speak to your director about your complete inflexibility and also your unprofessionalism in wandering around with this..street urchin in tow."

"Ok," said Harrison, "tell the director that you 'as bin chattin' wiv Harrison from rights of way and he'll be cool about that."

"Oh..just.....bugger off the pair of you," said Peter Knowles, turning on his heel and marching back across the yard.

A mile or so from the farm I pulled into a gateway next to a footpath signpost and asked Harrison to walk a short distance up the path to see whether a cattle trough was still leaking by the stile. Some time ago I had asked the farmer to stop the leak but I had never been back to check. Once Harrison had set off across the field I thought that I would give Nancy a ring.

"Hi Nancy, how's things?" I said, "I've got Harrison with me for the day."

"That's nice, just like old times then," said Nancy.

"Well, old times of a few months ago but I know what you mean."

"Say hi from me."

"He's just gone to check something but he'll be back in a mo."

"That's nice, what a luxury being able to ask somebody to go and check something for you. Has he got any friends?"

"Goodness knows," I said.

"Have you heard the rumour about the director?" said Nancy.

"No, I never hear any gossip, how exciting, do tell."

"Well apparently he's been suspended for refusing to remove a green cap with a red star on it when he's at work. He claims that he is not being politically provocative but he just likes it and even keeps it on in bed. Didn't Harrison give you a hat like that?"

"He did," I said, "but I never wear it in bed, what's got into the man? No you're dead right, I bet Harrison's given him one of his Cuban souvenirs. The director should never have been let out to meet the employees or, more specifically, the one non employee."

Harrison opened the van door and slumped down into his seat.

"Nancy says "hi" by the way," I said.

"Hi Nance," said Harrison.

I quickly conveyed the information about the director to Harrison who frowned and continued to stare down at his boots.

"I've just told Harrison the juicy gossip."

"Sorry I should have rung and told you earlier Victor, I found out yesterday afternoon. Anyway, I hope that you have a good day, I'm just off to see a man about a dog," said Nancy.

"Sounds intriguing?"

"No, I am off to see a man about his nutty dog that keeps biting people but fortunately it's got no teeth. Come to think of it the owner sounded a bit gummy when I spoke to him on the phone, bye."

After Nancy had rung off I asked Harrison about the leaking water trough and he tilted one of his Dr Marten safety boots to the side to demonstrate a muddy sole.

"They was clean," said Harrison.

"It's what is known as an occupational hazard although you can hardly call this your occupation and it's not really a hazard. I must remember to give the farmer a call."

Whilst we were out this way I also had to check on a report that somebody was living illegally on a byway in a vehicle.

I parked at the end of a byway that was one of the many broad interconnected droves in this area and this one still had a healthy covering of grass which was encouraging. All was quiet and there were no barking dogs as we approached the two vehicles that were parked a good two hundred yards up the byway. One vehicle was an old diesel van that may have belonged to the general post office in a previous life whilst the other was a handsome old coach painted green with a short chimney poking out of the roof at the back. I knocked on the door of the coach and the van but there was no answer. I took a few photographs and I would extract the registration numbers of the vehicles from the photographs later on back in the office.

"Oh well," I said to Harrison, "there's not much else we can do here."

I took a longer look at the front of the coach.

"No destination on the front of the coach then just the number eight? That number seems to crop up everywhere these days," I said.

"Does you want a cup of tea boss?" said Harrison.

"Pardon?" I said.

Harrison darted off into the hedge and returned with a small key and after unlocking the door to the coach he slid it open. After thoroughly wiping the mud from his boots on a doormat he climbed the steps and disappeared inside.

"Who lives here?" I called out, before cautiously peering into the vehicle.

Harrison was pouring water from a plastic water container into a kettle and he placed it on a small gas ring after lighting it with a cigarette lighter.

"My bruvver and he would make you a cup of tea for sure. You can come in."

I climbed the steps and looked about the very neat interior of the old coach that was now a home.

"Is this vehicle roadworthy?" I asked.

"Yeah, it's wicked but it stays here and don't go nowhere."

"Who lives in the van next door?"

"My bruvver's mate."

"No names?"

Harrison shrugged and continued looking on shelves and in a small cupboard for the right ingredients to make a cup of tea.

"I fink this it it," he said shaking an old tin.

The kettle creaked as it neared boiling point and Harrison nipped outside and returned with a pint of milk that had been kept cool somewhere underneath the coach. I sat down on a comfortable bench seat in anticipation of receiving a cup of tea from Harrison.

"You must let it brew," I said as he was poised with teapot and tea strainer in hand. He waited for a short while and I was then presented with a mug of tea.

"Thank you," I said.

We sat in silence as I took small sips from the tea that was too hot to drink.

"Have you got any sugar?" I asked thinking that it might mask the curious musty flavour of the tea. Harrison found some honey and I added a good dollop and stirred it in.

"Very nice," I lied, "and worth the wait."

"That's ok boss," said Harrison who had started to clear up the tea making process.

I decided that the best thing to do was to gulp down the tea when it was cool enough to do so as it was definitely not to be savoured.

Harrison continued putting some tins back in the cupboard and opening and sniffing at the contents of other tins. He then lifted the lid to look in another small teapot.

"Right, thank you," I said handing the mug back to Harrison, "I think we ought to get on. Please thank your brother, whatever his name is and I shall have to come back and talk to him on another occasion."

"Yeah," said Harrison who began pacing up and down and looking almost agitated, "I fink we should wait for a bit boss."

"Are you alright?" I asked.

"Yeah, is you ok?"

"Yes, thank you," I said.

"Cool, I needs to talk wiv Dolores boss, can you ring 'er?"

I found Dolores' number and when it rang Harrison took my mobile phone and stepped off the bus. I watched him pace up and down on the byway talking to Dolores and he then jumped back up the steps and handed me the phone as I stood up to leave.

"Fanks," said Harrison, "Dolores is comin' over."

"Ok, why's that?"

"Can we wait for 'er?"

"Well, I suppose so, I was getting rather peckish."

I had a strange metallic taste in my mouth and I seemed to be producing an unusual amount of saliva that I did not know what to do with. I remembered that I had some sunflower seeds in a twist of cling film in my trouser pocket and I sat back down to chew on these.

"Sunflower seeds?" I offered them to Harrison.

"No fanks."

After eating the seeds one at a time I rolled the cling film up into a ball.

"Is you ok?" said Harrison breaking the silence.

I had been mesmerised by the hedgerow outside the window and now diverted my attention to Harrison.

"Yes, interesting hedge, well, we can always have a nice little chat," I said, "let's start with Cuba, how on earth did you get invited to Cuba?"

Harrison continued to look agitated and peered back down the byway out of the coach window.

"'As you 'eard of free runnin'?" he said doubtfully.

"Is it like jogging? That's free unless you join a club I suppose. I never liked running even at school, walking's more my game and it's free."

"Nah, never mind, easier to show you boss, maybe in town sometime."

"Ok," I said, "well what about the coppice? I must be due a visit soon as I am some sort of a trustee?"

"We was goin' to have an open day and invite the director but maybe not after today," he said.

"What about the little shits in the wood or the crop circle and then there's fridgehenge?" I said but I could now hear a vehicle approaching and Harrison ignored my accumulating questions.

"We've been overtaken," I said as a small car passed the window bouncing along the byway.

Harrison disappeared to talk to Dolores and then Dolores climbed the steps and sat down opposite me whilst Harrison still paced up and down.

"Hi Mr Wayland," she said.

"Hi Dolores, that was quick."

"How do you feel?"

"Harrison keeps asking me that, I really ought to get back to work."

"Well you are working aren't you? You're engaging with your

volunteers," said Dolores.

"That's true," I said.

Harrison began to fiddle around with a small stereo system causing a repetitive ticking sound that must have been some sort of music.

"Look, a sheep," I said, "out there on the drove. Hang on it could be the vanguard of the two thousand sheep heading to the sheep fair."

I got up quickly and stepped down from the coach.

"I'll get my camera," said Dolores following me and dashing to her car.

There were a handful of sheep passing by being herded by a man driving very slowly on a quad bike.

"Oh, that's a shame, I was expecting two thousand sheep massing to the annual sheep fair," I said to Dolores.

The man on the quad bike cut his engine as he drew level and confirmed that this was in fact the much anticipated droving of the gigantic sheep flocks of yesteryear that had taken months of preparation.

"Yes, nine sheep," said the shepherd, "well by the time we took into account the highways, the police, the licensing, the animal welfare and movement of livestock issues. We've ended up by sticking nine sheep in the back of a truck and letting them have a run occasionally."

"So even the sheep are using the rights of way for recreational purposes," I said turning to face Dolores' video camera.

"Mate, you're a natural," said the shepherd, "do you live here?"

"No, no, not me but my friends do," I said, "well, they're people I haven't met yet."

The shepherd started up his quad bike and raised a hand as he pulled away after his straying flock. We could now see a truck positioned at the end of the lane waiting to receive the nine sheep on their momentous journey.

"Let me make you a proper cup of tea Mr Wayland," said Dolores, "and I promise that it will not taste like the one that Harrison made you earlier."

"That's a relief, no offence Harrison but stick to you guns in the future. No tea no sirreee."

We returned to sit in the coach and Dolores made us both a very nice cup of tea and asked me again whether I was feeling alright. I noticed that she had picked up the ball of cling film that I had left on the small table and was slowly unravelling it. I watched as the fine gossamer wrapper from my sunflower seeds was stretched and flattened and then smoothed out over her knee. This smoothing was an automatic action, over and over again.

"You're coming to the end," I said to Dolores.

"Pardon," said Dolores who laughed and looked at Harrison, "What does he mean?"

Harrison shrugged.

"What about lunchtime in the van?" I said.

"Well it's not exactly scintillating conversation but hey, as long as I can have some fruit and few oat cakes I'm happy. We've tried to get them to sit outside on a nice day," she said, "but they're not very keen are they?"

"They won't sit outside," I said. I reached forward and pinched a corner of the square of clingfilm and slid it out from under Dolores' hand and then held it up.

"What about this?" I said.

"Hmm," said Dolores.

"What's goin' on?" said Harrison.

"What should I do?" asked Dolores.

"Do not sit there in the drivers seat, swap with Harrison, do anything but don't do that," I said.

Harrison walked over and snatched the clingfilm and screwed it into a ball.

"Talk about sumfink else," he said.

There was now a silence inside the coach whilst Dolores looked pensive and Harrison was not one for starting conversations.

A motorbike could be heard approaching and it stopped outside. Shortly afterwards a man who looked remarkably like Harrison climbed the steps and glanced towards me as he placed his motorcycle helmet down. He was thicker set than Harrison but not much taller and was a couple of years older. He nodded to Dolores but did not say anything and the silence inside the coach continued.

I was suddenly reminded of the photograph of the Harrison look alike that I had cut out from the old Examiner newspaper and checking my trouser back pockets I found the creased up article about the cannabis scandal at the old folk's day centre. It had obviously been through the wash as it was now pale and delicate and I opened it up very carefully to show Harrison and Dolores.

"Doesn't he look like the chap in the photo?"

Like an ancient relic the damaged fabric of the newspaper began to come apart in my hands.

"I'm not sure Mr Wayland," said Dolores, "let me see, oh I'm sorry it's in bits, oh what a disaster, was it important?"

"Well it was ..I'm not sure," I said.

Dolores tried to gather the pieces together and held them in her hand.

"Hi I'm Marlon," said the man that looked like Harrison as he walked along the coach to introduce himself, "I'm Harrison's brother."

"Hello Marlon Harrison," I said.

"No, just Marlon. This is my coach, I live here."

"Oh, does he live here to?" I said pointing to Harrison.

"No, just me," said Marlon.

"So where does your special number eight bus service run to?" I asked.

"Not far," said Marlon smiling, "it's a very local service."

"I came here to tell you that you cannot stay here in this lane. It is in fact my job to tell you that. Harrison made me a cup of tea."

"Yes I know," said Marlon, "I think he used the wrong teapot."

"Where will you live now?" I said, "now that I have told you that you can't live here?"

"I don't know," said Marlon, "actually I was quite happy here."

"That's a shame," I said, "I wonder what you could do about it?"

"Well, I could just stay here I suppose," said Marlon.

I thought about this for a while.

"What shall I do with this?" said Dolores holding the remnants of my newspaper cutting in the cup of her hand. Marlon gestured for her to pass it to him and he opened the door to the little unlit stove and tossed in the crumbs of the article.

"Oh well, we'll never know now will we," I said.

I then started to think about feeding my cat.

"What time is it?" I asked.

"Half four," said Dolores.

"Is it?" I said, "how did that happen? Instinct will start to direct me home very soon. Old habits die hard."

Dolores picked up her video camera.

"Oops silly me, it's been filming ever since the sheep went by."

Marlon suggested that Dolores gave me a lift home and he would follow in my van.

"Are you sure? That seems like a lot of effort for everyone."

"I think it's best," said Marlon.

Harrison travelled in the back of Dolores' car with me in the front and Marlon followed behind in my van.

Once we reached my house the van was parked and the neighbours were left wondering why I had been driven home.

I entered my house and was greeted by my cat, waiting to be fed.

"This is Leadbelly," I said, whilst Dolores, Marlon and Harrison clustered on the doorstep and I gestured for them to come in.

The trio shuffled into my living room whilst I made a fuss of the cat.

When I turned around they were standing there looking at me. I was not accustomed to people standing in my living room when I got home from work and I did not know what to say.

"You've had a bit of a strange day," said Marlon, "but you're home now and it's ok. Sometimes it's interesting to have a wrong teapot sort of a day."

My stomach audibly churned over and I suddenly felt very hot.

"You'll have to go," I said.

"Ok Mr Wayland," said Dolores, "we just wanted.."

"To make sure that you're ok," continued Marlon, finishing

Dolores sentence.

I looked at Harrison and he starred back at me impassively.

I returned to the front door and held it open.

"Goodbye," said Marlon.

"Goodbye Mr Wayland," said Dolores.

Harrison scratched his head and looked like he wanted to say something but remained silent and followed the others outside.

"Goodbye," I said closing the front door.

At that moment the cat ran up my trouser leg and I cried out as its claws pierced my skin. Immediately there was a knock at the door and it was Dolores.

"Are you sure that you're alright, I thought I heard something?"

"It was the cat," I said.

"Ok," said Dolores turning away slowly, "bye Mr Wayland."

I watched as they all got into Marlon's car and crept away.

I fed the cat and spent an inordinate amount of time considering and then neglecting to undertake a few everyday tasks until I realised that I was hungry. I made scrambled eggs on toast and afterwards scribbled down a lot of notes that made very little sense in the morning.

The next day I felt fairly normal after the tea from the wrong teapot and when I got to work the chap from the other end of the building popped his head around the door.

"Dah dah, you're back in the tea club..if you want," he said excitedly, "but you'll have to pay five pounds up front."

"Ok," I said.

"Well have a think about it."

"I am thinking about it."

"You know that young chap who comes in here from time to time, el comandante or whatever his name is?"

"Harrison?"

"Yes that's him. He called in pretty early this morning to return a pair of boots. I put them over there."

I looked across at the black Dr Marten safety boots beside the radiator.

"Did he say anything else?"

"No, just the boots. Don't forget, tea club, you know how much you like your tea?"

After he had gone I walked across and picked up the boots and Harrison had obviously looked after them very well. I hoped that there might be a note inside but they were empty. I inspected the barely worn tread on the soles and confirmed to my satisfaction that Harrison was very light on his feet. I placed the boots back down by the radiator for the time being.

19
SKINNY DIPPING IN THE PRIMORDIAL SOUP

"MESSED THE BED?"

I looked up to see the chap from the other end of the building poking his head around my office door.

"No," I said, "I haven't quite reached those levels of incontinence yet. I just need to make a start on clearing out the office."

"Oh, I see, it's not often that you get into work before me Victor. I thought that you might have experienced some kind of abrupt and unscheduled awakening."

"Ha, ha, I shall miss your witty interventions, or whatever they are."

"No, I don't think you will, but this place won't be the same without us. Who'll run the tea club and the lottery and then there's your input into office life. What is your input again?"

"I'm just here and have been forever."

"Yes, roll on the day, not long now. It will take me about five minutes to clear my desk then it's hop aboard that old voluntary redundancy bus and off we go into the sunset. Any plans?"

"Not really," I said, "perhaps do some walking in another county and then complain about the state of their paths. It's what retired rights of way officers seem to do from my experience."

"That's the spirit. Oh and I nearly forgot, very heavy rain expected this evening."

The head disappeared and I could hear his tuneless and ebullient whistling retreating back to the other end of the building.

The offer of voluntary redundancy by the council had been announced suddenly a few weeks ago. It was an attempt to shed the burden of some of its workforce and to save money regardless of the great gaping chasms that would be left in the front line services after the scramble for the door. It may not be offered again and to stay would only be further cuts and decline. I had enjoyed the best of it and now at my age I did not have the stomach for the chronic worsening of it.

Looking out towards the rear of the staff car park I was conscious that I still had not managed to sort out my accumulation of rights of way maintenance detritus. I had purchased an expensive pair of Dr Marten safety boots for Harrison but the clearing up of the yard was a task that had never even got started. The boots had been returned after the wrong teapot incident and there had been no word from Harrison or Dolores during these last couple of months. We had now slipped into winter and it felt like a simple choice to turn my back on it all and walk away.

I had not yet informed Nancy of my decision to take voluntary redundancy and I admonished myself for acting cowardly about this as she really ought to be the first person to know. I continued unpinning curled up photographs of ploughed fields from my notice board and after a while the office telephone rang.

"I was just thinking about you," I said to Nancy.

"Good thoughts I hope Victor but actually don't answer that."

Nancy informed me that for some reason a cardboard box had arrived at her depot even though it was clearly intended for me and she had given it to someone in highways that was coming over to the west later on today. Initially I could not imagine what it was but then I remembered the walk leaflets that had been ordered a couple of weeks ago.

"That's great, I had no idea that you were doing that," said Nancy.

"Well to be honest I haven't had much to do with it, there this chap called Richard Fountaine who approached me fairly recently with the whole idea. I just gave him a bit of guidance on a few of the routes and supported a funding bid from some health promotion budget. I reckon that he's a bit of a loner, anyway he's not interested in coming out with me to do any practical stuff."

"Not like your Harrison then?"

"No, not like my Harrison," I said glancing automatically at the pair of safety boots that remained beside the radiator, "that was a very brief era wasn't it? A glimpse of how things could have been."

"Yes, shame that it sort of fizzled out," said Nancy.

"Hmm, I have now reverted back to my default position of lowering expectations whenever the public ask me anything, which actually is a pretty good long term strategy. Another useful thing is knowing what not to do, it took me years to work that one out. Oh and finally, always keep a toilet roll in the van."

"What's with the helpful advice all of a sudden Victor?"

"No reason," I said.

I returned to dismantling the many years of my disorganisation within the office until Peter Knowles rang to inform me that his wife had left him and it was all my fault.

"Brilliant Wayland, I hope that you're bloody satisfied. She says she's not returning from London until that wretched footpath has been got rid of."

Apparently more and more people were walking through his yard and he was damn sure that I had been encouraging them to do so. I recalled to myself that at my suggestion this route had actually been included in one of Richard Fountaine's new walk leaflets but as these had yet to be circulated I strenuously refuted this accusation. I also added that as of next week I was taking voluntary redundancy and so in the future I would not be the person dealing with this matter.

"Well bloody bully for you Wayland, retiring with a fat wad of tax payer's money, my money. Good riddance I say, to you and to that bloody street urchin as well. I just hope that your replacement will be more reasonable."

After he had hung up on me I was left wondering whether Mr and Mrs Knowles were after all genuine in their aim to establish a long term family home and they were not solely property developers after all. It made no difference to moving the footpath as there was nowhere to move it to but it left me questioning my own judgement. It was perhaps another indicator that I had outstayed my welcome in the best job in the world.

In the rush to get to work early this morning I had left my reading glasses at home and I began squinting at documents and letters largely guessing at their content before stuffing them into a black bin liner for shredding and recycling. I considered returning home to pick up my glasses but with the news that very heavy rain was expected tonight I now changed my plans. I decided instead to clear some ditches on the most vulnerable steeper tracks as due to the lack of resources they had not been visited this winter.

I returned to the slope where a few months ago Harrison had worked out the difference between a spade and a shovel. It was a gloomy, gusty and generally discouraging sort of a day and the wind blew with more determination as I slowly worked my way up the track clearing out some of the ditches as I went. There was no way that I could dig out all the points where the water could be diverted away from the surface of the track so I concentrated on those key ditches on the steeper gradients. Before I started digging I had strapped on my neoprene back support and with all this bending and exertion I now felt constricted with a pressing urge to empty the bladder. Answering a call of nature in a strong wind with no shelter requires a bit of tactical nous and it is normally something that an experienced countryman can undertake without dampening their clothing in the process. Facing the verge and committed to the task a capricious wind then conspired against me by swirling unexpectedly and I was forced to turn out into the track to combat this unhelpful buffeting. At this critical moment I neither saw nor heard two mountain bikers approaching at speed down the steep gradient.

"Put it away," shouted a man as he swerved his bike across to the far side of the track to avoid me.

"Yeah, perve," called back a female voice as the second cyclist rattled on down the hill.

As I throttled the flow and tried to pull my clothing together and yank the neoprene strapping back into place my crossly muttered excuses went unheard as the cyclists disappeared from view. This situation would never have occurred when I first started this job all those years ago. Back then you could go all week without meeting a soul out on the more remote rights of way network but that has all changed now. I knew this to be a national trend rather than a personal professional triumph but I lamented that there was no such thing as solitude any more particularly when you require it most.

I wiped my hands on the back of my trousers and grumpily carried on casting out the silt from the drainage ditches in preparation for the expected heavier downpour later this evening.

By the time that I returned to the office feeling cold, stiff and damp, the box that had been redirected by Nancy was now sitting on my desk. After washing my hands I rang Richard Fountaine and left a message to inform him that the leaflets had arrived and when convenient he could call by to collect them. Without my reading glasses I was squinting tiredly at the computer screen when the chap from the other end of the building wandered into my office.

"I think that I might take up walking when I leave this place. It'll get me out of the house at least. Any suggestions?"

"Just get yourself a decent map," I said, continuing with my laboured pummelling of the computer keyboard.

"Yes but with all your years of plodding about Victor, you must have some favourites?"

In a move to get rid of him so that I could finish up in the office and go home to soak in a hot bath I ripped open the cardboard box and handed him a couple of Richard Fountaine's leaflets.

"Here, try these and let me know what you think. Now if you don't mind I have to get on."

"Ok, I get the message," he said drifting away again with the new leaflets, "time is money and all that."

I was still feeling stiff the next morning and arrived to work later than usual. The chap from the other end of the building greeted me at the door and followed me through to my office.

"Oh dear, oh dear, oh dear."

"What is it now?" I said.

"Oh dear, oh.."

"Ok, get to the point."

"Victor, your leaflets."

"What's wrong with them? There should be three different leaflets. "Classic Country Walks", "Walking From Church to Church" and "Five Vigorous Walks"."

"Sounds great, but it doesn't read like that," he said shaking his head slowly.

"Can I see?"

"Ah, hang on," he said, withdrawing the leaflets from my grasp, "let me put it like this, every time the word "Walk" appears in the title the L has been replaced with an N."

"But you don't spell walk that like, that would be.."

"Exactly."

"But it must be a spelling mistake, you know, a typo. Please let me see."

"Wait a mo, that's what I thought at first, but then there's the text, here we go: "Having gained this hard won elevation.." and a bit further on "..it is a great place to unburden yourself of all the strains and pressures of modern life."

"What's wrong with that?" I said, "exercise and a bit of solitude are a great combination."

"I'm not convinced Victor. A fiver says he's a merchant banker."

"I don't know what his profession was..oh I see and you can spare me the vigorous hand gestures. No, I'm sure that there's a simple explanation. Where is the box of leaflets anyway?" I said looking around my office.

"He called round this morning to pick them up but you were late in and missed him."

"Richard Fountaine?"

"Ha ha, is that his name? Yes he was very excited when I gave him the box."

"Great, thank you," I said, crossly grabbing the leaflets from his hand, "I'll ring him now and recall the lot. It must be the printer who messed up."

I studied the front of each leaflet and it really was an unfortunate misprint. I continued to leave messages for Richard Fountaine but had still received no response by the end of the day.

"Any word from old Dick Fountain?" asked the chap from the other end of the building as I washed up my tea mug.

"Richard Fountaine," I said, correcting him.

"He'll be out there somewhere casting his long shadow."

I could not be bothered to respond and went home. I had now had two days off in an attempt to use up some of my outstanding annual leave and I had promised to stay with my sister to bleed her radiators.

I felt in better spirits after a break from work but on my return there was still no word from Richard Fountaine. I continued to answer some old e mails before I would finally turn off my computer in less than a week's time.

"Oh, it's you," I said, as the chap from the other end of the building appeared in my office with an irritating smile on his face and something concealed behind his back.

"I hope that you brought that extra fiver in today Victor. It's amazing what you can find on t'internet."

He dropped a paperback book onto my desk and I picked it up cautiously to read the title.

""'Skinny Dipping in the Primordial Soup"?"

"Yes, and look who it's by."

"Richard Fountaine."

"Exactly, it's old Dick Fountain..," he took back the book and thumbed through it to find a double page illustration and held it up in front of my face, "...up to his old tricks again."

"Whoa," I said recoiling, "take it away."

"I certainly don't want the thing, it's all yours," he said, casting the paperback book onto my desk as he wandered out of the office, "it cost me about a fiver so I won't be out of pocket once you settle up."

I threw the book in the bin and then left a more strident message on Richard Fountaine's answer phone urging him to return all the leaflets at once.

Before I rang Nancy I retrieved the book from the bin and warily flicked through it to the end in an ultimately fruitless search to glean any more information about the author.

Nancy asked straight away about the walk leaflets and wondered whether Richard Fountaine could do the same sort of thing in her area.

"I don't think so," I said, "it hasn't quite turned out as I hoped and our Mr Fountaine seems to have another agenda."

"Oh?" said Nancy.

"Well, he's got a bit of a fixation, he's what's called a merchant seaman in cockney rhyming slang, you know, he likes a bit of a tug?

"I'm confused, I thought the leaflets were intended to get people out walking and this all sounds a bit... nautical."

"Sorry, I'm not explaining things very well, not seaman I meant banker. Put it this way, he believes that if we all went about masturbating alfresco it would set us on the path to world peace. I know this because he's published a book called "Skinny Dipping in the Primordial Soup" which is extremely weird and all the illustrations are very..spurty.. do I have to spell it out to you?"

"Is he a bit of a wanker?"

"I think we can be more generous than that and call him a complete and very dedicated wanker and it seems to be a predominantly phallic endevour from the evidence."

"Oh well, perhaps when the boys are busy with that, the women of the world can take over."

"Maybe that's the plan, anyway these wretched leaflets are out there encouraging folk to pleasure themselves all over my patch. What's more each bloody leaflet has got my name and contact details printed on the back so that's a great legacy isn't it? Foolishly I didn't check them before he picked them up."

"I'm sorry."

"Yes, well nobody has seen hide nor hair of old Dick Fountain as he is now referred to in this office. Bloody people, bloody volunteers, well not Harrison, why did he have to just disappear like that? Anyway, that wasn't why I rang. I've been putting off telling you something."

"Telling me what?"

"I'm leaving. I'm taking voluntary redundancy."

"Oh Victor," there was a pause and I could detect Nancy trying to stifle her tears before continuing, "they won't replace you.. and I'm going to have to look after the whole of the county on my own aren't I? I hoped somehow that you hadn't heard about the wretched voluntary redundancy thing."

"I didn't think you'd be pleased."

"Well," said Nancy sighing, "I'm pleased for you, goodness knows you've done it for long enough."

"Yes but I've not been so..effective..these last few years," I said, "and it just seems like the right time."

"What will you do with yourself?" said Nancy.

"Well hopefully I'll be able to go for a walk without there being a problem at the end of it."

I went on to tell Nancy that I would ring her in a couple of days and that perhaps we could meet up quietly before I left and I stressed that I definitely did not want a leaving "do" of any description.

Two days later and an envelope appeared on my desk containing a retirement card. Nancy had obviously arranged this hastily but her sentiments on the card were heart felt and very touching. The remaining comments were largely from people I did not know and ranged from "get well soon" to "happy birthday Victoria."

Today was decision day with the final e mail to submit confirming acceptance of the conditions of my voluntary redundancy. Before sending it I set myself the target of clearing my desk completely and in doing so I uncovered a dvd in a flimsy plastic wallet that Dolores had given me some months ago. I played it on my computer and it was a short film of how to cut a hazel stick that I had demonstrated back in the early summer. I could not believe how old I looked or how odd my voice sounded. Just before the film ended the camera panned across to capture Harrison very briefly and I paused the video to study his image more closely. It was not a face to stand out in the crowd and it betrayed nothing of his character. I then tried to consider what his character actually was and found myself struggling to come up with any apt descriptions apart from his silent confidence that had struck me when we first met.

My reverie was halted abruptly by the chap from the other end of the building who strode into my office holding aloft a small box of chocolates.

"It's D Day Victor, so... there you go."

"After Eights, thank you. I haven't got you anything."

"Why?" he said.

I glanced around my room for something that I could give him as a retirement present.

"Hang on, I know."

I left the office for a moment to retrieve the hazel walking stick from the cupboard in the gents toilet that he had stowed there some months before.

"Here you are," I said, "you will find this very useful if you do actually get around to walking anywhere."

"Is that it?"

"Yes, it's a very handy tool."

"Hmm," he said, raising a weak smile, unable to ignore the opportunity to goad me further about the leaflets, "on the subject of very handy tools..," he began before losing interest in the easy pickings on offer, "oh forget it, what about my fiver?"

I could not be bothered to argue with him and counted out all my loose change and the stray coins that were still legal tender that I had found in odd crevices and under things whilst clearing the office.

"Thanks, now I've got to lug this lot around," he said pocketing the various coins. He then pointed to the frozen image of Harrison on my computer screen.

"That's the pancake roll kid, I saw him the other day."

"Harrison? did you, where?" I said, unable to suppress the interest in my voice.

"It was a couple of weeks ago in town. He was sat on a bench with what looked like a can of strong lager in his hand. It was before midday Victor, so that's not a good sign."

"Are you sure it was Harrison?" I said, "he's got a very nondescript face, there's a lot of young people who look like that."

"No, it was him alright. Well, to be honest he was always a bit of a no hoper wasn't he so I can't say that I am particularly surprised? Enjoy the chocolates," he said, jangling the change in his pocket and looking disparagingly at the hazel stick as he wandered off.

For a moment I sat in my chair staring at the image on the screen before picking up Harrison's boots from their place beside the radiator and hurrying out of the depot in the van.

I went first to the byway where Harrison's brother Marlon had parked his old number eight bus but the grassy lane was uninhabited. They must have moved some time ago as there was barely a sign that anything had been there at all. The next stop was the coppice and I carried the boots for ten minutes or so from where I parked up but the wire gates were padlocked with no evidence of any recent activity. At lunchtime I walked around the town with the Dr Marten safety boots that I wanted to return to Harrison so at least he would have some decent footwear for the winter. It was a cold day and I found no one drinking on any of the benches in the town centre and had now run out of ideas of where to look for him. I tried Dolores' mobile phone but was informed that the number was unobtainable. Similarly Harrison's old mobile phone number drew a blank.

In the time that I had been searching for Harrison I had made a decision. When I got back to my office I rang Nancy but it went straight to answer phone.

"Oh hi Nancy, I guess you must be at your office Christmas lunch, ours was a couple of days ago and I managed to dodge it. Thanks for organising the retirement card, very touching but I'm not leaving after all. I've decided that Harrison needs me here, well more specifically he needs rights of way for direction in his life. There's me thinking that he's this and that but he is just as vulnerable as anyone so I'll keep the retirement card safe for when I actually do retire and then at least you won't have to bother with that again.

Can I take you up on your offer of coming over to you on Christmas day for lunch even though I am not retiring after all and as long as Joe doesn't mind? Perhaps we can celebrate my non retirement? Bye for now."

There were a couple of messages on the office phone that I considered not listening to but curiosity got the better of me.

The first was from the lady in human resources who wanted to talk to me about a report of indecent exposure on a steep hill in my area and did I know anything about it. She thought that it was probably a matter for the police and I quickly skipped to the next message;

"Hi, it's Dave Barlow here from comms..you know we used to be the old press thingy? Anyway, there's a bunch of fresh tweets about these new themed walks in your area, organised by a really cool guy called Richmond Fontaine? Apparently you're involved so we definitely want a piece of it. Just ping it over and we'll do the rest, cheers Vic, ciao."

Retirement or not I still had quite a few days of annual leave to use up so I hastily turned off my computer and slipped the retirement card into a desk drawer. As I was about to leave I spotted the paperback book "Skinny Dipping in the Primordial Soup" that I had retrieved from the bin and I opened it and wrote in thick pen "this book belongs to Leonard Shaw" on the inside cover. Before I left for home I wandered up to the other end of the building and surreptitiously concealed the book under a battered box of potpourri on the table of donated prizes for the office Christmas raffle.

On Christmas eve I found an envelope on my doormat with "Mr Wayland" written on it and I instinctively opened the front door but there was nobody there. Inside the envelope was a short note and another of Dolores' dvd's.

"Dear Mr Wayland,

Thought that you might be interested in this. It is my latest video filmed on super 8. H says that it might explain a bit about what he was doing in Cuba?? Happy Christmas and see you in the new year with the van back on the road. X Dolores."

I fumbled with the disc, hurrying to get it into the tray in the side of my lap top.

It opened with a logo that said "super 8 productions" and I recognised the soundtrack instantly as The Mississippi Boweavil's Blues by Charley Patton. The video began with Harrison sitting on a bench cradling a can of something and taking the occasional sip. Passers by crossed in front of the camera obscuring the bench and I recognised the large building behind as the multi storey car park in town. I caught a brief glimpse of the chap from the other end of the building who walked by, glancing across at Harrison but not stopping. With the interruptions of passing shoppers the figure of Harrison seemed very static and forlorn as he starred blankly ahead. I was begining to wonder what the purpose of all this was when a special constable approached the bench and pointed at the can whilst Charley Patton continued to holler. I thought that this must be an alcohol free zone and Harrison was now about to be moved on or arrested. Harrison rose slowly from the bench and handed the can to the special constable. As the camera zoomed in on Harrison he suddenly sprang backwards, back flipping away towards a high brick wall. Turning and running at the wall he was now running up the wall and levering himself by his fingertips he landed with ease on top of the wall.

"Get down from there," I found myself yelling at the laptop screen, "or you'll ..break something."

This was just the beginning of a series of upward propulsions amongst the many layers of the brick built multi story car park, interspersed with heart stopping sprinted leaps from narrow wall to narrow wall with no regard for the great urban chasms below. The film camera continued to track this suicidal progress but there were also edited flashes of close up action where other fish eyed lens cameras had been installed at key points on this precarious route. With its saturated colours and the jerkiness of a hand held camera the overall impression was that of a home movie from a bygone era but there was obviously a great deal of craft and planning that had gone into this exercise.

A crowd had quickly gathered next to the special constable, all craning their necks to look skyward. Harrison was now running the length of the highest wall of the multi story car park before skimming down between the floors and the mezzanine stairwells on his rapid descent. This breakneck momentum continued as he leapt across to an adjacent roof with the impact on landing cushioned by a tumbling roll before he was back on his feet with no interruption to the pace of this assault. After a gratuitous headstand upon a ledge, Harrison reappeared again on the high wall behind the bench and before the camera could zoom in fully he had already slipped down out of sight inside the multi storey car park. There was a silent applause from the crowd of Christmas shoppers and the camera focussed upon the special constable's bewildered face as he sniffed warily at the can in his hand. At the conclusion of the Mississippi Boweavil Blues the film ended in rapid flickering frames as if the spool had run out on a film projector.

I sat back open mouthed and watched the video again. Was this what Harrison had meant by "free running" and had he been invited to Cuba as some sort of anarchic street gymnast? I was equally amazed that Harrison had remembered the Charley Patton song from the time that I had played it in the van all those months ago. I began to laugh to myself, initially with relief that Harrison was not habitually drinking strong lager on a bench in town before midday as had been reported. I then chuckled out loud, watching again the expression on the face of the special constable with his nose hovering over the confiscated can. Finally I roared with helpless laughter until the tears rolled down my cheeks at the thought that I had declined an attractive voluntary redundancy package in order to save Harrison from a life of despair.

THE END

Lightning Source UK Ltd.
Milton Keynes UK
UKOW05f0947161216
290177UK00012B/220/P

9 781906 978341